MW00849346

IGNORE SCOTT

BOOK 1: THE MILTON WOMEN

LEIGH DONNELLY

Copyright © 2021 Leigh Donnelly
All rights reserved.

The characters and events portrayed in this book are fictitious. Any similarity to real persons, living or dead, is coincidental and not intended by the author.

No part of this book may be used or reproduced in any manner whatsoever without written permission from the publisher except in the case of brief quotations embodied in critical articles and reviews.

Cover Art: Leigh Donnelly

ISBN: 978-1-7362068-3-6

❀ Created with Vellum

PROLOGUE: JACKIE, 10 YEARS EARLIER

"Shit. Hold up, guys. I'm stuck," Jackie called to her friends. Her heel was jammed into a crack in the sidewalk and she couldn't get it out. As she bent down to undo the strap so she could properly yank it out, she heard the bus doors close and the engine roar as it rode off without her.

She looked up at the bus with her mouth hanging open. Sam and Becky must have been too drunk to notice she wasn't with them. No longer in a hurry, she took her time undoing the intricate strap on her heel and then gave a final tug with enough force to send her flying backwards once it finally jerked free.

Jackie closed her eyes and braced herself for the impact. She was certain there was some sort of metal bench behind her that was about to jab into her back as her arms flailed helplessly at her sides.

And while she did slam into something hard, it wasn't the bench. It was Scott Davis. The guy that drove her wild through all of high school and who, up until they'd graduated the week before, had been her flirty seatmate in English class for all of senior year.

"Easy there, Strauss," his voice said into her ear as he held up. "You don't want to spend your summer in a cast, do you?"

She went to steady herself but forgot that one foot, thanks to the heel still in her hand, was four inches shorter than the other and she stumbled again slightly.

"Scott." She found her footing and reluctantly stood up again on her own. "Thanks for catching me." Inwardly she cringed. Stupid, stupid. Why was she unable to be witty or clever around him? Likely it was due to the way his wavy brown hair fell just so around his face along with the way his dark brown eyes would catch hers and make her feel as if she was the only person in the world who existed.

"I would never let you fall, Jackie." He put out one of his toned arms for her to hold onto as she worked her heel back onto her foot and she accepted.

"Where's your crew?"

"Brian and Mark are back at the place with a few other people we met on the beach today. We're having a small get together. I was sent out to get some much needed supplies." He held up the bag with a few drinks and a bag of chips.

"Where's *your* crew?"

"On that bus down there, without me." They both looked down the road but the bus was long gone by then.

"You should not be out here on your own. Is your place nearby? Want help tracking them down?"

It was sweet to hear him concerned about her, and it was a legit concern. Each June a large portion of high school graduates in Maryland descended on Ocean City for a week of excessive drinking and poor decisions. Underaged drunk teens with raging hormones flooded the streets – it got ugly sometimes.

"No." She took her phone out of her purse to text Sam. "I'll wait here for the next bus, and I'll catch up to them. You go. Enjoy." She noticed she was still holding onto his arm and let go.

"Or you could hang with us tonight." Was it her imagination or did *the* Scott Davis actually blush when he said it?

She felt her face redden to match his, but she tried to play it cool. "I mean...yeah...I guess I could hang with you all for a bit."

Many hours and many drinks later Jackie was sitting on Scott's lap at the table as they finished the last hand of poker for the night. It wasn't a team sport, but somehow she'd ended up there with his hand around her waist. His fingers occasionally gripping every so slightly into her skin as if it was taking all his effort to keep himself from claiming her right there in the living room.

Someone Jackie didn't know, likely from another high school, won the pot and the party began to die down. Still sitting on his lap even though every other seat at the table was now available, Jackie turned to Scott and reached for her phone.

"I guess I should text Sam and Becky to let them know I'm on my way back."

The hand around her waist gripped again, his thumb rubbing up and down against her tank top. "Or you can stay here and sleep it off."

Without looking down at her phone she tapped out, *staying out tonight,* to her friends.

"I don't want to put anyone out -"

"It's fine." He licked his lips and then looked down at hers. "You can take the couch." His eyes moved back up to hers and he reached out to tuck a bit of hair behind her ear. "Or you can crash with me." She felt his fingers in her side again as he said it and knew what he was offering.

Why not? They both wanted it and had been flirting for

the past year in class. Why not enjoy a night of hot sex before he went off to some intensive summer writing course for school, and she made her way to start her new life in Philadelphia?

As an answer to his offer, she leaned in and pressed her lips to his just as she'd fantasized doing for so long. It was even better than she'd imagined. Soft full lips on hers and his fingers now under her shirt as he caressed and stroked her skin with his fingers.

She moaned into his mouth when he reached her bra and started to rub and lightly pinch her nipples through the cotton. Yup, she was finally going to sleep with Scott. But she didn't want any attempt at a relationship. Long distance never worked. She wanted to make sure they both saw it for what it was, a one-night-stand before they went their separate ways, never to see each other again.

"Just this one night," she managed when she pulled her mouth from his. He looked a little hurt, so she clarified. "We're both leaving for college in a few days. Let's just enjoy this one night without any promises."

"Just one night," he agreed. "We better make it a good one."

JACKIE, PRESENT

"*We're* going to lose all our money at the penny slots while we get sloshed on dirty martinis," a sloshed Aunt Olive had promised a then sixteen-year-old Jackie Strauss. Inappropriate? Absolutely. But that along with her eclectic style and bright yellow hair was part of what made Aunt Olive such a force to be reckoned with. They never did make it out to Atlantic City, though. Poor Aunt Olive had had to cut back on the booze and travel plans after a few health scares, and then just when they'd finally purchased their bus passes up to the casino, she'd passed away unexpectedly.

Just as unexpectedly, Jackie found herself the new owner of Aunt Olive's house on Christmas Lights Lane. A street nationally renowned for its massive display of Christmas decorations. Every house on the street put on an impressive, meticulously curated collage of holiday décor with the extravagance of a big city on the backdrop of a tiny town on the Eastern Shores of Maryland.

For Jackie, a twenty-eight-year-old woman who dreamed of finding a career that made use of her artistic abilities, being part of Christmas Lights Lane was the opportunity of a lifetime. Especially since that year, the event was being filmed for a documentary. Ever the optimist, Jackie was sure she was approximately one year away from her big television debut as the next big do-it-yourself television personality.

Even though the display wouldn't officially open until the day after Thanksgiving, the first committee meeting was held in late August at the Holy Church of Milton on the corner of Christmas Lights Lane and Main Street.

Jackie said a little prayer to Aunt Olive, took a deep breath, and headed for the basement stairs towards the meeting. As soon as she reached the landing, she could hear the pause in conversation and see the eyes of a few dozen people on her.

"The new Ollie's here," someone said. Their voice was a bit more accusing than Jackie would have expected from someone she was meeting for the first time.

"Am I late?" Jackie asked as she pulled her phone from her back pocket.

There was a man in his mid-thirties standing on a small, elevated platform that served as a modest stage in the basement. He stepped down and began to walk towards Jackie with his arms outstretched for a hug as if they were old friends. Unsure how to react, she accepted his embrace. She didn't know if they'd begun filming yet or not, and she didn't want to come off in the documentary as too frigid or unapproachable. Besides, it was a pleasant contrast to the comment from her neighbor and he seemed nice enough. Having a good sense of stranger danger had never been one of Jackie's strong points.

"Jackie, it is so nice to finally meet you. My deepest sympathies about your aunt. She was one hell of a woman," he said before he turned back to the group with his one arm still around her shoulders.

"Everyone, this is Jackie. As most of you already know, she inherited Ollie's place last month."

"And you're Tiny Tim?" Jackie guessed. She'd received multiple flyers dropped in her mailbox about the upcoming holiday season. Mostly it was tentative, minor changes from last year along with a detailed calendar for the upcoming year. All of them were signed, *Tiny Tim.*

"Excuse my manners. Yes, I'm Tim. And no, you're not late. We just like to get started a little early around here sometimes. Eager to get another season going I suppose."

Why didn't she think to show up early? She allowed herself a few seconds of self-loathing before she put it off to the side to focus on putting her best foot forward going forward. There was plenty of time for her deep self-hatred over the seemingly minor error that night when she was tossing and turning, unable to sleep. The memory of showing up "late" to the meeting would nestle in nicely between the memory of that time she accidentally cut off the sweet old lady in traffic a few years back, and that time as a child when she accepted five dollars in change when she was only due back one. It was a miracle she found any sleep with the string of regrets she agonized over each evening in bed.

She let it go for the time being and instead scanned the group for any familiar faces. The only thing she saw was a group of strangers dressed head to toe in Christmas attire. *Crap*, she thought. *I look like I'm dressed for the beach while everyone else is ready for Christmas in July.* Another few seconds were devoted to her berating herself before she mentally added it to the list of nightly regrets. The optimistic part of herself hoped that maybe her fashion faux pas would help her to stand out. That was what she really wanted, after all. To be the stand-out of the group, the one offered the future do-it-yourself series based off her stellar DIY skills and unbeatable personality.

Well, she was still working on the personality part. Being "on" for the camera even when she wasn't feeling it would be the most difficult challenge for her. A challenge she hoped she was up for. No, it was a challenge she *knew* she was up for. It wasn't optional.

Tim guided her to the group and pointed to an empty chair sitting front and center. "We reserved this spot just for you. Being new and all we knew you wouldn't want to miss a thing," Tim said before leaving her to take the one small step up needed to be back on the stage.

"Now that everyone's here, let's address the elephant with a boom mic in the room. Lana, Scott, and Lizzy, can you all come up here please?"

Jackie was caught off-guard at the sight of Scott Davis on the stage with a video camera. Her high school crush, the one that got away, Scott Davis. In itself it wouldn't have been that surprising given that she was back in her old stomping grounds and running into old classmates here and there the past few weeks she'd been in town. But they both had left after graduation and never looked back. How were they both randomly back in Milton and part of the lights event?

If he was surprised, or in any way affected by seeing Jackie, he didn't show it. It had been over ten years since that amazing night at the beach. The night they stumbled back to Scott's room only to find four people were already passed out there. Scott improvised and created a place for them out on the balcony. They made love and slept under the stars. Her lady bits jerked to attention at seeing Scott and remembering that summer night.

She felt her jaw swing open as if attached by a hinge to her head, while he gave a quick smile and nod of acknowledgement before turning his attention back to Tim.

Next to him stood Lana, who looked to be somewhere in

To Auntie Gwen
Thank you

her forties if Jackie had to guess. She looked down at her iPad and then back up at them again before speaking.

"Good evening. It's a pleasure to be here with you all. I honestly can't tell you how excited we are," Lana said as she referenced Scott to her right and Lizzy to her left, "to be here filming this unique and festive community event." Lana made a point of scanning the crowd and making eye contact with each individual as she spoke. "I know you all have a lot to cover tonight, so I'll try to be brief."

The smile from her mouth diminished and she turned solemn. "We're not looking for staged, reality television. We will not be prompting you to say or do anything. If there is a dangerous situation, Lizzy and Scott will get involved. But beyond that, they are merely spectators. In short, ignore Scott and Lizzy." Scott mocked an expression of hurt with his hand to his heart and got a few chuckles from the crowd for his efforts.

Jackie's heart jumped in response. He was hot in high school, but grown man Scott was almost too perfect. His previously long brown hair had been cut short, his facial hair was trimmed into a neat scruff that gave him the irritatingly sexy look of not caring too much about his looks while still being undeniably attractive. Lugging around cameras all day had been good to him, too, as she took in what she was sure were clearly defined muscles underneath his t-shirt and jeans. And based on the brief gesture he'd made to the crowd, he was still incredibly, irresistibly charming. She was supposed to ignore Scott, the Adonis on stage before her, for the next three months?

Originally Jackie's biggest fears had been accidentally swearing (she knew they'd bleep it out, but she was going for the wholesome Chip and Joanna look) and coming off as too cold or impersonable. Her potty mouth fears took a back-seat after seeing Scott on the stage. Instead, she worried she'd be daydreaming about sexy naked time with Scott and accidentally nail her hand to a board. Not a good look for her.

While Jackie's inner monologue ran wild, Lana continued talking: "The documentary we're creating works best when the people who are the focus of the documentary go about their work as if they aren't being recorded. Now, as with most things in life there are exceptions. While we don't want you looking into Scott's camera or speaking to Scott or Lizzy, we do want to hear from you during pre-determined interviews and during something we call reflection sessions. After today's meeting we'll ask you to do a quick, five-minute reflection. I won't tell you word for word what to discuss; we don't want to prompt you outside a few general topics. But I will say anything off the topic of the light festival will likely not make it into the documentary."

"Okay. Thank you, Lana, Lizzy, and Scott," Tim said as reclaimed his spot center stage. The three took their cue to go back to their stations. Lana set herself up by the stairs and prepared to tap away at her iPad throughout the rest of the meeting. Scott settled into a spot not too far from where Jackie was sitting, and Lizzy was next to him with her boom mic at the ready.

"It's a little after six now," Tim said. "We'll shoot to have the meeting over by seven. Around that time an order of Pete's pizzas will be arriving so you all can mingle and eat while you're waiting for your turn in the reflection...box?" he said with a puzzled expression aimed at Lana.

Lana looked up from her iPad and paused her tapping as she said, "Today we'll be in the room in the back with Scott and Lizzy filming. Going forward, you all will be in a room we'll set up in your garage, Tim. If that works for you."

"Absolutely. Whatever you need, Lana. Reflection *rooms*, then. Sounds good. So, just act completely natural, everyone. But keep in mind the cameras are there -"

"No," Lana called out. The audience swiveled in their seats to look from Tim to Lana. "The best advice I can give you is to ignore the cameras. Never look at them. Don't break the fourth wall by trying to speak to your potential future audience. Don't attempt to play some made-up character or try out that British accent you've been working on. Please, I know it's difficult, but act as though we're not here. Run into us if we're in your way. We're paying attention; we'll move."

They all turned back to Tim and a voice from somewhere behind Jackie called out, "I just watched a documentary about jazzercizing with Richard Simmons and they spoke to the camera the whole time. He even had a cameraman come out from behind the camera to get some one-on-one help with his squats." The man next to the woman nodded and furrowed his eyebrows as if he too had seen that documentary and was thoroughly confused as to how and why this would be any different.

"We won't be doing that here," Lana said prompting the audience to again turn to look at her. It was like a tennis match but worse because the audience was in between the two people lobbing comments back and forth and therefore needed to turn their entire bodies each time they wanted to face the new speaker.

Lana looked down to her iPad in thought and then looked back up and said, "Think more of the Real-World style where the only time you speak to the camera is during quick isolated sessions in a small portion of Tim's garage."

Jackie felt for Lana. By Jackie's estimate, her neighbor's children may have grown up watching MTV, but most of the people currently living on Christmas Lights Lane had no idea what Lana meant with The Real-World reference.

"I can't offer your crew any of my oatmeal cookies?" a neighbor from the back of the group asked. Before anyone could answer she added, "Fine. I'll just leave them on the table, and I want you to know you can have them whenever you want them. I won't say anything into the camera about it. I don't want to ruin your movie."

"You can talk before we begin filming your segment," she offered. "I'm merely requesting everyone here ignore us once we get started," Lana said, the tone of her voice inching towards frustration.

"And we will certainly do that for you. Right, everyone?" Tim asked his neighbors. The crowd turned back to Tim and mumbled random words confirming they would ignore the crew. Tim carried onward with a bit of extra enthusiasm in his voice when he said, "Okay, gang, let's do this!"

"I'll start recording then," Scott said as he hoisted the camera on his shoulder and disappeared behind it. A red dot blazed on the camera to show he was recording, and the neighbors all obediently turned from the camera back to Tim.

Tim rubbed his hands together and made a big to-do of giving the official welcome to the group.

"Welcome, everyone, to the first meeting of the Milton Christmas Display Committee for the season!" Tim announced. Everyone cheered as if they'd all just arrived and hadn't had a somewhat tense conversation about the documentary moments before. A few rows behind Jackie, a pair of older women wielded festive cowbells bedazzled with green and red gems to show their support of the momentous occasion.

Jackie's first thought was, *those cowbells are fabulous.* What came next was panic. *Holy shit. This crazy group of neighbors is my people.* While she had only intended to live in Aunt Ollie's old house for the event, the idea that she could stay longer began to form in her mind. The scene in the church basement could be her indefinite future.

Most of the meeting was an overwhelming blur for Jackie. She'd come in way too overconfident given her lack of experience in comparison to everyone else in the neighborhood. It didn't matter that in a past life she'd taught herself to cut and sew intricate patterns to make her own clothing, or that she'd had a semi-lucrative side-hustle doing interior design in Philly. The Christmas lights event in Milton was a whole new beast in the way of design and DIY.

The final part of the meeting was the house rundown and binder distribution. Each house had a binder of information which Tim had kept for safekeeping during the off-season. Tim called on each neighbor to give a quick summary of how their planning for the upcoming season was going. The neighbor then went to the front stage to receive their binder in a ceremony not dissimilar to that of a high school graduation. The binder was formally passed on and the hand-off was lauded as cheers erupted from the audience.

"And last but not least, our newest committee member, taking over for the sorely missed Ollie Hoffman, is Jackie Strauss!" Tim announced. A few kind souls cheered while some, the cowbell couple included, held their applause until Jackie proved herself worthy of it. Harsh, but it made Jackie like them even more.

"Thanks, Tim. I'm excited to be here." She looked around the room nervously and then looked straight into Scott's camera. She slapped her hand to her forehead and cringed at how quickly she'd broken Lana's only rule. "Sorry, Scott," she called out before realizing she was still doing it and adding in Scott's name to boot. "Shit...sorry..." She turned back to Tim begging him to do or say something that would take over control of the situation and help her to stop mucking it all up.

"Fantastic. We're excited to see Ollie's shoes filled with a family member. Family and community is what it's all about."

Enthusiastic nods went through the crowd before it was time to get down to business. "Let's hear where you're at with your planning."

Jackie stood up to address everyone even though no one else had stood. She stopped standing at that realization and ended up in a half squat. In her mind an image appeared of Richard Simmons cringing and shaking his head at her pathetic form. She decided she might as well just stand up since she was halfway there. Things could be worse, they likely would get worse, she needed to buckle up and let it all happen. Salvage what she could and never look back. She'd be the only one to stand, so be it. Just another way that she would stand out in the crowd.

She cleared her throat and said, "I've decided to go with a different theme this year – change things up a bit."

Tim kept a smile plastered on his face, but his eyes deceived him as they widened like a nocturnal creature caught in the middle of the street as two headlights barreled towards him.

"I'd like to do a nautical theme -"

"It's the Eastern Shore. We're all doing some sort of nautical theme," a man called out impatiently. Again, a smattering of chuckles rippled through the crowd along with a few mumbles and grumbles between neighbors.

"I understand that, thank you," she said to everyone since she couldn't pin-point the disgruntled neighbor at the moment. Her palms got sweatier by the second as she tried to organize her thoughts while reminding herself the moment was key in scoring a spot as the main focus in the documentary. This could be her first impression and in her mind everything that followed would hinge on the few precious minutes before her.

"I'll be doing an *underwater* nautical theme. I've decided to dig up the grass on my front lawn and install a temporary beach and ocean floor by spreading sand where the grass used to be. My main display will be a four-foot tall, animated Santa crab named Santa Claws." She'd spent the last few weeks doing little unpacking. Her time was devoted to the job she'd found in town as the front desk clerk of a marina, and to researching and planning out the new intricate house design she'd dreamed up.

Her efforts and hours upon hours of planning looked like they were going to pay off. Tim appeared to be warming up to the idea. "Okay...it sounds like you may have something here. Though one of the reasons this neighborhood has been so successful over the years is because we create a *cohesive* display with each house blending and working with the houses next to it," Tim explained. "Before you start digging up your yard, let's sit down together with Margaret, Evelyn, and Mort. Then we can discuss how your house will incorporate with the others."

"Absolutely," Jackie beamed. "Looking forward to it," she added for good measure before she ascended the stage to officially receive her house binder.

The meeting adjourned with everyone singing an original verse to the tune of "Rockin' Around the Christmas Tree."

Rockin' around Christmas Lights Lane
  We're the best holiday display
  Join us for a ride, on our train
  We'll beat Bal'more any day

Midway through the chanting Jackie pondered the very real possibility that she hadn't just inherited a house, but had also unknowingly joined a cult. When the camera wasn't trained on her, she sneaked a few glances at Scott. One of which

Scott intercepted and they shared a quick look that said, "How the hell did we end up here?"

During the brief song, the neighborhood clapped to the beat, and everyone pointed at Mort for the train reference. She didn't know anything about that, but she had a feeling the Baltimore line was directed to Baltimore City's own holiday lights display on 34th Street. The two Maryland locations had been battling for the title of best holiday display in the state for the past decade. The Baltimore location often beat out Milton on convenience alone since it's located in a heavily populated area with Interstate 95 cutting directly through the city. But Milton had been gaining traction for years and, according to the locals, Tim was the leader they needed to put them ahead of Baltimore in the upcoming season.

The pizzas arrived, as promised, and were set on a few tables along the wall next to the stage. After their song, some went straight for the free food, while others lined up for the reflection room in hopes of getting out of the meeting sooner rather than later.

Jackie grabbed a slice then took a seat at the edge of the stage which was really just one long step. She planned to sit back and take in the dynamics of the group as she ate. Her neighborhood analysis was put on hold when Tim sat down next to her. Not just next to her, but practically on top of her. An interesting move given there was at least five open feet of step on either side of her. He was white hot, too. Their thighs touched and she could feel the heat coming from him through both his khakis and her capris. She hoped the heat was a result of the hideous knit Christmas vest he was wearing even though it was well over eighty degrees in the church basement, and not due to some sort of attraction to her.

"How are you holding up?" he asked her. If he noticed

she'd inched away from him to create a modicum of space between them, he didn't mention it.

"I'm fine."

"A little overwhelmed?"

"Not at all." Lies. The cameras weren't anywhere near them, so who was she trying to fool? Herself, likely. Fake it till you make it was a well-known saying for a reason.

"I have no doubt. Your mother gave me a bit of a run down about you at Ollie's funeral. You'll be great. I'm sure of it."

Jackie thought back to the day of the funeral and was more than mildly disturbed to hear Tim had been present and had been asking about her. She was serious about the event, but she was also weary of letting it take over her life the way it seemed to have taken over poor Tim's life.

Unsure of what to say in response, Jackie merely thanked him for the vote of confidence and excused herself to get in line for her reflection session.

"Right," he said. "Well, I'd better keep circulating around the room. Don't want people to think I have favorites."

Despite herself and everything she'd just thought about his lack of a social life and hideous outfit – a vest and a Rudolph tie complete with blinking red-light nose – she shamelessly checked out the view from behind as he walked away. She couldn't honestly say Tim was a hard no for her. The man clearly worked out and he was organized and motivated. It didn't help that she hadn't been laid in months.

Get your head in the damn game, she thought to herself when she realized what she was doing. *You are here to win. To be the best of the freaking best. So what if it's been a while since you've been properly shagged. Get over it. You will not let any guy – not Tim and especially not Scott – interfere this life-altering opportunity!*

With her mind back on track, Jackie tried to psych herself

up as she waited for her turn in the reflection room. It could very well be her introduction to everyone if they decided not to include her section of the binder presentation at the meeting in the documentary.

Lana said her documentary wouldn't be like everyone else's, but Jackie wasn't buying it. She'd been watching nothing but DIY shows and various documentaries since she found out she'd be a part of this one. She knew that with this large of a crowd and this big of an event, they would have no choice but to narrow in on the most interesting stories and people within the event. Lana was sitting in on the reflections and was likely already outlining on her iPad whom they would be focusing on. She needed to rock this reflection to secure a position as one of the main interests from the start.

Mort smiled at Jackie as he left the reflection room and she heard Lana call from within, "Whoever's next, we're ready for you."

SCOTT

The temporary reflection room was set up in the back of the church basement with a couch on one wall, a small table pushed off to the side, and a few bean bags placed sporadically around the room.

Scott sat in a wooden chair facing the couch with his camera on a tripod. Lizzy was off to his side with her boom mic on a stand as well since the interviewees were stationary. She had a smaller camera she was running to get another angle of the interview since she didn't need to do much with the mic beyond the initial set-up. Lana sat in the corner at a table with her iPad at the ready.

"Hi," Jackie said as she entered the room.

Scott had already seen her throughout the meeting and knew that she'd be coming in at some point to do a reflection, but his breath still caught when she walked into the tiny room and sat down on the couch in front of him.

Over a decade later and she hadn't changed much in that time. She'd had a smattering of freckles on her nose and cheeks that seemed to have disappeared. But seeing her up close in the reflection room he saw that if he looked hard enough he could just make them out. Curly brown hair still framed her face and fell to just above her shoulders.

As a teenager she'd been all elbows and knees, but since then she'd filled out. So much so that he'd already caught himself staring more than a few times in the brief hour and a half that they'd been in the church basement together. Good thing he wasn't too religious given the impure thoughts that had flooded his mind that evening.

"Jackie Strauss," Scott said. "What's it been? Ten years? High school I think?"

How embarrassing. He was a grown-ass adult and yet for whatever reason he was playing games with her. Acting as though he couldn't remember the last time he saw her had been in Ocean City, Maryland, for senior week a few days after their high school graduation.

"Yeah, something like that," she said as she played it equally cool. Either that or she genuinely didn't remember which he hoped wasn't the case. "How have you been? How long have you been back in town?"

"I've been good."

Lana, however, was not having it. "Let's begin. Shall we?"

"Right," he agreed. "We'll catch up another time. Since this is your first reflection, Jackie, we'll give you a quick summary of what we're looking for. But going forward, you'll be in a room with a camera already set up; it will just be you and the camera."

"Okay."

"In general, we're looking for feedback from you about how things are going. Are you on schedule? Do you have concerns? What's working or going well? What's not working or isn't going well? That sort of thing. You're reflecting on the project and your role within it."

"I can do that."

"Great." He ducked back behind the camera. "Whenever you're ready." The red light lit up.

"Hi, I'm Jackie." She gave a half-wave into the camera.

Scott could see her tense up as she caught the image of herself in the camera. Everyone else did, too, which was why he was able to spot it so easily. From behind the camera, he gave an encouraging thumbs up he hoped she noticed.

"Um. I'm happy to be here. Tim seems like a really nice guy. We'll be meeting up soon to go over the event...Not as a date though. He doesn't want to date me..."

In his periphery he could see Lizzy quietly chuckling behind her camera, and he wondered if Jackie noticed it as well. *Oh, shit. She's losing it,* Scott thought as she watched Jackie's eyes widen and her mouth fall slightly open. He popped out from behind the camera, locked eyes with her, and pantomimed taking a deep breath. Or at least he'd meant to pantomime it. He found out it's easier to actually take in the deep breath than only pretend to do it.

She followed suit and took a deep breath herself, looked back into the camera, and started again. It worked. She clearly articulated her excitement at being a part of the team, shared her memories of walking through the majestic display as a child, and talked about her determination to create similar magic of her own as the newest member of the team.

Afterwards, as Jackie rose to leave the room, she turned back and mouthed, "Thank you," to Scott before she shot him another sweet smile and walked out.

Fuck me, he thought as he ran a hand through his hair and rubbed the back of his neck. He abruptly moved his hand back to his side when he noticed Lana's gaze on him from the corner of the room. Her one eyebrow cocked ever so slightly to show that his actions didn't go unnoticed. Scott gave Lana a shake of his head to tell her it wasn't what she thought, then turned his attention back to his camera and his thoughts back to Jackie.

At first, she'd been adorably nervous during the meeting and during her interview, but at the end she'd nailed it. He had no doubts that she was going to blow all their minds with her new displays. There was also no doubt in his mind that he was going to have a hell of a time focusing on his work with Jackie Strauss around.

What are the odds we'd meet up again like this and then spend months working together? he thought that night. He didn't believe in fate or signs, but he also didn't believe in coincidence.

Not that he was looking for anything serious. His recent marriage had been an absolute disaster. Fighting about everything followed by a long, drawn-out divorce that in the end, Corine had never agreed to anyway. In the months since their divorce officially went through, Scott had been on a few dates here and there. He even casually dated for a few weeks when he was in Florida.

And while he'd enjoyed the company of the women he casually dated, he hadn't met anyone he could see himself getting serious with again. But Jackie…there wasn't anything casual about the way he felt about Jackie.

His first day of working the actual event included Jackie's meeting with Tim and some of her neighbors. On his way to her house that morning he'd been like a teenager trying out different lines for when she opened the door.

His options mostly included various ways of greeting her while adding some comment or other about her house or outfit or hair. He shook his head in frustration that he couldn't come up with anything worthwhile. Anything beyond what he'd say to most any other neighbor on the block. Jackie was not just any neighbor.

He also didn't have time for mediocrity with Jackie. The timer was already up and running for how long he'd have with her – until January second, likely – so he needed to start the wooing and charm immediately. Because as much as it terrified him to date anyone beyond a few weeks, he never could resist her.

Scott ran his hand through his hair one last time before he rang the bell. A few times during their brief stint as seat-mates in English class she'd commented that he was funny. Maybe some sort of joke was the way to her heart. That and a little bit of flattery.

When she answered the door he said, "If it isn't the lovely Jackie Strauss. I'm here to shoot your date with Tim."

Jackie gave a genuine laugh at the comment. "Hi, Scott. I knew I would do something horribly embarrassing on camera. I just didn't expect to do it on the first day of filming." She shook her head as if to dismiss it. "Anyway, come on in. It really is good to see you again."

"Yeah, you too, Jackie." He gave her a quick hug with care-fully placed hands on her waist and center back. It probably wouldn't have been completely out of the question to give her a kiss on the cheek given all of the other places he'd kissed that one night, his nerves got the best of him. Besides, he was there for work. He should be keeping it professional for both their sakes.

He noticed her outfit, black pants that hugged her hips and showed off her toned legs with a black and white blouse, and said, "You look nice for the meeting. Anyone in partic-ular you're trying to impress?" Could she tell he'd been refer-ring to himself with that question? It had been a while since he'd put any actual effort into flirting and dating. He had a feeling it showed.

"I'm trying to impress everyone. I don't think you realize what's at stake here, Scott. I've dreamed of having my own DIY or interior design show on one of the streaming networks or any of the cable channels. I'll take PBS if they'll have me." She glowed as she spoke, and he couldn't help but get wrapped up in her enthusiasm.

"This documentary has the ability to make or break my dreams. And, coincidentally, my good buddy Scott," she said as she nudged him with her elbow to drive home that she was indeed referring to him, "happens to be on the film crew."

"Coincidence? I don't know about that." He set his case down and began to set up his equipment. "But I do vow to do my best to perfectly capture your displays when I'm filming. Nothing but the best lighting for you, Jackie."

She eyed him up as if to assess the commitment level of his vow.

"You doubt me?" he asked in mock concern. Or at least a mixture of mock concern. Was she fucking with him or was she skeptical? Impossible to tell. How well did he really know her? Teenaged Jackie was likely to be at least a little different than adult Jackie – he knew he'd changed drastically since high school. A failed writing career and a failed marriage didn't mesh well with his previous optimistic and carefree attitude.

A smile eased across her face and as if she read his mind she said, "I'm fucking with you, Scott."

"I knew that." He shot her a smile then rummaged in his bag again. "You know, I'll request the same from you, too."

His hands deftly moved about the case arranging and connecting various parts as he spoke. He set up partly because he needed to, and partly because he got a little timid talking about his plans for the future and found it easier to discuss if he had something else to focus on.

"I'm hoping to get out to LA and want to use my footage here as part of my portfolio to get my foot in the door with a production team. Either that or follow Lana again to whatever she finds next."

A few more adjustments to the camera and he was ready for the next step.

"Alright, Jackie. Ready to mic up?" he asked as he held out a small mic on a clip along with the transmitter which was a black electronic box the size of a deck of cards.

"This is your lavalier microphone, and this is the transmitter. The mic pins to your shirt, close to your mouth is preferable so it can pick up everything you say, and the transmitter we can attach to your belt or the top of your pants."

He walked towards her with the mic and transmitter, and her large brown eyes beamed as if she couldn't believe it was all really happening. That she was going to be a part of the documentary and it wasn't all some crazy dream.

"I'm ready," she breathed. "Whatever you guys need, I'm on it."

"Then let's do it. Do you mind?" he asked in reference to the mic as he approached. His nerves were getting the best of him. The mic clip and transmitter were already sweaty in his hands, and he couldn't bear to hand them to her and see her cringe in disgust as she wiped the excess moisture off. Would she really do that? Probably not. But he wouldn't blame her if she did, and he didn't want to chance it.

"Not at all." She pushed her hair back behind her ears and tilted her head high to give him as much room as possible.

"Easy, tiger," he chuckled at her eagerness. "I don't need *that* much room for this tiny clip."

"Oh, right." Jackie gave a little laugh as she dropped her

head back down to her normal position which happened to place her mouth just a few inches from his own. Not that he'd noticed. Much. Scott had mic'd up plenty of people over his short career as a cameraman, but being in Jackie's personal space left his fingers clumsy and unable to properly function.

What normally took him a few seconds took considerably longer. He tried a few, what he hoped were nonchalant, deep breaths to calm down, but that only resulted in his nostrils filling with her soft, sweet coconut scent which left him mildly light-headed and no more relaxed than when he'd started. Scott cleared his throat and gave a quick prayer to someone, anyone, that his mouth still worked and his words wouldn't crack like some prepubescent teenager.

"In a minute I'll show you how to put it on so you can do it yourself from now on. I'll be leaving it here with you so I can swing by with the camera as needed without worrying about if you're mic'd or not. Lana's already changed Lizzy over to camera work, too. Without the boom mic, we'll need everyone mic'd."

"Why'd she move Lizzy to camera work?"

"Even Lana's doing some camera work too, I think. Whole thing is a bit more than she'd realized. Not enough cameras going to film everything she wants to film."

Fuck! his mind screamed as his fingers slipped once again and the clip slammed shut on itself instead of her collar.

"Is that a good thing or a bad thing in terms of pitching the documentary?" Like a pro, Jackie was focused on work and unmoved by the fact that he was in her personal space and, given his occasional stooped posture to mic her, practically having the conversation with her boobs.

"Neither?" His fingers slipped yet again. He wiped them on his jeans to dry them off before trying again. "Maybe good since there's a lot of material?" he guessed. Not only could he not think clearly, he also hadn't really thought about it like that. Whether or not he would still be working with Jackie had been his top concern. Mercifully, the clip finally snapped shut onto the top portion of her blouse and he was ready to go.

"Now, check out how this looks in the mirror here." With his hands on her upper arms, he guided her a few feet to the side and turned her towards the mirror while he stood behind her and pointed to the tiny mic on her collar.

"I wanted to start by showing you the wrong way to mic up. See how this wire is hanging down the front of your shirt? We don't want that. It could catch on something and in general it looks sloppy. It takes away from the documentary since it tells the audience you know you're being filmed."

"But I *do* know I'm being filmed," she challenged with a half-smile. Was she flirting with him?

He gave a light laugh in case she was, but he also wanted to give her an answer in case she wasn't. "I know, and so does the audience. But just like in a movie when you suspend disbelief, people do that with documentaries, too. We believe we're watching something totally natural even though we know at the heart of it no one can *act* completely natural when there's a camera on them."

"Right. That makes sense."

Not flirting, she just had a genuine question. Damn.

He started to undo the clip to show her the correct way to set up the mic while still in front of the mirror so she could clearly see what he was doing. Unfortunately, he'd overestimated his ability to function in front of such a beautiful and intimidating woman while trying to watch himself in the mirror.

"I don't think I can do this from behind you. But I still want you to see in the mirror here what I'm doing..." He moved around to stand in front of her and face her as he

23

worked. The purpose of him stooping down slightly and moving off to one side was for her to still see what he was doing even though he was between her and the mirror. He hoped she knew that and didn't think he was eye-level with her left boob, yet again, because he was a pervert. Though honestly it did feel debatable that morning given his inability to focus on anything beyond how badly he wanted to run his fingers through her hair while enjoying what he was sure would be the deepest and most intimate kiss of his life.

He cleared his throat again as if that would in any way help to clear his base thoughts of him and her together doing naughty things and wearing limited amounts of clothing.

"To hide the wire," he somehow continued, "you can loop it like this through the clip so that the clip guides the wire down behind your clothing." His thumb grazed against her collar bone as he worked, and he could have sworn he heard an almost inaudible sigh from her. Or maybe it was a sigh out of annoyance because she could tell he was struggling and that it was taking longer than it should.

Scott couldn't remember the last time he'd been so nervous and unsure around a woman. As much as he found it unnerving, it was also deliciously addictive. It gave him the sense of being alive in a way he hadn't felt in years.

"That is harder than it looks," she laughed. Her hands fumbled around his as she tried to get the mic from him while watching herself in the mirror. Maybe it was a nervous laugh since she too felt the intense chemistry between them?

"Okay, I think I've got it now. Let me take it off and try it on my own."

Scott stepped away to give her space to work and to admire her in general. After a few tries, Jackie formed a nice loop that expertly caught in the clip and then she guided the falling wire down the inside of her shirt just like he'd shown her. The end of the wire dangled in front of her belt buckle and the zipper of her pants.

"Perfect," he said. He held up the transmitter for her to see. "This has a hole at the top where your wire connects." He connected the wire to the transmitter. "And a clip on the back to hang comfortably on your belt or waistband, like this." Scott lifted the bottom of her shirt up just enough to get to her belt. Again, his hand brushed against the skin right above her pants. Once it was secure, Scott noticed she was blushing and took a few steps away from her.

"Sorry. You probably could have done that one on your own."

"It's fine. First times can be hard." Was that a reference to their first time together? Adorably, the slight cringe on her face led him to think she was feeling as awkward and clumsy as he was.

The night before, Scott had wanted to ask Jackie out for drinks, but the moment never seemed right. The evening had been busy with lots to get through to be sure they'd have a solid start to their documentary.

There, in her living room as they finished getting ready for the meeting, he felt his chance slipping away again. His mind vacillated between all of the reasons they shouldn't: Lana explicitly forbid any hanky-panky between documentary workers and those being filmed for the documentary, he was still thoroughly messed up from his divorce, and she was probably in a serious relationship with some giant buff model-looking dude who was fluent in Italian. There were more but the longer he thought about it the more outlandish (but were they *really* that outlandish?) his ideas became. Before the moment could slip away, he went for it regardless of everything his mind was telling him.

"Let's grab a beer after we're done here. You can tell me more about what you've been up to since high school."

"Yeah, that sounds good. You ready to go?" she asked as picked up her binder, a notepad, and a pen.

He hoisted up his camera and hid behind it to cover up the ridiculous smile that he knew took over his entire face.

"Let's do it."

JACKIE

*T*hat evening, Jackie and Scott were nestled into a booth at The Cut and Run, a restaurant and bar a few blocks from Jackie's house. Earlier in the day she'd meant to eat lunch right after her meeting with Tim, but she'd felt the pressure of the neighborhood's expectations weighing on her and instead dove further into her planning. By the time she'd made it to the bar to meet Scott, she was famished.

"I'll get the California roll, and a beer. Flying Dog," Jackie told the waiter.

Scott ordered a burger, medium-well done, and a beer. He then gave Jackie a concerned look after the waiter left their table.

"Sushi? Here? Are you trying to get food poisoning?" he asked with one eyebrow cocked impressively high on his face.

"It's fine," she laughed. "California rolls aren't even raw and I'm starving. Besides, we're on the water. I'm not ordering sushi from some restaurant in a landlocked state."

He nodded his fake approval. "Makes sense. You think

27

because we're on the water that Bruno over there," Scott said pointing to one of the bartenders whose name tag did indeed say Bruno, "got up early this morning, caught some wild tuna from the Chesapeake Bay, and then expertly filleted it for their sushi special this evening."

"California roll has imitation crab meat. Not tuna. I'm also pretty sure you can't catch tuna in the bay."

He made a face of mock disgust. "Even worse. You're eating imitation crab in Maryland." He moved the large stand that held the drink specials for the night over to the end of the booth as if he could hide behind it. "I don't want anyone I know to see me with someone eating *imitation* crab meat."

"You're a food snob," she countered. She'd remembered having similar flirty banter back in their high school days in English class. Even though over a decade had passed, she suddenly felt like a teenager again sitting with him in the booth. Except this time instead of wondering what it would be like to kiss him, she was wondering what it would be like to have his now muscular body pressed up against hers as his rough, calloused fingers explored every inch of her bare skin before slinging into...*Nope. Inappropriate. Get back to the witty banter and get your mind out of the gutter,* she told herself.

"I'm *not* a food snob," he defended. "Any sane person will tell you ordering *sushi* from a suspect restaurant, nay, more of a bar, really, like The Cut and Run is risking near-death illness." He moved the specials stand back against the wall.

"Good thing I didn't order the raw fish then." Their eyes locked during the brief pause in their conversation. Their intimate, but way too brief stare down, was interrupted when the waiter returned with their drinks.

They each gave a quick thank you to the waiter and Scott raised his glass up to toast. Like a heathen, she'd almost taken a drink before she'd noticed.

"To old friends," he said.

"To old friends."

They clinked glasses and each took a drink. While he looked lax and at ease as he drank, her mind raced with all the conflicting thoughts circling around one main question: If they'd just toasted to friendship, was there any hope that this could be a date? Did he really *just* want to have a drink with an old friend? Not that dating Scott was even an option for her. She was going to spend the next few months locked in her house with her plans and lights while he was going to spend his time behind his camera. No time for romance, or sex even. Sad. But then he'd leave and life would go back to normal for her, sans heartbreak, as long as she kept ignoring any and all feelings she had for him.

Before she could get too lost in her thoughts, he set his glass down and said, "From what I remember about you in high school, you were artistic, somewhat athletic – I think you were on the softball team? – and intimidatingly smart." *Holy shit,* Jackie thought, *Scott knew me beyond our one shared class.* "I want to say AP Chemistry or something insane like that." *He knew – and remembers now? – what science class I took?!*

In a cool tone Jackie didn't even know she was capable of using in Scott's presence, *thank you, Flying Dogfish beer,* Jackie responded, "Close. I did take art, but I was on the field hockey team, not softball. And yes, I took AP Chem."

"And since high school? Did you become an artist? Are you coaching field hockey somewhere? Have you discovered any new elements to add to the periodic table?"

The conversation tipped back into flirting again. Was this his attempt at playful banter? Much like she thought Tim had been hitting on her, she had trouble distinguishing between friendly and flirty. On more than one occasion she'd nerved herself up to ask someone out only to find they had zero interest in her and were merely being polite. Each time the poor guy had rejected her with a heaping amount of pity in his eyes and written all over his face. Their expressions lamented, "Poor woman can't read a situation to save her life."

Regardless of his intentions and her qualms about dating him, whatever was happening between her and Scott at The Cut and Run, she was there for it. "Nothing quite as exciting as all of that," she said with a bit too much batting of her eyelashes. *Just be confident and flirty while making it look effortless*, her thoughts instructed as if it were possible for her to do so, and she just hadn't considered it up until that moment.

"Some artwork, I suppose. Right before I moved back to Milton, I did some interior design work in Philly. Nothing you would have seen or heard about. Very low-key. I left field hockey behind as soon as I left high school. And all the naturally occurring elements in nature had already been discovered a few decades before we were even in chemistry class."

"Did they teach us that in high school?" Scott asked with a sheepish look on his face.

"Probably, though I don't remember much about high school chemistry. Most of my chem knowledge comes from my under-grad degree in organic chemistry from John's Hopkins. After that I spent a few years in the research and development lab of a pharmaceutical company. In the end, I hated the work and the work environment. It just wasn't for me. What about you?"

The strong beer on her empty stomach sent a stream of bliss straight to her head. That, on top of Scott's face which showed nothing but admiration, caused her to get light-headed. He was impressed by her. The night could end right there and she'd still be on cloud nine.

"No way. I'm not following that," Scott said with a laugh.

"Oh, come on. It sounds impressive, but it's not as if I did anything with it. I'm working the front desk at some local marina. My friend Cici in high school had the same job as a teenager."

Their waiter appeared with their food and fresh drinks. As Jackie used a fork to eat her California roll – they didn't have chopsticks – Scott mimicked concentrated concern as if she could keel over at any point from some fatal food poisoning.

"It's fine," Jackie said with a laugh. "Now, you really won't tell me?"

Scott shook his head no as he slathered his burger in ketchup.

"Okay. I'll guess. Let's see what *I* remember about *you* from high school." Jackie pretended to think about it. She knew almost everything about Scott from high school. He was her high school crush. The only reason she went to school some days. But what could she say that would sound nonchalant as if she hadn't been stalking him for those four, glorious years?

"You played the drums in the marching band, right?"

"Snare. Yes. Although to be honest I only did that to get closer to Rachel something or other." He chuckled. "Strange, I can't even remember her last name now."

It was Rachel Cassell. She'd been a few years ahead of them and a goddess around school. She was also still in town, still single, and still very attractive. Best to move on and let him continue to forget about Rachel.

"You're not a famous celebrity drummer now? That's surprising." She tapped her pointer finger against her temple to help drive home how much of her mental capacity she was using as she attempted to remember. "Okay...you were in yearbook, weren't you? So maybe you're a writer now?"

"Not yearbook. A reporter for the school paper. And no, I haven't written any novels or published any articles."

"Yet or you never will?" She had fond memories of

reading his exposés on the myriad of banal high school topics: Will Milton High ever have a female football player? Why are the sophomores petitioning for a dress code and is it a possibility?

But her favorite piece of his writing came from an English class assignment. They'd each had to write an original poem and then critique with the person sitting next to them. In her case, Scott. He'd overachieved with a well-written villanelle about insomnia, while she wrote a mediocre haiku about painting. Even in high school she could tell he was talented. At the time she'd been convinced he'd end up in a band, writing the songs that would make them world famous. It hadn't surprised her to hear he was skipping summer break to attend a writer's class a few weeks after graduation.

"You think I can write a novel?" he asked. His tone was so sincere that she couldn't help but believe he would take her answer to heart.

"Yes," she'd said with way too much confidence. In an effort to reign it back in she added, "I'm assuming you could. I don't know you that well, Scott." So many lies. "That's why I'm asking." Jackie smiled at their conversation as it seemed to spill into the type of discussion most people would have on a date. It probably wasn't a date. But if everything about their evening together resembled a date, perhaps it would end like one, too. Her eyes fell to his soft lips for a few glorious seconds before she forced them back up to his eyes.

"True," he conceded. "Okay. I'm going to blame the beer on a mostly empty stomach for this one, but, I'll tell you. I graduated from Arkansas Tech with my bachelor's in creative writing. My beyond supportive and patient parents offered one year's rent and minimal expenses while I focused on writing my novel. It was...awful. I made it all of six months before I started looking for a backup plan."

Scott chuckled as he spoke, but Jackie could sense a sadness behind it.

"I thought I wanted to be a writer, but it was a miserable existence." He looked out into the bar as if he wanted to look anywhere but at her and he finished the rest of his beer.

"I get it," she offered. "Sometimes you don't know until you try it." It was easy for her to understand since she'd felt the same way about working in R and D. Some people loved it, but it wasn't the right fit for her. And just like Scott, she usually didn't tell people that. In a way it made her feel like a failure to work her way through school only to find she'd hated the career she'd chosen.

There was a comfortable silence as they both took in their ever-changing surroundings. When they'd first sat down it had had more of a restaurant vibe to it. Since then, the lights had dimmed, the waiters had started closing out their tables for the night, and the volume of the music turned up to something resembling a club.

"Looks like we both spent a fortune on degrees we'll never use," Scott said.

"Cheers to that," She raised what was left of her beer to his empty glass.

The waiter returned one final time to close out the tab. Jackie insisted on paying her half and then wondered why the fuck she hadn't let Scott pay when she wanted so badly for their night to turn into a date.

With the tab settled and out of the way, they chatted for a bit about how they'd both ended up back in Milton and where they'd been during the in-between time of high school and their recent return. She was dying to ask about the random photos he'd posted the past few years on Facebook– how does one even become a scuba diver in the shark tank at Mandalay Bay? – but she didn't dare tip her hand that she'd been keeping tabs on him.

"Any marriages?" he asked.

"No," she said in the same tone she would have answered if he'd asked her if she'd murdered anyone lately. It's not that it was an outrageous idea. She was in her late twenties. Plenty of her friends were married with kids. It only seemed like an unreachable goal for her because she'd never dated anyone for more than a few months. Jackie knew she was not the marrying type and was thrown off guard a bit when anyone assumed otherwise.

"Have *you* been married?" She knew he never got married. She asked only because social mores insisted she ask.

"Once. We split a while back." Her eyes landed on his left hand. He said they'd broken up a while ago, but she still checked for any signs of a ring. None.

It took Jackie a few long seconds before she got over her shock and could offer up a response that was appropriate for the given situation.

"I'm so sorry, Scott. I didn't realize…"

"You couldn't have known," he said with a hand waving off and dismissing her apology. He looked down into his empty glass.

"Do you want to talk about it?" she offered. She herself was torn about the whole thing. On the one hand she was fascinated about this portion of his life she was completely unaware of. What kind of woman won over Scott Davis? And what kind of woman would then allow him to get away? On the other hand, she was blindingly jealous of this stranger who didn't even have Scott anymore.

"No, I don't want to talk about it. Thanks, though."

"Okay. But I'm here if you ever do. Want to talk."

He nodded.

Shit, find something else to talk about, or he's going to leave.

"I forgot to ask how your afternoon with Tim and Lana

went. Reflection room all ready to go?" Once he'd left Jackie's meeting, he'd had to film a few other neighbors before heading over to Tim's to set up the reflection room in the garage.

"Working with Tim and Lana was...intense."

"I can see that. Tim with the decorating and Lana planning out the logistics. The two of them together are a force to be reckoned with, I'm sure. Though I bet it was nothing but merry and bright perfection once they'd finished."

"It is."

She took a sip of her beer and they both sat lost in thought for a moment.

"It was a bit...weird, too," he added.

"Well, yeah. It's Tim and Lana."

"No, not like that. It was weird because I kind of felt like a third wheel."

"What?" Jackie snorted an unexpected laugh.

"Did you just snort?" Scott asked, his eyes as wide as the smile on his face.

Jackie's mouth went tight-lipped. "Don't change the subject. Is there something going on between Tim and Lana? Should we be calling them Tana or Lanim?"

Scott put his hands up. "I don't know for sure. I'm just saying there was a lot of touching and giggling for two over-achievers who should have been focused on setting up something as important as the reflection room."

"I can't picture it. I don't know them that well, but flirting at work doesn't sound like them."

"I agree. I've known Lana for years and I've only seen her relax a handful of times. But I also know flirting when I see it."

"Do you?" Jackie teased as she downed the last of her beer.

Scott narrowed his eyes at her. "It's like that, huh? Let's

35

get another round and I'll prove to you, beyond a doubt, something's going on with them."

She waited a few excruciating beats so as not to appear too eager at his offer of another round of drinks before accepting his challenge.

When Scott went up to order their drinks, the bartender flicked her long blonde hair one too many times for Jackie's comfort. To his credit, Scott appeared to be immune as he grabbed their beers and returned with the booze along with a gorgeous smile.

"Thank you." She intentionally brushed her hand against his in the beer hand-off.

"My pleasure." He sat back down, oblivious to her intentional touch, and began his speech on the ins and outs of how to spot flirting. "We were all working together in the garage for about an hour or so. I would say the last half hour though was rife with sexual tension."

Jackie gave him an incredulous look. Not only was he incapable of noticing any of her flirting, but he also completely missed the bartender's advances, too.

"I'm telling you; I could have cut it with a knife." Her expression remained so he said, "Okay, let me think for a minute how to describe it."

Scott looked down into his pint glass as if he could see scenes from the reflection room set-up playing out within the contents of the glass. With his attention focused on his drink and his memory, Jackie took the opportunity to shamelessly take him in. She wondered what his short hair would feel like as she raked her fingers through it, and if his toned abs would contract and tense at her touch in anticipation of her fingers reaching down below his belt. His tongue licked his lips as he thought, and she wondered how it would feel moving over the most sensitive parts of her body. It had been so long and they'd both been just teenagers for that one night they were together.

.

"Alright. I guess I need to start back when Lana and I were in Florida for our last documentary. She and I were eating lunch one day and I was scrolling through my Twitter feed. It's mostly full of work stuff, but I also follow random people and groups on there, too, like Milton."

Jackie gave a small chuckle. "We have a Twitter account? Who's running it?" Jackie wasn't on Twitter herself, but the whole thing seemed too modern for the sleepy, traditional, small town of Milton.

"Who do you think?"

"Tim?"

"Exactly. Mr. Christmas Lights Lane is Milton's biggest cheerleader in all categories, not just Christmas. I'm assuming that it's part of an effort to get the word out about the event in general. And maybe to help him sell houses. Did you know he's a real estate agent?"

The waiter had closed out the tab but left their plates, so Scott continued to randomly munch on his left-over fries as they talked and drank. She joined him after he slid his plate towards her as an offer to share. No words. It was like they were already so close that they were sharing the food on their plates like it were second nature and expected.

"I should have known it would be Tim. Though I didn't know he was a real estate agent. Makes sense since he'd need a flexible job to run the lights event." She grabbed another fry off the plate and dipped it into his ketchup before she realized she may have taken their food sharing to another level. But he didn't seem to notice or mind.

"Anyway, continue with your story. Sorry I interrupted."

"You didn't interrupt," he said with a reassuring grin. "So, Lana sees a post from Tim and starts asking me about it. Then she starts following Tim and reaching out to him about the event. And for the next two weeks, I swear I could always tell when she was getting or sending a message to Tim. She had a slight smile as she typed out responses on her phone."

Jackie had to interrupt again. "A *slight*," she raised her hands up to put air quotes around the word slight, "smile is nothing. She was probably happy to have a new documentary subject to work on. It was a career smile, not a flirty smile." Her confidence in her opinion surprised even herself given she knew next to nothing about Lana or Tim.

Scott shook his head. "Nope. I know Lana's smiles. Mainly because she rarely does it and since she is, 99% of the time, a robot devoid of emotion."

"Why is that?"

"I'm not sure. Maybe a combination of some sort of tragic past and a strong determination to keep her social life away from her work life?" He shrugged and then pointed to the last fry as a question of whether she wanted it or not. She did, but it was already so sweet of him to share that she wouldn't dare take the last one. After she declined, he popped the fry into his mouth and carefully stacked their plates to place at the end of their table.

"But my point in mentioning any of this," he continued, "is that I've thought for a while there was something going on between them – at least on Lana's end. And in the garage last night I'm pretty sure I confirmed my suspicions. They kept it professional for the first thirty minutes or so. But then at one point, Lana was helping to move some of Tim's old fishing stuff out of the space where we were setting up and she got herself completely tangled up in the fishing line. Her hands, the buttons on her shirt, her earrings. I don't even know how she did it, but it was a mess."

"Sounds very sexy," Jackie said in a mock serious tone.

"*I* did not think so, but Tim's a fishing kind of guy so maybe having someone snared in his line *is* sexy to him. I don't know. I offered to help her, and I swear," he said as he held up a hand like a witness in a courtroom, "Tim practically checked me into the wall in an effort to get there first."

"No way…" Jackie imagined the man in a Christmas vest and Rudolph tie charging at Scott as he tried to stake his claim on his prey.

"I said *practically checked*, and I know what I saw," he insisted.

"Okay. Let's say that's what happened. Carry on. What happened next?" Things were getting interesting in the story, and between her and Scott. She knew her face had the goofiest grin on it, but his did too, so with a bit of help from the beer she accepted it and let herself get caught up in the moment.

Scott put his beer down and laid his rough, calloused hands on the table between them. "Here. Give me your hands."

Jackie put down her beer as well and braced herself for the feeling of those perfect hands on hers. But as soon as she placed her hands in his, he started to move and pose her so that her fingers all pointed towards the ceiling and were spread apart. To anyone else in the bar it looked as if she was waiting for him to high-five her with both hands.

"In order to adequately show you this next part, we're going to role play."

"Kinky," Jackie said before she could stop herself.

He laughed as a deep red covered his face and then he continued, "You're Lana all tangled in line, and I'm Tim. I start here, with your pinky. And because I'm Tim, I have no boundaries." Jackie giggled at their shared observation. "And I'm right in there as if I can't see further than an inch or two in front of my face." He mimicked it and Jackie was again giggling as he investigated her fingers up-close.

With her hands still in his, Jackie shook her head in

disagreement. "You already killed your argument by acknowledging that's just Tim's awkward self. He's not flirting." She didn't bring up the fact that she too had already questioned if he'd been flirting with her since embarrassingly the answer was no. Tim had not been flirting with her.

"I'm just getting started. As he's untangling her, only one of his hands is working while his other hand, his thumb in particular, is massaging her other hand, like this."

His eyes never left hers as he pretended to untangle non-existent line with one hand while the thumb of his other hand formed slow, lazy circles along the back of her hand. No, that's incorrect. His eyes did leave hers for a split second as they darted down to her lips before jumping back to her eyes as if they'd never left.

No longer laughing, Jackie admitted, "This feels pretty intimate." Her eyes remained locked on his even though much of her focus was on his lingering hand which continued to massage hers.

"Exactly," Scott breathed. After clearing his throat, he continued. "Once Tim successfully extricated her hands from the line, he moved on to the section that was caught in her earrings."

He let go of her hands and asked, "Will you humor me?"

Lacking the ability to speak at that moment, Jackie nodded back.

"Stand up for a second, please. It's difficult to demonstrate this one with the table between us."

Once they were both standing, Scott said, "We've already acknowledged that Tim's a close talker. So even before he's helping her, he's already standing like this." Scott moved closer to her so that their bodies were almost touching. Even with the strange smells that filled the bar, she could pick out his fresh linen and citrus scent. She wondered if he'd taken the time to go home and shower before meeting her.

"And then Tim leans in like this." Scott leaned down and forward so that if Jackie moved at all their cheeks would be touching. He began again but this time he was whispering in her ear in a husky voice. "While Tim was unhooking her earring – which must have been quite entangled because it took a really...long...time for him to finally free her – he whispered in her ear making her giggle like a smitten schoolgirl."

The tickle from his stubble and the feel of his breath on her ear and neck caused a little giggle to escape Jackie.

"Just like that," Scott whispered into her ear. Then he pulled away with a smirk on his face and sat back down in the booth, reaching for his beer. "I'm right, aren't I? There's something going on between them."

"Yeah, totally," Jackie said as she finally exhaled and joined him back at the booth. How was he able to turn it off that quickly and fall right back into the booth and their conversation as if they hadn't almost fucked in the middle of the bar?

Jackie took his lack of reaction as a sign of defeat. Because while she felt like she almost mounted him on their table, it seemed he'd felt no effects from the role-play whatsoever. It was not a date. Scott was not interested in her. He was telling a story and he was an animated storyteller. She figured that made sense, after all, since he is part of a documentary crew that was literally telling a story using visuals.

"I will say that I'm surprised, though, because Lana gave Lizzy and me a long, drawn-out speech about how we shouldn't get too involved with anyone in the documentary."

"Why not?" Her mind still felt a bit sluggish coming down from the rush of being so close to him and hearing his deep voice whispering into her ear.

"She doesn't want anything to get in the way of our work," he said with a shrug.

41

"Oh." She took in every detail of his response knowing she would want to analyze it later to try to pinpoint how he personally felt about getting involved and if he thought it would interfere. She could flat-out ask him and get her answer immediately, but she hadn't had enough beer yet for that kind of courage.

Instead, she asked him about the other documentaries he'd filmed. Maybe he'd divulge on his own if he'd ever mixed pleasure with work.

"I did one in Vegas." He picked at the label on his beer. "It was backed by the Vegas Tourism Visitor Authority or something like that. Whoever is in charge of tourism there. I think portions of it still play in various hotels and airport lounges."

"That sounds interesting."

"It wasn't. That was my first documentary with Lana. She and I also did one at a nursing home down in Florida which was the last one we did before this. That one was very interesting – though a bit sad at times, too."

Jackie knew it was customary for her to ask more about it, but she didn't want to discuss anything sad. Maybe it was selfish on her part, but the night was going so well. She didn't want to chance a change in the mood.

"This is your big break then? Hopefully?"

"Hopefully. As long as Lana keeps her head in the game and doesn't let whatever's happening with her and Tim distract her."

Jackie wasn't sure how to respond to that. She sipped her beer and nodded her head. She'd wanted to know how Scott felt about dating while creating a documentary with someone. Turned out he thought it inevitably led to issues at work and was too distracting. Damn.

"Though I guess whatever is happening is working out just fine so far." Scott pulled his phone out of his pocket and gave a couple taps on the screen. "Check out the finished reflection room."

Or maybe not…

He extended his phone out for her to see. The screen showed a small corner of a room with red and white striped walls, lights hanging down from the ceiling, a small elegantly decorated fake Christmas tree that could have been done by Martha Stuart, and an oversized green chair. It looked like a mini winter wonderland. Anyone else seeing it would never have been able to guess it was part of a garage.

The image was on his Twitter account, and she noticed it already had a few hundred likes. "You got a few hundred likes in the past few hours?" she asked. She had attempted to get her own name out there by using Instagram regularly for the past few years. Up until she saw Scott's numbers, she'd been pleased to have amassed 328 followers in that time. Scott must have been well beyond that to have so many likes on one photo in such a short amount of time. She was more than impressed with his social media usage and kicked herself for not looking for him anywhere besides Facebook and Instagram during her previous online stalking sessions.

He shrugged. "It's just something I do for Lana to help spread the word about the documentary. Build up the hype before we start officially pitching it."

"May I?" Jackie asked motioning towards the phone. She would undoubtably create a bogus Twitter account as soon as she had the time so she could more thoroughly get a look at the past few years of Scott's life. In the meantime, she wanted a quick preview.

He could fill a gallery given the quality and quantity of pictures he posted online. It was entirely possible the followers he did have had no interest in any of his documentaries and simply followed him because they enjoyed his captivating photos alone – without any story or reasoning behind them.

Scrolling back up to the top before handing it back to him, she noticed a photo of the side of her house that made her pause. Leaning against the siding was an old-school sled, a wooden Flexible Flyer, which was the focus of the photo. Unused for a decade or two, vines had started to overtake it as they wove their arms in, out, and around the various parts of the sled as if reclaiming the wood. Above the photo was the words, *Ivy League*, with a few various hashtags mentioning the town and the upcoming event.

She looked back up to him and said, "You're really talented."

One side of his mouth turned up into a slight smile as if he was suddenly bashful and unsure of how to accept her compliment.

"Thanks." He took his phone back and shoved it into his pocket. They chatted a bit more about the event in general before the conversation began to die out. A few seconds of silence followed before he said, "Anyway, we should head home. Long day of filming tomorrow."

"Yeah, me, too." She smiled and then blushed with embarrassment. "I mean I have a lot to do. I won't be filming anyone."

"Let me get the tab for the drinks – I insist," he added as Jackie began to get up. This time she didn't try to stop him.

From the booth Jackie finished her beer and stole a few glances at Scott while he was at the bar paying. While he waited for a free bartender, she started plotting out what she'd say as he walked her home. Her tipsy mind was ready to overlook all the reasons she shouldn't make a move on Scott: she didn't want to get involved with anyone while she was bogged down with event preparation; she didn't want to potentially mess up the documentary if they did hook up and it ended badly; and Scott had just told her Lana, his boss, forbid him to get involved with anyone in the documentary. Not to mention that she still wasn't completely sure he was even interested in her. And yet all the reasons she'd reminded herself of each time she saw him just didn't seem that important once alcohol blurred her judgment.

But she had to put all thoughts of dating Scott to rest yet again when she saw the blonde bartender (where was Bruno when you needed him?) slip her number on a cocktail napkin to Scott who happily accepted it and tucked it into his back pocket.

It was mildly immature to not give him a proper goodbye, but she was mildly drunk, so she gathered her things and slipped out the door with only a quick goodbye wave to Scott as he signed the receipt. At the time he'd seemed dismayed at her unexpected exit. But as she walked by the window, she saw he remained at the bar to chat with the bartender rather than go after her to walk her home.

That was fine. She needed to sleep off the booze. She needed to put in a full eight-hour shift of work each day and then spend each evening and night starting to build her giant aquarium to fill the bay window on her first floor. She had major goals to achieve, and it was best that nothing distracted her along the way.

SCOTT

*H*e'd laid it on thick with Jackie at The Cut and Run. Layer after layer of flirting: the touching, whispering, laughing. And she'd mocked *him* for not being able to spot flirting! Or maybe that was the problem – she did pick up on his flirting just fine, but she wanted nothing to do with it. Why else would she dart out of the bar without even letting him walk her home? Without saying goodbye beyond a quick wave as she bolted out the door?

Sure, she *may* have gotten the wrong impression *if* she'd noticed him taking the bartender's phone number. But he was only being polite. It takes balls to give a phone number to someone. Also, he was terrible at everything related to rejection: either being rejected or rejecting someone else. Either way, he avoided it at all costs. Hence his reluctance to make a move on Jackie the night before. Though in his defense he would have found the courage on their way back to her house if she'd hung around and let him walk her home.

Even though he was feeling thoroughly rejected after

their night out, he was somehow still hopeful when she'd called the next day. Even if it was only a work-related call. The sudden optimism was throwing him for a loop. Ever since his divorce he'd been siding more with the people who claim true love was a myth and not worth the hassle. No one would have characterized him as optimistic in the ways of the heart.

"Hey, Scott. It's Jackie." Her voice came through the phone as confident as ever.

"Jackie, hey. How's it going?"

"Fine. A little slow at work, but I guess that's kinda nice in a way."

"Yeah. Slow at work can be good, sometimes." He cringed hearing the unoriginal, banal garbage coming out of his mouth. Along with rejection, phone calls were not his thing either. He was about to start filming at Tim's house – shouldn't even have answered the call, but he couldn't resist hearing whatever it was she had to say. He made a motion to Tim to give him a minute and Tim gave a thumbs up back as he walked into his kitchen to give Scott space.

"Tim knows I'm working on my tank this week and he asked me to schedule a few days with you to film it."

Scott had been kneeling at his case. He stood up to pace as he talked. "Okay. Can you give me some dates and details about what to expect?"

"Yeah, sure. After a bit of research, I've changed up my plans to two long tanks with one above the other which means I need shelves, too. I'm running around a bit this evening gathering materials. I'm thinking tomorrow would probably be better to film."

"Tomorrow works." He would have made any day work for her. "And you're going to all of that? The building and assembling?"

"Yes, Scott. Women are capable, too."

Shit. He always stuck his foot in his mouth on phone calls. It was no surprise he'd managed to insult her in record time.

"I didn't mean it like that. I'm not embarrassed to say that *I* am not capable. I'm impressed *anyone* can do it regardless of gender." He held his breath hoping that his explanation wasn't too sarcastic. Something he'd been working on with himself for a while. Occasional, scathing sarcasm was another unpleasant side-effect of his somewhat new, recently-divorced personality.

"Oh, right." Her voice relaxed which allowed him to relax a little as well. "Then I suppose I can admit I've conferenced with more than a few of my neighbors, and I had a very long conversation with one of the local Home Depot associates."

"I'd have to do the same, and then some."

She paused for a moment, and he wondered again if he'd done or said something else to offend or upset her. He had the feeling she was contemplating something. He really hated phone calls. Facial reactions and expressions were crucial for him during conversations.

Tim poked his head back into the living room and Scott held up his finger requesting yet another minute on the phone. He put his hand over the phone and down at his side as he lightly said, "It's Jackie. Scheduling times for the week." That Tim understood. He disappeared again to leave Scott to his work.

"My Mom has been at my house a lot lately," Jackie added. "She'll probably be there more often than not when you all are there filming."

"That's good." He wanted to put her at ease since she clearly sounded uncomfortable about it. As though it may be seen as a hardship for him or Lizzy that her mother would be there. "It makes it more interesting to have another person there to talk to and work with since you're not really supposed to interact with me at all – or with Lizzy when she's around."

"It will be interesting, that's for sure. Mom brings her cat, Tom, with her when she visits."

Scott rubbed the back of his neck as he tried to figure out the correct response to what she was trying to say. Nothing came to mind, so he improvised.

"I get it. Tom the cat. Tomcat. Clever."

She sighed. "It would be clever, except it's not a play on words. It's just Tom. As in my father, Tom."

"Huh…" he said, refusing to elaborate before hearing more about the situation.

"Dad died my junior year of college."

"Oh, shit. Jackie, I had no idea. I'm so sorry." How had he not known that? Social media had its flaws, but he really did need to be on it a bit more to keep up with everyone. He couldn't believe how much time had passed without him knowing. Poor Jackie. And there he was on the phone with her with what felt like an insurmountable void between them since he was unable to physically reach out to comfort her.

"Thanks. It's okay; it was a long time ago now. I'm fine." He imagined her pacing her house as well and using her hands in conversation even though it was a phone call. At that last comment he could see her flicking her wrist and hand as she dismissed his no-longer-needed concerns.

"But back then, Mom was devastated," she continued. "When a stray cat showed up at the house a month later, Mom insisted it was Dad's spirit trapped in cat form."

Jackie paused to allow Scott to comment. He did not comment. He could not comment. He said the wrong thing with normal, everyday conversations. But this – this whole scenario was way out of his league.

Luckily, she began talking again and bought him a bit

more time to better understand the situation and come up with a better response.

"She was a wreck. But when she had Tom the cat, she wasn't anymore. We couldn't tell if it was a healthy outlet for her grief or not, but it seemed cruel to argue with Mom about it."

"Okay," he said as a weak way to buy a few more seconds. In the end, he decided not to comment or weigh in on his opinion about the cat at all. "You're right. This sounds like it will be interesting. What time should I swing by?"

He could hear the relief in her voice when she asked, "Is five okay?"

"Five works."

"Good." Except it didn't sound final, so he let the conversation fall into a comfortable silence again as she organized her thoughts. She'd just told him about her father being reincarnated as a cat – what else could she possibly be holding back from saying?

"Since Mom's going to be here, she and I planned to have dinner together afterwards, too. I know you're probably busy and catching up with old friends and everything. But if you'd like to stay for dinner, we'd love to have you."

"Dinner with the lovely Jackie Strauss? How could I say no to that?" A huge grin spread across his face again and for once he was glad they were speaking on the phone so that she couldn't see how dopey he knew he looked.

They would be together a lot in the upcoming weeks and months, but most of that time he would be hiding behind a camera, and she would be working her ass off trying to earn herself her own DIY show. Any time they spent together outside of work, even if it was in the company of other people, was priceless.

"Wait. I don't want you to feel obligated to give me a yes

or no for dinner just yet. Please experience an hour or two with Mom and Tom before you commit to staying and breaking bread with them. I love them to death, but...I just want to make sure you know what you're getting into here."

"Okay. I understand. But know that I'm going to stay for dinner, even if I'm not officially confirming just yet." He was going for charming, but he was walking a fine line between endearing and overly eager, possibly even desperate.

Lucky for him it seemed she did find it charming as she gave a slight laugh and said, "Alright then. I'll see you tomorrow."

It was the perfect ending to their conversation and Scott hated to turn back to work, but that had been the whole reason for her call to begin with.

"Wait. Before I forget," he added, "don't *you* forget to do a reflection session or two this week. Definitely one before I see you and probably at least one during the week after I see you, too."

"Crap." He heard a muffled thud and wondered if it was the sound of her hand against her forehead. "Thanks for the reminder. I completely forgot. I'm not the last one, am I?" He could hear the concern in her voice and imagined her wincing as she waited for his answer.

"'Fraid so." He knew exactly how she felt and found himself empathetically wincing himself even though she couldn't see him. "But you're also one of the few people on the block who's not retired, and the *only* one who is starting this year's display from scratch. I'd say you have a good excuse."

She let out a deep breath. "Thanks, Scott. I'd better get to it. See you Tuesday."

. . .

Jackie said she would start working on the tanks at five. Scott texted that morning and asked if he could show up a little before that to make sure he didn't miss anything or get in the way of her starting on time. It wasn't absolutely necessary given how long he'd been in the game and how versed he was in setting up and taking down his equipment, but he couldn't pass up on a little extra time with Jackie without the camera between them.

When he arrived that evening it was exactly as he'd thought it would be. Similar to their night at The Cut and Run, conversation came easily. The casual mood left as soon as Jackie's mother arrived. It was the signal for him to hoist his camera up and the signal for Jackie to once again ignore Scott.

"Hi, Mom," Jackie greeted her with a hug.

"Jackie, sweetie. How are you?" But before Jackie could answer, the woman moved straight to Scott. "And you used to go to school with Jackie? How nice," she said into the camera since Scott was buried behind it.

Tom jumped from her arms and made himself at home as he rubbed up against Jackie's legs.

"Hi, Dad." She stooped down to pet him.

Clearly this would not be making it into the documentary, so Scott put his hand out, poked his head out from behind the camera, and said, "Yes, ma'am. I'm Scott. Nice to meet you."

"Call me Babs, hon. Nice to meet you, too," she cooed as she shook his hand with both of hers. Her fingers were covered with large-jeweled rings and the tips had long nails painted a rich red-orange color. It was all very fitting given her eclectic outfit that he, with his lack of knowledge about anything fashion, couldn't even begin to describe. Everything was colorful and flowing and perfectly fitting based on what he knew about her so far.

"Mom, we're supposed to ignore Scott while he's shooting," Jackie said, her face wincing a bit at the harsh words. Babs looked distraught so she added, "It's fine. He understands. He's used to it."

Regardless, Babs's hands still holding his captive, she furrowed her brow in disapproval.

"But he's adorable. How can you ignore him?"

Had the camera not acted as his buffer, he was certain she would have reached out and pinched his cheeks. Scott blushed as he set his camera down and reached into his bag to get another mic. He couldn't tell what Lana would be looking for in this particular documentary, so he wanted to capture every possible sigh and breath hitch from everyone involved just in case. He figured it was as good a time as any to take a quick break and mic Babs up as well. Lana had given him an extra handful of mics; he might as well put them to good use.

"Mind if I mic you up, Babs? Your voice would probably have been picked up on Jackie's mic, but this way gives us the best sound quality."

"Yes, yes. Please. Check me out, Jackie. It's like I'm a movie star."

"It's glamorous alright," Jackie confirmed before pointing at Babs's bag and the leash hanging from it. "Is that leash for Dad?"

"It is. Now I can take him for walks." She was holding up the leash as if it were a trophy she'd won. "You know your father loves the outdoors and getting exercise and fresh air."

Scott worked to secure Babs's mic; a slightly tricky endeavor given that she was an animated talker who frequently gestured during conversations. Just like her daughter.

"And what's with the golf club?" Jackie asked, referring to the putter Babs had brought with her and set by the door.

"I can't stand going for walks. I've refused for years, but Tom's upped his complaints." He considered asking what Tom had been doing by way of complaining: Unruly and unrelenting meows? Clawing at the door? Hissing? Scratching? Pantomiming going for a walk as Babs was lounging on the couch watching tv?

Babs sighed, "I finally gave in. We go for walks now. Then I figured I'd better use this leash so people don't complain when I'm out in public. Some people will call the police if you have an unleashed pet. I've seen the cell phone videos of it. Have you seen the videos, Scott?"

He connected the mic to the transmitter. "I have seen them, Babs. Some nasty stuff out there. I think the leash is a great idea." She smiled at his praise and confirmation. Scott held up the transmitter. "Attach this to your belt or the top of your pants, usually on the side or back so it doesn't bother you when you sit, and you're good to go."

"Thanks, dear," she said as she connected the transmitter and hooked it onto her belt in the back.

"Yeah, I get the leash," Jackie said with nothing but patience in her voice. "But why do you have a golf club?"

"Juggling. I've started juggling while I walk to keep my agility up and to keep my boredom at bay. Tiger Woods does it. Did you know that?"

"I did not know that," Jackie said. "I didn't know anyone could juggle golf balls with a club." She looked to Scott for confirmation, but he'd already hoisted up the camera again and considered himself officially out of the conversation. It was a lonely job, sometimes.

Her mic attached and ready, Babs grabbed the club and effortlessly juggled a golf ball she'd produced from one of her pockets. *Tap, tap, tap.* There was a steady rhythm as she gently hit the putter against the ball.

Scott did his best to get it all on film – Babs was pretty

fast – even though he had serious doubts Lana would want any of it for the Christmas lights documentary. A shame it would be cut. He personally could watch the mother-daughter duo go back and forth all night.

"Pretty impressive, Mom," Jackie conceded with admiration in her voice. "Can any of the other girls do that?"

"Fran and Gilly are too busy with their adorable grandkids to waste time trying to perfect their technique. Millie's tried but she can't quite get the hang of it. I don't do it around them very often; no need to rub it in. I happen to enjoy the challenge of it and have the extra time, that's all."

"Well, feel free to brag in front of me. I think it's pretty amazing."

"Thanks, sweetie." Babs caught the ball mid-air and set it and the club down. "Now, let's focus on you and *your* talents. Tell me again what you're building tonight?"

Before Jackie could get through even the basics of her plans, her doorbell rang again sending Tom off into another room. When Jackie answered the door, Scott immediately recognized Sam, Jackie's best friend from high school.

"Hi!" Sam said to Jackie. "I was talking to Babs earlier today and she told me you were doing some filming for the documentary. Thought I'd swing by to see what's happening in person and maybe get my fifteen minutes of fame." She ran her hands through her thick, long blonde hair as she spoke and adjusted her clothing to make sure she was presentable. "Do a little name-dropping of the Smith vet clinic if you know what I mean." She poked her head into the house and looked around for evidence of camera crews.

"Subtle, Sam. Come on in." Jackie moved aside for her to enter.

"Scott," Sam said as she went straight for the cameraman. "It's been years. Didn't know you were back in town." Her wink and glance back at Jackie suggested she did indeed know he would be there.

He popped his head from behind his camera again and found Sam right in front of him with Jackie mouthing behind everyone, *I'm so sorry*, with a pained look on her face. If only she knew what he'd seen at the neighbors' houses already and in his job in general doing documentaries. It was refreshing in comparison to most of what he'd seen on tv and on social media – those carefully crafted and curated stories that showed only the best of everything. Documentaries were grittier: the good, the bad, and the ugly. Though in his opinion, when he saw Jackie's crew, he could see only a loving, though quirky, family. Nothing worthy of apologizing for on Jackie's end.

He gave Sam a hug as best he could with the camera still in his hand. "It's been too long, Sam. I'm only in town for the documentary. I'll be heading out again after New Year's."

"You guys can catch up during dinner, Sam," Babs offered. "Jackie said Scott is staying to eat with us."

Before Jackie could say anything, Sam clapped her hands together and said, "Perfect. I'll stay for dinner, too." Scott found yet another mic in his bag and got to work getting Sam set up.

Jackie had her hands on her hips and turned to Babs to ask, "This is everyone, isn't it? You didn't call up my old dentist and invite her over, did you?"

"Don't exaggerate, Jackie. Sam called me to follow up about Tom's FLUTD and I just happened to mention I'd be here with you and Scott tonight. Besides, it's not always about you. I enjoy seeing Sam outside of the clinic."

"What's a FLUTD? Is Tom okay?"

Scott noticed the playful annoyance drained from Jackie's tone as concern took over and she searched the room for the cat.

"It's the cat version of a urinary tract infection," Sam explained. Sam's father had been the town vet for as long as he could remember. Scott assumed she must have carried on the Smith vet tradition.

"It's my fault." Babs's previously bright and bubbly disposition turned morose within seconds. "You know how your father has a deep-seated aversion to moist food -"

"Eww, Mom. Please don't use that word."

"Fine. However you want me to say it." Like mother like daughter, Babs's hand fluttered in the air as if to shake off Jackie's issues with Babs's word choice. "He doesn't like wet food. Not as a cat and he didn't as a human, either. Always thought it was too mushy. A texture thing, I don't know. Now Sam's telling me that as he gets older it could be causing him to get kitty UTIs. It's my fault. I should have forced the canned food on him."

"Babs, you cannot blame yourself. We don't know for sure what caused it. Regardless, you noticed the signs and brought him in immediately. Ya did good," Sam said with a comforting side hug to Babs. Scott finished mic'ing Sam himself by slipping the transmitter clip into the waistband of her shorts. He hoped she didn't mind. They were in the middle of a serious conversation, and he didn't want to interrupt them or hold things up any longer than necessary.

Tom reappeared on the coffee table and trotted over to Jackie to be petted.

"Hey, Dad. Burns a little when you pee, huh? I've been there, too." Tom purred in appreciation of her commiseration.

Scott picked up his camera again. It was a lonesome feeling sometimes disappearing behind the camera and watching everyone else interact and carry on without him. He'd felt it on some level and to some degree each time he lifted the camera up. Sometimes, especially during disagreements between retirement home residents and their families, he was grateful to escape and become a wallflower. Lately that hadn't been the case. Since he'd arrived back at Milton he'd started to inch towards feelings of dread at the thought of easing out of the scene and back behind his camera. At least he had dinner to look forward to.

"Right," Jackie said, noticing the bright red light had once again appeared on the camera. "Let's get this started."

In the two hours that followed, Jackie transformed a pile of tools and wood into the basic frames for her tanks while chatting with Sam and Babs. Scott had been entranced the whole time. Jackie consulted some notes on measurements here and there, but mostly it was like she was on auto pilot and knew exactly what she needed to do. She was able to hear about Sam's dilemma at work – her father had recently hired a vet tech and Sam's convinced they are stealing from the clinic though she can't prove it – while effortlessly switching back and forth between drilling a pilot hole and driving a screw into the wood, at an angle, using a pocket hole tool. Not that Scott knew anything about that before Jackie explained it to her mother as she was setting up her tools.

By the time they'd all unmic'd and sat down for dinner, there were two, solid rectangular frames sitting on two temporary shelves in front of her bay window.

"Now, Scott," Babs said as she passed the dinner rolls to him after they'd all settled in at the table. "Why haven't you and I crossed paths before tonight?"

Jackie beat Scott with her reply. "We were just school friends, Mom. We didn't really hang out outside of school."

"Not usually, no," Scott added. "Though there was that one time during senior week..." He shot a smile at Jackie.

"Right. Aside from that." Jackie's face turned bright red. He'd simply meant that time they'd hung out together outside of school, but her mind must have immediately gone to the specific part of the night they'd spent on the balcony in the make-shift bed he'd made. That was promising. He wondered how many times Jackie had thought of that night since then.

Sam's eyes bulged and Scott could tell that Jackie had told her about it. All good things, he'd hoped. Though at the time he was only eighteen; he'd learned a few things since then.

Oblivious to it all, Babs said, "When Tom and I were at Milton the high school was much smaller than it is now. My graduating class was only a few dozen students, and my family knew all of them. Spent all of our birthday parties together through grade school and junior high. Nothing like it is now, I suppose."

"That sounds horrible, Babs," Sam said. "Knowing every person and moving through the grades with them? How did you break up with someone and successfully avoid them in school if they were in each of your classes?"

"You don't," Babs said flatly. "Speaking of dating," she added with what Scott was beginning to see was her usual positive energy, "are you seeing anyone now, Scott? I know like Jackie you've just moved back to town recently."

"Ugh, Mom," Jackie said as she let her head fall back in exaggerated annoyance. "I'm sure Scott's own parents are harassing him enough about his love life." She turned to Scott. "Do not feel obligated to go down this rabbit hole with her."

There was no way he was going to risk getting on Babs's bad side by refusing to answer her innocuous question about his current dating status, though he did appreciate Jackie's attempt to give him an out. It was comforting to think she knew him well enough to know he wouldn't want to discuss his love-life at the dinner table with someone he'd met only a few hours prior.

"Um, no. I'm not seeing anyone at the moment." He felt his face turn red which unfortunately made him blush even harder.

"Not even that cute bartender that slipped you her number the other day?" Jackie said with just a slight amount of sass in her tone.

Crap. She'd noticed that. But at least he knew for sure the reason she'd bolted from the restaurant so fast that night.

"Cute bartender? Tell me more," Babs said as if she were gossiping with her best girlfriends.

"Well, yeah. She gave me her number. And I accepted it because it felt rude not to. It takes a lot of guts to slide your number to someone like that. I couldn't slide it back to her." He looked at Jackie as he explained what happened and was pleased to find what he thought was a hint of a smile as she tried unsuccessfully to keep a straight face.

"Why weren't you interested?" Babs asked. "No personality? Bad breath? It's not her job, is it? Because you really need to be more open-minded if you're looking down on service industry workers."

Babs's pressure for more details as to why he wasn't interested caught him off-guard. He didn't mind admitting he didn't want to call her, but he had no intention of telling Jackie's mother that he didn't call because he was interested in her daughter instead. And saying he was interested in someone else, but not saying who wouldn't work either. He could tell that conversation would go south quickly.

"I don't think it's a good time for me to be seeing anyone. My work times are sporadic, and I'll just be moving again soon anyway." He finished the last of his drink and said, "I'm going to get some more tea. Anyone else need a refill?"

Was it blatantly obvious he was skirting her question and hoping Babs would move on to something else? His own immediate family, his mother and father since he had no siblings, was timid and private. No one would hound anyone about their love life and conversation remained on the pre-approved topics of weather, traffic, and the general aches and pains his parents gained year after year. Most of the sounds at their dinner tables consisted of the clatter of plates as they were set or cleared and the soft clanking of forks and knives hitting the plates as they ate.

Heads shook no in regard to Scott's refill offer. Babs said, "I'm good, but can you get Tom a dish of water? They're in the cabinet to the left of the fridge."

"Sure. I'll be right back." He moved about slowly in the kitchen to give them enough time to find something else to discuss. His pace quickened when he realized the new topic may be him in general, or in particular the night in Ocean City which had been mentioned but not thoroughly explored.

"Did Tom get any food?" Scott asked as he walked back into the dining room and placed the water dish on the table in front of the cat in Babs's lap.

"Yes, but he won't eat it. It's too moist." Babs ignored Jackie cringing next to her at the mention of moist again. "Tom's always been a stubborn, stubborn man."

There was a comfortable silence as Tom gently purred under Babs's magical touch. If he did understand her comment he wasn't acknowledging it in any way.

"Scott, did you know that I was listed as one of the top five psychics in Milton?" Babs asked apropos of nothing at all.

"No, I did not know that. I honestly didn't know there

were that many in the area." He was happy to have the change in topic and wanted to encourage Babs to elaborate.

"We're everywhere, Scott. Not all of us cheapen our gifts by hanging glowing tarot cards in our window and offering five-dollar readings."

"Easy, Babs," Sam said with a gentle, reassuring squeeze to Babs's arm. She turned to Scott. "There was an incident a few years back. A feud, if you will, between some of the psychics in the area. Still a bit of bad blood about it."

"I just want to make sure Scott understands I'm not one of those clairvoyants who's going to hit my knee on the table and pretend it's a dead relative trying to communicate from beyond the grave."

Before he could stop them, Scott's eyes darted down to Tom, Babs's dead husband reincarnated as a cat who happened to be sitting in Babs's lap, and then went right back to Babs's eyes again. "I would never think that about you," he said with as much sincerity as could.

"I'm legit, Scott."

"I believe you."

"I'm glad you trust me, Scott. Trust is important when conducting a tarot reading,"

Scott opened his mouth to object, but Babs was already out of her seat and rummaging through her cavernous bright orange purse. Tom trotted off to find something more interesting in another room in the house.

"I have a safe place for them in my purse. We have to respect the cards if we expect them to offer us spiritual guidance." Babs returned to the table with the tarot deck. "Jackie and Sam, can you clear the table? Getting ketchup on the Papess does not show respect."

Jackie and Sam did as they were told. From his spot at the table Scott could overhear them exchanging a few words in the kitchen in hushed voices. He thought he'd heard his name once or twice.

Babs gave him the rundown of what to expect during the reading she was going to give him. She warned him that contrary to popular belief, the cards do not predict the future. Their purpose was to offer spiritual guidance.

"Now," she said as Sam and Jackie took their seats at the table again, "while you're holding the deck, Scott, ask it a question. Something that's currently on your mind and is in the near future, preferably."

His palms broke out in a sweat, and yet he couldn't bring himself to deny Babs her reading. Her eyes lit up the same way Jackie's did a few hours before as she was creating her displays. When the Strauss women slipped into their element, their enthusiasm was infectious. He couldn't bring himself to be the one to dim the light in either of their eyes, regardless of the negative impact it may have on him in the process.

Sensing his discomfort, Sam added, "Babs has read my cards dozens of times. You're in good hands."

"You don't have to - " Jackie began to say before Babs cut her off.

"He's a grown man, Jackie. He'll tell me if I'm making him uncomfortable."

False. He couldn't even muster up the courage to ask Jackie out or turn down a phone number from the bartender. He definitely wasn't going to admit to being uncomfortable with Babs's impromptu reading. The problem wasn't that he believed in the cards, but that regardless of the personality he portrayed when out and about for work, he was a private person – a product of his family.

"No, it's fine," Scott said, discreetly drying his damp hands on his jeans underneath the table. "I guess I could ask something about my career." He thought for a few seconds and then asked, "Will the documentary get picked up by a network?"

"That's a *future* prediction – a destination prediction if you will. I'm here for *guidance* on your way to your destination. I can't tell you how things will end; I can only help you get to your desired ending," Babs reminded him. "I'd also like to point out that I specialize in relationships and readings about love. I'm best able to guide you in those areas rather than your career."

He'd already insisted that it was fine for Babs to do his reading, so he took a deep breath and said, "Okay, I guess I can do a relationship question."

"Perfect. Let's see," Babs said, eyeing him up to determine her next move. "Were you seeing anyone before you moved back to Milton?"

"No."

"And you're not seeing anyone now because you'll be moving again soon?"

"Right."

"That sounds like a convenient, perpetual excuse to not get into any relationships. From the outside, it looks like you're using work to avoid getting too close to anyone." The three women stared blatantly at him as they waited to see what reaction he had to Babs's assumption.

He turned the question over in his mind as he tried to decide if and how he would answer her. He'd already spilled about his divorce to Jackie – had even brought up the topic of marriage with her. He could do it again, with a somewhat wider, less intimate audience.

"I got married a few years back. It was a mistake. Ended badly. I haven't really dated anyone seriously since."

"I see," Babs said. Her voice was full of patience and empathy though he couldn't fathom how she could under-stand a miserable and failed marriage. According to everything he'd seen and heard so far, Babs and Tom were high school sweethearts who literally made it till death did they part, and then had an additional few years beyond death with cat Tom.

"Then if you're comfortable with it," she continued, "you can ask, 'How can I move past my divorce in order to find someone new?' I'm assuming that's what you want to do? Find someone to share your life with?"

Sam and Jackie were on the edge of their seats waiting to hear Scott's answer and Babs's impending reading. He didn't think they'd hold it against him if he changed his mind and declined the reading, but something in his gut told him to keep going. It was somewhat horrifying yet comforting the way Babs pegged his past and saw through him within a few hours of meeting him. In a way, he wanted more.

Lana had found him in Vegas, and he'd clung to her and the job to save him from the painfully large hole he'd jumped headfirst into by marrying Corine. He went from Vegas to Florida to Maryland. Even there in Maryland he already had a departure date looming in the distance. As much as he somewhat wanted to explore what Babs was saying, he also didn't need Jackie to know all the details of his sordid past. He'd like to think he still had a chance with her. Especially after seeing her wield her power tools with as much confidence and finesse as an artist with a brush. Quite possibly the hottest thing he'd ever seen. Ever.

"Maybe I've been using work to avoid relationships," Scott acquiesced. He shifted in his chair and went to take another sip of tea before he realized he had already finished his second glass.

The reassuring smile never left Babs's face as she said, "Well, let's give it a try just in case." She was on to his bull shit, and she was not having it. "Repeat the question I gave you while holding the cards. You'll be sending the question into the cards so they can reveal insights into how you can achieve your goal."

"Okay. We're really doing this," Scott said with only a slight tint of red in his cheeks. He refused to meet eyes with Jackie or Sam as he asked, "How can I move past my divorce in order to find someone new?"

"Good. Now, carefully shuffle the cards. Not like a poker dealer, please," Babs said as Scott prepared to riffle the deck. "We don't want to bend the cards." He stopped and changed it up to a general overhand shuffle.

"Okay, that's good. I'll take the deck now. I'm going to do a basic reading with just one card. We could use more cards, but then we'd also get an abundance of information from the abundance of cards. We don't want that; I can tell you barely wanted the reading to begin with. Let's start off small, shall we?"

"That sounds good," Scott said as if he had been the one to request the reading in the first place.

Babs cut the deck and pulled one card from the top of the newer, smaller deck. She placed it face up in the center of the table. Everyone leaned in and stared at the image of a tall burning building with one person on each side plummeting to their deaths. A look of sheer panic and terror on each of their faces.

"The Tower," Babs said.

"That doesn't look good," Scott said. Despite how he felt about the reading initially, he found it somewhat disturbing to see the macabre card staring back at him from the table.

"There really isn't good or bad with tarot," Babs offered as she took in his reaction. "You're gaining insight and guidance. In your situation, this tower represents your current ideas about love and relationships. This," she pointed to the lightning bolt hitting the tower, "is attacking your current ideas and burning them to the ground. It's a good thing.

That's what needs to happen for you to start again successfully. We look at the burning tower and the doomed man and woman, possibly lovers, and we think it's a bad omen. But sometimes things aren't working, and old ideas need to be broken down before you can start anew."

"Interesting. I'll keep that in mind," he said. Scott hoped that would be enough to satisfy Babs. He had been trying to go along with it and be a polite guest, but this was miles outside of his comfort zone.

"You know if you elaborate on your previous marriage, I could maybe give you further guidance," Babs pushed.

"Mom," Jackie cautioned.

"No, thank you. You've been more than generous already giving me the reading. I'm generally a very private person. That's probably why I prefer to be on the back end of the camera rather than in front of it."

"Okay," Babs conceded, "But I'm always around if you want to -"

Before she could finish Sam was up and helping to collect the cards. "That's enough, Babs. We should really get back anyway. I think it's time for Tom's medication. Do you need a ride home or did you drive?"

"I guess you're right. Tom, we should get going." She gathered her putter, leash, and bag. "I don't need a ride; I drove. You're not going to offer Scott a ride home?" Babs asked, sensing, like Scott was, there was something more to Sam's insistence on ushering Babs, and only Babs, out the door.

"Nope," Sam replied. Scott noticed Sam gave a quick wink to Jackie and then called for Tom. Within a minute of when Sam had initially stood up, two minutes max, Sam had all but pushed Babs and Tom out the front door while promising to be in touch soon for drinks and to help more with the decorations.

Was Sam attempting to be his wingman? No. Not likely

since they hadn't seen each other since high school, and she knew nothing about his feelings for Jackie. But maybe she was being Jackie's wing man. Either way, he'd have to send that woman a fruit basket or something for ending the impromptu reading when she did.

"You were right," Scott said once he and Jackie were alone in the living room. "That *was* interesting."

"Never a dull moment when Babs and Sam are involved. You want a beer?"

"Sure, if you're having one." His phone vibrated in his pocket, and he reluctantly checked it. A text from Lana. Work. He couldn't ignore it. Jackie went out to the garage to fetch a few beers.

Where are you? she asked.

Jackie Stauss's house, he texted back.

Perfect, I'll be over in a few

When Jackie returned with the drinks Scott said, "This is going to sound weird given the time, but I promise it's completely normal when it comes to Lana. She's at Tim's house and wants to swing by really quick to go over a few things with me. Do you mind?"

It was late, but once Lana was into a project there were no time restraints or boundaries between work time and down time. Work and documentaries were her life. He'd found that if he tried to put up boundaries with her, she just kept pushing until she got what she wanted. It was easier to agree to meet with her rather than text back and forth for a while before finally giving in and meeting with her anyway.

"No, that's fine. Does she mind that you're here with me? Drinking? This late at night?" They were old friends and off the clock, but he could understand how it still felt weird for some reason, since it did for him a bit, too. As if they were teenagers and a teacher was about to bust them for drinking and making out in back theater room.

"I don't see why she would. I'm not working the rest of the night. Besides, you already know my theory about Tim and Lana. And anyway, we're just hanging out, as friends." Scott regretted it as soon as he'd said it. His reasoning had been to not dampen the evening they were about to spend together, alone. And yet with those few words he'd practically picked her up and physically placed her down in the friend zone, a safe three feet away from him at all times, with that one damn comment. That one word.

"Good point," Jackie agreed. If she was disappointed by his comment, she didn't show it. His confidence faded a bit. Where was Sam when he needed her?

Jackie opened the front door and there was Lana already making her way up the porch steps.

"Hi, Lana. Come on in."

"Thanks, Jackie. Looks like you've been busy. Have you done a reflection recently? If Scott filmed you today, it's ideal to have a reflection that same day and with the same clothing."

"Right. I keep forgetting about those. I will. I promise."

"Good. See that you do." Lana took one last look around the disheveled living room and said, "Well, I only stepped in to take a peek around and give you a reflection reminder. Scott, I need a few minutes with you out front. Jackie, nice to see you." Without waiting to hear a response from Jackie or Scott, Lana moved out the door with the expectation that he would follow her.

"You, too, Lana," Jackie called out to Lana's back.

Scott mouthed *sorry* to Jackie before following Lana out to the porch and then down the walkway a bit.

In typical Lana fashion, she turned and got straight to the point: "I looked at the footage with Muriel and she's still talking to you, into the camera, the entire time." To the average person it may have sounded aggressive, but Scott knew it was Lana's style to identify whatever the problem may be and lay it out on the table. It wasn't meant to be overly critical or aggressive. It was the way she approached any issue with work. Acknowledge what was happening, find a solution, and then move on from there. There wasn't time to consider if someone's feelings may be hurt in the process.

"Yeah, I've been working with her about it. She's lonely, Lana. I've tried going over thirty minutes before filming starts so we can eat together and talk, but she continues to talk to me the entire time I'm there."

Lana nodded her head in understanding and thought on it for a beat.

"I could set the camera up somewhere and then just be on camera talking to her instead," Scott offered. He hated being in front of the camera, but he'd do for Muriel if that's what it took.

"No. I want you to get different shots. Nothing stationary. No tripods. I'll talk to Tim and have him there with her when you're filming."

Again, it sounded harsher than it was. It had taken their first two documentaries for Scott to learn not to take it personally.

"No family? Friends?" Lana asked.

"Yes, she has family and friends. But she's not comfortable putting them out. There's a lot going on in everyone's lives and Muriel doesn't want to impose on them."

"I'll work with Tim on it," Lana said ending that part of their conversation. "How'd tonight go here?" She motioned with her head towards Jackie's house.

"Good. I got some good footage of Jackie framing out the tanks and assembling her shelves."

Lana narrowed her eyes at him. "You're here late. Didn't you start at five?"

"Big project," Scott offered as if that gave any explanation as to why he was still there drinking a beer with Jackie while neither of them was working.

"Is there something going on here? Do I need to be concerned?"

Scott turned back to the house to verify that Jackie was nowhere in sight and that the windows were all closed. Lana had not bothered to lower her voice for any part of their conversation.

"With Jackie?" Scott gave a small laugh. "No. Nothing. She's an old friend. More like a sister."

He'd never had relationship conversations with Lana. Their previous documentary had been in a nursing home – no threat of inappropriate work relationships there – and before that they'd done the historical documentary in Vegas. Back when he was at the end of his marriage and then newly divorced. Scott hadn't even told her he'd gotten divorced. His ring wasn't there one day, and he happened to notice Lana notice it. But nothing was said.

Scott studied Lana's face and found no hint as to what she was thinking. The woman was a stoic machine. Yet another reason he'd been so surprised to see her openly flirting with Tim on the job the other day.

"Keep it that way, please," she said as she turned to walk back towards her car parked out front of Tim's house. "Nothing can interfere with the integrity of the documentary."

"Not a problem, Lana," he called as she continued to walk away from him.

He remained outside for a few more minutes thinking about what Lana had said and how he felt about it all. When she'd first broached the subject about not getting involved with other people in the documentary, he hadn't thought too much about it. There was no chance he and Lana were going to be falling in love anytime soon, and he certainly wasn't falling for anyone during his divorce in Vegas or during their senior center stay in Florida.

Being in Milton with Jackie changed everything. Lana was right to think that something was up, and he doubted he could ever keep a relationship hidden from her given how many cameras and mics were around to catch every glimpse and seemingly innocuous comment.

If he went back into the house with Jackie, he was sure something would happen between them. Could he risk his job to see if something *could* work out between him and Jackie? And what happened if it did work out? He was leaving in a few months. It wasn't fair to start something he had no intentions of continuing long-term. He hadn't been able to make it work with Corine when they were in the same state. How was he going to do a long-distance relationship with Jackie when they were on opposite sides of the country?

With a heavy heart he went back into the house and called out to Jackie, who was in the back kitchen. "Jackie, I need to take a rain check on the beer. I have a few things I need to work on tonight after all."

She walked out of the kitchen and back to the living room with an empty trash bag for her left-over scraps and other crafting detritus that littered her floor.

"Oh. Right, of course," she said. He could tell she was trying to hide any disappointment from her face. She didn't want to make him feel bad for having to pick work over hanging out with her. He hoped that ff the situation was reversed, she would have picked work over Scott as well.

They said their goodbyes and he drove back to his parents' house. He almost considered calling up the bartender and reverting back to the dark days following his divorce where he'd filled his lonely nights with one-night-stands. But everything about that old life had lost its appeal.

Maybe he was getting too old for that sort of thing, but he doubted it had much to do with maturity. He had a sinking feeling that pooled heavily at the bottom of his gut that the real change had been Jackie. Sharing his bed with some stranger was no longer an option when it came to easing the loneliness he felt.

JACKIE

A holiday playlist including hits from N*Sync, Mariah Carey, Celine Dion, and Ariana Grande was set on repeat for the past two hours as Sam and Jackie worked together to plan out how the soon-to-be-famous Santa Claws lawn decoration would come together. It felt odd in late September to have Mariah on, but the season in general was growing on her more and more as she got deeper into the event.

"Jeremy's a saint for putting up with this tonight," Jackie said as she watched Sam calculate the specifics of the electrical work that would need to be done to make their display wave its claws and its Santa hat.

"I don't know about all of that," Sam replied as she studied the paper in front of her.

"Trust me," Jackie insisted. "I've seen what else is out there. Jeremy's a keeper."

"That's what I hear." Sam still kept her eyes glued to her paper as she wrote down a few numbers and calculations.

"Hey," Jackie said with a wave of her hand in front of Sam's eyes to snap her out of it. "You okay?"

Sam looked up at her with a smile on her face. "You know I'm teasing. He is fabulous and I tell him all the time. But let's keep the saint comment between us. Don't need his head getting so large it won't fit in the doorway anymore," she teased.

They sat in silence for a bit as Jackie made a few notes in her sketch pad and Sam finished up her work as well.

"So," Sam said as she slid her work to Jackie for review, "what exactly happened with Scott after I left?"

Sam had texted her later that night asking for details, but Jackie had only texted back that he left shortly after and nothing had happened.

"Like I said in the text. Nothing at all." Jackie took the paper and placed it into her notebook to review later. They'd been at it for hours and she no longer had the mental capacity to look at anything event related.

The music cut off and Jeremy walked into the kitchen to start making dinner.

"No luck with Scott, huh?" he asked, having clearly overheard the first part of their conversation, even under the cover of the holiday music.

"It kind of felt like we were cock-blocked, to be honest. By Lana of all people."

"That doesn't surprise me," Sam said. "I saw her do an interview with the local News 57 crew, and she was terrifyingly cold. I got shivers listening to her, Jackie. No joke."

"What'd she do?" Jeremy asked. He gathered supplies and set the oven to preheat while they were talking.

"I finally had Scott alone, in my house. I went to get us a couple of beers from the garage and trash bag for cleanup, and by the time I got back to the living room, she was practically on my doorstep. Stopping by unexpectedly and working all hours of the night are apparently typical for her. She and Scott stepped outside for a few minutes, and then when he came back in, he said he had more work he had to get to."

"That sucks," Jeremy commiserated. "But that just means he *had* to leave, not that he wanted to."

"Maybe you're right," she agreed. Jeremy was well aware of Jackie's infatuation with Scott back in high school. It wasn't an option to keep it a secret when Jeremy was permanently affixed to her best friend's side once they'd started dated. Jackie had kept the continued social media stalking to herself, but she never could have hidden her high school crush from Jeremy.

"How was the rest of the week working with him?" Sam asked.

"Hard to say. Mom's been there each time, too. So it's never just the two of us."

"I bet Babs loves him. He's catnip for parents with his charm and boyish good looks," Sam said.

"Sounds like you want to date him, too," Jeremy said to Sam. There was something off in his tone and Jackie couldn't tell if he was joking or not.

"You're funny," Sam said flatly. "You weren't there the other night to see him in action. He has this ease about him when he's talking to just about anyone. And he's generous with his compliments, but he's also sincere about it. You have to see him work Jackie's neighborhood to understand."

"That's exactly how it is. And yes, Babs loves him, too," Jackie agreed. She'd seen the effect Scott had had on her street and heard the way her neighbors reveled in his presence.

"I do all of that, too," Jeremy interjected. "Babs loves me."

Jackie was familiar with the way Jeremy often teased and joked about such things, but his voice in the kitchen was sincere. There was an edge to it that showed he really was concerned that Sam was more impressed by Scott than she was by her husband. She looked back and forth between the married couple trying to decipher what was happening below the surface of what she was hearing and seeing.

"You've charmed Jackie's neighbors? I'd love to hear about it," Sam challenged.

Where was the playful banter between lovers? The conversation they were having was bordering on bickering and likely to turn to an all-out argument if it continued.

Sensing the looming argument himself, Jeremy didn't answer Sam and instead turned the subject back to Jackie and Scott.

"Babs being there is probably why he hasn't tried anything. It's different from friends being around. Guys don't want to hit on someone right in front of their mom."

"Maybe…" she conceded. "Or maybe it's for the best anyway. He's temporarily living at his parents' place for the few months he's in Milton, then he'll be leaving again. It doesn't make sense to get into anything serious with someone who's traveling around all the time."

"It doesn't have to be serious. It has to be fun. And I bet a few nights with Scott would be very, very fun," Sam said.

Jeremy gave Sam an odd look that Jackie couldn't quite work out as he placed three wine glasses on the island.

He turned to Jackie and asked, "Are you staying for dinner, Jack? We're having my legendary homemade mashed potatoes and meatloaf."

"Yes, stay. We've barely gotten a chance to talk."

"I can't -"

"You won't," Sam corrected.

Jeremy had filled two glasses already and hovered over the third waiting for a definitive answer on whether or not Jackie would be joining them.

"I *can't*," she reiterated. "There's a team-building activity for the lighting event that I *cannot* miss." She glanced at her phone for the time and added, "I only have a few more minutes before I need to head back."

Jeremy put away the wine and extra glass, then handed Sam her drink.

"I get it. You'd rather spend all your waking hours with your new best friends and your unrequited love than to have dinner with your actual best friend and Jeremy."

"Hey," Jeremy said, "Jack and I are friends, too. Aren't we?"

"Meh," Jackie teased as she made a motion with her hand to show it could go either way. Then she turned back to Sam. "Please tell me you understand how deep I am in this neighborhood and in this event. It's for work. Of course I'd rather be here with you. With both of you."

Sam stood up. "Come on. I'll walk you out."

Jackie said bye to Jeremy, gathered up her things, and followed Sam to the front door.

"I'm sorry I've been guilt-tripping you so much lately. I do understand and I think you're making the right decision to put this as your top priority."

"Thanks, Sam."

"I miss you. Ya know. You're back but it's almost like you're not back." Sam looked back to Jeremy who was in the kitchen doing something on his phone. "The only time we see you is if we're helping out – which we don't mind doing. At all. But I miss us just hanging out or going out and doing something. When's the last time you went out to the bar or went dancing?"

Jackie felt a pang of guilt as she said, "I'm still doing those things, but lately they're all related to the event."

"What's the team-building activity?" Jackie could hear the renewed annoyance in Sam's voice.

"Christmas Lights Lane Olympics followed by happy hour," Jackie said meekly.

She nodded slowly and said, "Well, have a good time. Just remember not to drink too much of the punch." She opened the door for Jackie to leave.

All that day Jackie's phone had been blowing up with texts from her neighbors. They'd discovered group texting the year before and on occasions like the neighborhood Olympic games, the smack talk was never ending. That morning, before she'd met up with Sam, there had been a ceremonious drawing of names to see which neighbors would be on which team. Once the teams were divvied up, the lines were drawn as to who was a foe and who was a friend for the day.

Margaret and a few other neighbors offered up their services to create team t-shirts for the occasion. Each team had their own color (red, green, white, or blue), team name, and saying. Jackie was on the green team along with Mac, Muriel, Otto, and Evelyn. They'd had to settle on a team name and motto on the spot to give Margaret and company enough time to get the shirts decorated by the games that afternoon.

Similar to her first event meeting, Jackie found the other four came to the table with ideas and suggestions while she spent most of the time just trying to catch up with what was happening and with what the overall expectations were. After thirty minutes of deliberation along with a hefty dose of playful bickering, Mac finally caved and agreed to Evelyn's suggestion: Awesome Balsam. Their motto was short and sweet: We're Fir Real. Mac didn't think awesome and balsam rhymed enough for people to get it, but he was outnumbered and out of time.

· · ·

When Jackie showed up again that afternoon for the official opening of the games, she picked up an oversized green t-shirt with a giant decorated balsam fir tree on the front and reluctantly pulled it over her head. She'd been going for athletic and cute with her yoga pants and matching sporty top, but that was all lost as everything above her knees swam in the sea of forest green cotton that made up her uniform.

"Looking good, Strauss," she heard Scott say from behind her. She turned to find him poised, camera phone at the ready, to snap her picture. It was likely for the Twitter page, so she played along giving him her best muscle man pose as she flexed what little biceps she had.

Then he looked back down at the phone to make a few adjustments while she looked over every inch of him. As the temperature got cooler, she found his wardrobe consisted mostly of plaid shirts and old faded jeans. In the past she'd always preferred something preppier or more business-like on men, but damn did it suit Scott. That along with his bit of facial hair all gave the appearance of a sort of mountain man who could be dropped in the middle of the woods with only the clothes on his back and he'd survive just fine using nothing but his bare hands to hunt and clean animals for dinner before retiring for the night in the hut he'd built with random materials he'd found in the woods. Jackie's insides lit up with heat and fire as she imagined the two of them in front of the fiery blaze mountain-man Scott would make. They'd have to share a sleeping bag, of course, to share their body heat and to keep from freezing in the night…

She snapped back to reality when he gave the phone a final tap before turning to show her the picture.

"I certainly wouldn't want to go up against that."

She gave him a playful punch on his arm – a lowly and desperate attempt to make any contact with his irritatingly perfect body – and said, "Don't patronize me, Davis. I'm probably one of the weakest ones here, which is really saying something given who I'm up against." She held her arms up for effect. "I practically got lost putting on this extra-large shirt."

It was an exaggeration that she was the weakest one in the lot, but she had trouble taking compliments from Scott for some reason. And even though she desperately wanted to impress him, she often downplayed any praise he threw her way. It was a bad habit she was working on but had yet to see any improvements with.

"I stand by my assessment," he said as he went back to his phone to type out a few lines on Twitter before officially posting the photo.

"Are you here on official Twitter business today?" She was thrilled to see that he was there without his video camera. They would have the entire afternoon and evening where she didn't have to ignore him. It was going to be glorious; she could feel it.

"Lizzy's filming while I'm on Twitter duty with a mandated posting of one picture per fifteen minutes. Minimum." He shrugged at Jackie's reaction to the large number of pictures he'd be posting throughout the games and during the happy hour that followed. "Tim's been filling Lana in on the shenanigans of the last few neighborhood Olympic events and Lana's convinced it will be at least an episode of the documentary. If not more."

"And who better to capture those shenanigans for the Twitter audience than you."

"According to Lana, there's no one better equipped for the job," he joked. His phone went into his back pocket and then he pulled from his front pocket a few sheets of folded up paper and an envelope of cash. A lot of cash.

"And, as a bystander who is in no way biased as to who will win, I'll be the photographer slash bookie today. Get those one dollar bills out, Jackie. I'm taking final bets up until 4:55 sharp." He tapped a nonexistent watch on his wrist.

"What? I didn't realize people were betting." She absently felt for any pockets she may have. There were none.

Scott looked at her skeptically. "Jackie, this is the same group that takes half a dozen bus trips to Atlantic City each year and religiously hits up the Wednesday night bingo games at the firehall. You're surprised they have pools set up?"

She shrugged. "I have a lot going on right now. Some of the details slip by me." Jackie reached for the proffered papers to see what the different categories were. As she skimmed she said, "Maybe you could help a girl out and spot me a bit of cash? I'm good for it. I promise." She looked back up at him and batted her eyes.

A blast from a bullhorn sounded from the other side of the road where the majority of the neighbors had gathered with their groups. Pods of green, red, blue, and white shirts all clumped together as they started to discuss strategy.

"Five-minute warning," Tim called using the bullhorn, regardless that it wasn't needed for everyone to hear him. He projected effortlessly and most of the neighbors had decent hearing or decent hearing aids.

"You're putting me in a tight spot here, Stauss. One, it's already 4:55 now which means I'd be breaking my hard deadline. And two...well...I don't know how to put this nicely...You're a bit of a flight risk. I can't guarantee you won't flee in the middle of the night once I come to collect."

He pulled the papers back from her hands as if he wasn't going to let her bet, and she grabbed his wrists playfully in response.

"Scott!" she called as he held the papers above her head while she attempted to jump up and reach for them.

"You'll need to give me some sort of collateral, so I know you're good for it."

"We don't have time, Scott," she managed between giggles. Despite her protests she was thoroughly enjoying his game and the feeling of his hard body against hers as she continued to press against him and reach for the papers. "My team is already giving me the stink eye as it is."

"No way. Not when you're with me. They all love me," he said more matter-of-factly than in an overly cocky tone. With good reason. The neighbors all loved him. It was no secret.

"Scott..." she tried one last time.

"Fine. But be quick about it and don't let anyone see. I have a rep as a bad-ass bookie and I want to keep it that way." Their loud voices and animated antics had already caught the attention of most of the neighbors. There was nothing subtle about anything they were doing. She wondered if he knew that as well.

The six mini games for that year's annual Olympics event went by in a blur of frenzied activity and high-pressured stakes. Jackie had a feeling that on an average year the competition was fierce for bragging rights alone. But with the cameras present and the surprise guest judges – none other than their very own Mayor Donne and Fire Chief Schmidt – there was electric energy in the air just as there always is the few moments before a lightning storm.

They began with the untangling of the light balls. Each team was given a large ball of tangled lights that they had to work on together to untangle and lay out down the middle of the blocked-off street. Snowbody Does it Better took the win for that event mostly due to Mort's small and agile hands. All those winters spent creating train gardens at the local historical society paid off big time as Mort led his team to sweet, sweet victory early in the games.

Scott's Twitter audience was treated to a picture of Mort on his knees holding up the string of lights above his head as if he'd just won a gold medal. Mort's mouth was mid shout and he looked like a rabid dog.

What followed was a barrage of games, each one faster-paced and with more to lose than the last: The Wrapping of Odd Shapes, Present Stacking, Gingerbread House Decorating, and Snowball Dodgeball. All were holiday-themed and set up in a way that required some physical movement, but nothing that would be considered too strenuous for any of the homeowners. They couldn't afford any injuries at the start of the holiday decorating season.

The teambuilding aspect of it was at an all-time high as they competed. Jackie learned that Otto was a bit of an origami wizard as he scored them a second-place ranking in the wrapping event.

Though it didn't help them at all during the games, the present stacking event triggered Muriel's memories of her childhood spent making playing card houses with her twin sister Maureen in the rural outskirts of Minneapolis. As they carefully stacked boxes, she briefed them on the different techniques they'd used for their houses and how there was a competition in town though they'd never won it.

Jackie showed off her design skills as she took on most of the gingerbread house decorating. They won that event, though just barely since Margaret, along with every other self-respecting neighbor living on a street called Christmas Lights Lane, knew her way around frosting and gum-dropping a ginger house.

By the time they'd arrived at their final game, a mere two hours after they'd begun though it seemed much later than that, Clause for Commotion and Snowbody Does it Better were tied for first place with two wins each, with Awesome Balsam in second place with one win, and Blue, Blue, Blue Christmas in last place with no wins to their name.

The final event was the Christmas Carol-Off: a play on a dance off and a caroling competition that required each team to sing and dance to a never-before-heard mix of popular Christmas songs. One last time, Mayor Donne and Fire Chief Schmidt took their positions as judges with their clipboards at the ready. For this event they moved to Tim's backyard where he happened to have a floating deck. Jackie guessed he'd built it for just such occasions since it awkwardly had three steps up from the ground to the top of the deck, and then another five steps up from the deck to get to the sliding back door.

Jackie would like to say that after an unprecedented chain of events her group stole the spotlight and somehow took first place even though each game was only worth one point and it was mathematically impossible to beat out Snowbody Does it Better and Clause for Commotion. She wished she could say that she finally learned to carry a tune and coordinate her limbs to move flawlessly with the beat. But that was never in the cards for her. Literally she had forced her mother's hand at a tarot reading about her vocal skills. She can still see the card on the table with the dead man who had ten swords sticking out of his back.

So no, Awesome Balsam turned out to not be awesome enough to pull first place. But it was, hands-down, one of the best nights of her life. She never would have guessed hanging out with a bunch of neighbors, who were on average the same age her grandparents would have been had they not passed years before, would be one of the highlights of her adult life. Although she had to admit that while the games were fun, the happy hour after was her favorite part of the night. And if she was really honest with herself, she knew that had less to do with her neighbors, and more to do with her time with Scott.

Tim set up a large bonfire in his backyard between the deck and the garage. Everyone brought chairs, food, and drinks to sit around and enjoy one-another's company. The upcoming months were sometimes hectic with decorating and planning – on top of the stress holidays tend to bring in general. The happy hour that followed the event games served as a final hurrah before life got messy again.

Jackie and Scott found themselves sitting together on a sort of outer ring around the fire pit. Lost in conversation about the games, the upcoming event, work, and everything else adults tended to talk about when conversations were kept light.

After her fifth yawn, Scott insisted he walk Jackie back to her house. She considered protesting since she didn't want the night to end so soon, but a walk home with Scott, in the dark, sounded even more enticing than the party.

"You know why I'm walking you home, don't you?"

Ummmm...is this a trick question? she thought. She'd had just enough sangria that she'd almost said something about how he obviously had a massive crush on her. Maybe if she'd had one or two more cups, but at the moment she wasn't quite there yet.

"Because you're a gentleman," she said confidently.

"A gentleman bookie," he corrected.

She swatted him on the arm playfully and somehow ended up with her arm hooked in his as they continued to walk.

"You are *not* walking me home just to collect your paltry five dollars," she insisted.

"Then you don't know me nearly as well as you think you do." They took a few more steps before he added, "I'm dangerous, Jackie. A force to be reckoned with."

"Uh, huh. Big tough guy. That's what all the neighbors tell me, too. Watch out for Scott; he's bad news."

Suddenly, they were at her house though Jackie barely remembered taking the steps to get there. All she was aware of was Scott's bare forearm against her own. Until that moment she'd never thought of that part of the body as being anything remotely sexy, but the feel of his warm skin brushing up against her own was doing crazy things to her body.

"Here we are," Scott said with a flourish as if he'd just presented her with some sort of gift.

"Yes, here we are." When they'd first started walking the short distance to her house, she imagined the sounds of the party fading as they increased the space between themselves and the festivities. But their departure had only encouraged everyone else to begin making their way home as well and the usually quiet street was flooded with her neighbors. She was certain Scott felt it, too. Because they both stood in front of the walkway to her house as if debating what to do.

After a glimpse at everyone still mingling in the street around them, Scott merely said, "Good night, Jackie."

"Good night, Scott." As she walked towards her house, she could tell that they'd just put another nail in the friendship coffin they were creating. A few more and it would be fully sealed – beyond anyone's ability to reopen it to the possibility of something more. As much as she knew that was the way it should be, it still made her toss and turn for a long time that night before she settled into a restless sleep.

SCOTT

*L*ate September Scott was at Jackie's again as she put the final finishing touches on her tanks and prepared to fill them. When he'd first arrived, Jackie apologized that they'd probably be making a late night of it. To make up for it, she'd ordered take out for them to pick at throughout the evening.

"That's perfect," he said. "With my hours and constant moving around I'm used to takeout." He set up his camera and she went about getting supplies together and putting on her mic.

"Where is everyone?" he asked when Jackie came back into the room with a bucket full of materials she needed that evening. "It's so quiet without Babs and Sam and Jeremy around."

"It is. When I was out in Philly, I didn't realize how much I missed everyone back here. How much I missed having a full house of family and friends for random dinners in the middle of the week. You know?"

"Yeah, I do." For a while he'd survived on filling his days with work and surrounded himself with people he encountered on the job. It wasn't cutting it anymore. He needed people in his life who knew him beyond work. He needed companionship and something that felt closer to family than the acquaintances he'd had here and there over the past few years.

"Sam and Jeremy have something going on tonight, and Babs is down for the count with strep throat." She started moving tools and supplies out of the bucket and lining them up on the large piece of cardboard she'd set out to protect her hardwood floors.

"I'm sorry to hear that. Does she need anything? Can I help?" *Help with what? What kind of comment is that?* He already acknowledged there wasn't a remote possibility for something to happen between him and Jackie, and yet he still struggled with basic communication when it came to her.

Jackie took his awkwardness in stride though and merely said, "That's sweet, but she's fine. I was over with her earlier today." Then she looked up at Scott. "Okay, I'm ready."

The red light went on, he figuratively left the room, and she got to work. The very beginning was quiet with only the sounds of her work filling the area. But as the time passed, she either got more comfortable in front of the camera, or less comfortable with the silence, and she began to talk to herself as she worked.

Little mumblings like, "No, that's not right," and "Come on, just a little more..." Through his work Scott found it was common for people to talk to themselves and noticed it more and more when he wasn't filming, too.

"Fuck, Scott, I cannot figure this out," she muttered miserably as she placed the plexiglass in place for the third time and it still wasn't lining up the way she needed it to.

"You will. If anyone can figure it out, you can," he said just loud enough for her to hear.

Jackie's hands remained in place to hold the pieces where

she needed them to be, but her head whipped around to the camera and her eyes widened in surprise.

"It speaks."

Scott couldn't take it anymore. He wanted – no, needed – to do more than stand by silently while Jackie worked.

He hit the audio button on the camera to make sure it was no longer recording. He didn't want Lana listening in on his conversation with Jackie even if there wasn't going to be anything scandalous about their topic of discussion. He was well versed with how much the lavalier mics picked up and was careful to keep his voice just low enough that his words would be nothing more than indistinguishable mumbles.

"Look," he said softly with his face still hidden behind the camera, "most of what Lana is going to keep will be sped up so that hours of progress can be captured in minutes, sometimes even seconds-worth of film. When that happens, there's no audio beyond some music or voiceover that's put in during editing. So as long as you're not looking at me and I keep behind the camera, we can talk a bit."

"Oh, thank god," she sighed still facing the tank in front of her. "I don't know if you caught me mumbling to myself for a bit there, but I don't do well in silence. I need some sort of conversation to help me concentrate even though I know that sounds contradictory." With an extra grunt of effort, she pushed once again, and the plexiglass fell into place. "See? I got it once I could really start talking again."

"I knew you'd get it."

Jackie hopped down from the ladder she'd been on and walked over to her make-shift workbench on the floor to start her next task. As she worked, she kept her eyes on whatever she was doing, but she continued to talk. Scott could tell she was careful not to look at him or to do anything with her hands or body language that showed she was engaging in conversation beyond the movement of her mouth. It was sweet that she was doing everything she could to make sure he didn't catch hell from Lana about her talking to him during filming.

"Jeremy is the friend of a friend of the owner of Preserve the Bay. You heard of it?"

"Sure," Scott said. "I get breakfast at Filler Up Diner a few times a week. They have an ad on their menus."

"That diner is dodgier than The Cut and Run. What kind of food snob are you?"

"Have you even been there?"

Jackie started to work on another part of the tanks, so Scott slowly moved about the room to reposition himself and to get a better angle of what she was working on.

"No, it's too dodgy. And don't even bother going into whatever speech you're about to make. I can't see you but I know you've got some sort of shit-eating grin on your face thinking about whatever witty comeback you have for me.

"Never, Jackie. I was merely thinking that you and I need to make time to grab a bite to eat at the diner."

Her hands stopped as if that hadn't been the response she'd expected and she wasn't sure what to say back.

"Anyway, tell me about the nonprofit."

She started to work again as she said, "Right, the nonprofit. They're main focus before has been research based and political – getting local politicians to sponsor preservation bills and that sort of thing. But now they're expanding. Just bought a large hunk of land on the Chester River where they're going to build an interactive museum and they're going to start a program to visit schools for assemblies and that sort of thing."

"That's cool. Are you going to volunteer there or something?"

"Not volunteering. But working there, in a permanent position."

"Permanent?" Scott asked louder than he'd intended. He imagined her helping to create some sort of touch-tanks that resembled the actual state of the bay versus a healthy body of water to help kids understand why Maryland and the surrounding states needed to get their shit together to stop polluting it.

"Yes. Year round with no looming end date. Isn't it exciting? Stephanie, the founder, is looking to add an additional chemical oceanographer with the new location and Jeremy passed on my name to her." Jackie continued with how her name got to Stephanie and what they'd discussed on the phone earlier that week about the position and expectations. Her face beamed at the thought of this socially engaging and creative science career, and it tugged at his heart a little. Without the camera he would have picked her up and spun her around in a big hug as he told her how happy he was for her and how awesome she would be.

But with the camera he was stuck doing the best he could to give an enthusiastic but still just-above-a-whisper response of, "That's awesome, Jackie. I know I would have paid a lot more attention during assemblies if you had been leading them."

That comment was the one that did her in. She blushed as she turned to the camera with a half-smile and said, "Scott..."

Since she'd already looked into the camera, that felt as good a time as any to pause and eat. He set the camera down, rolled his shoulders a bit to loosen them back up.

"Let's take a quick break to eat. You can tell me all about your new dream job."

Similar to the way Jackie talked about crafting and do-it-yourself projects, her eyes lit up with excitement as she explained how she would have to study up on oceanography again because she hadn't done much with it since a course in college, how she would be tasked with leading the design team to create the layout of the new space they were building, and how she would design craft projects to complete with students at schools.

Most of the tables around the first floor were covered with materials and tools, so they were on the couch with their plates of food. The far end of the couch where there was a bit of room for them both to fit as long as they squeezed in. Not a problem for Jackie. Ever since he'd walked her home from the Olympic games, arm in arm, she'd become more comfortable around him. Walking with her arm linked into his, leaning on him for support, and in general finding ways to touch in a way that bordered on friendly and more than friends.

On the couch one of her legs was draped over his. He was certain that if he closed the small space between them by leaning over to kiss her that she'd let him. That she would even pull him in closer as they discarded the food and filming for the night. But that wouldn't be fair if she was staying and he was merely passing through on his way to his next job.

"Then you're going to stay in Milton?" he asked between forkfuls of the Chinese takeout that had been delivered earlier.

"Maybe? I'm talking about all of this as if it's a done deal. It's not. This potential position is still way, way up in the air. Nothing official." She emptied a few packets of duck sauce onto her plate and generously coated an eggroll in it before taking a bite. He could tell she was thinking something through as she chewed.

"I didn't think I'd stay," she said after she swallowed. "I've barely settled into the house here assuming I was just going to sell it after the season was over." Jackie looked around the room as she spoke, taking it all in as if she'd arrived for the first time that day. "But I like it here. I like being closer to

Mom and Sam. And if by some chance I do get the opportunity to have my own show somewhere, I'd want to do it here. Filming on the weekends or something if that's possible."

Scott nodded his head. He understood, though aside from Jackie he didn't have anything like that pulling and drawing him towards the town. Scott's parents were traveling most of the time, and many of his friends had moved away like he did. He envied Jackie's ability to see herself staying in Milton long-term. As an adult he hadn't felt that about any place he'd lived.

"Also, I think something's going on with Sam and Jeremy," she added. "I want to be here for them if they need me."

Again, he nodded as he took a bite.

"And you're definitely *not* staying?" she asked him.

"I like traveling and seeing all the different parts of the country. Maybe the world if that's ever a possibility." He didn't want to get into how he struggled to find somewhere that felt like he belonged, where he wouldn't feel the urge to up and leave after only a few months had passed. Besides, what could he possibly do in Milton? It wasn't a documentary hot spot and as far as he knew very few movies had been filmed on the Eastern Shores of Maryland. Probably half a dozen over the past few decades.

Even without the added explanation, Jackie nodded her head as if she understood his viewpoint as well. The conversation lulled a bit after that as they both got lost in their thoughts and their food.

What had he expected her to say? As crazy as it sounded, he almost expected her to ask him to stay. To not leave. But casual friends don't really do that, do they?

JACKIE

When Jackie had first unveiled her plans, it felt like she had forever to make them a reality. The day of the first meeting, it had been over eighty degrees outside. It wasn't until late October that Jackie started to fold under the pressure of it all. There was an actual countdown of days leading up to the unveiling, and she was quickly running out of time.

On top of the minor and major setbacks with her holiday displays, Scott was always around. Her mind threw logic at her at all times as to why it wouldn't work, and her heart was on board as well knowing that his leaving would be devastating if they took things to the next level. But her body would hear none of it.

Each time their eyes locked, her knees felt weak. Each time he reached out to help her and their hands, or any other parts of their bodies touched, a build-up of anticipation and longing settled between her legs. Like one of Pavlov's dogs her body began prepping for a wild night between the sheets each time they touched – regardless of anything her heart or mind had to say about it.

And she was pushing the boundaries as well. She randomly linked her arm in his as they'd walk, picked stray (nonexistent) threads from off his clothing, and practically sat on his lap a few occasions when they were on the couch together. She couldn't help herself. Once he didn't pull back the first time, she took it as the green light to not only continue, but to up the occurrences and duration of each infraction.

The day before Halloween he and Sam were helping Jackie shovel out the grass in her front lawn so she could replace it with sand to create a temporary beach. Every now and then he'd put his shovel down and film a bit of them shoveling and talking (without him), but mostly he was by their side and more than pulling his weight with his efforts.

It was perfect weather for intense physical labor: overcast and in the high fifties. And to Jackie's credit, she only occasionally checked out Scott in his sweaty, tight, gray t-shirt that clung to his abs. His usual plaid uniform tossed to the side once he started getting down and dirty with them. The view itself made the strenuous digging worth it. *He's not a piece of meat. Stop drooling over him and help him*, Jackie reminded herself.

Halfway through their work, Sam's stomach gave an audible roar prompting Jackie to head into the house to get a bit of food together for them. "Be right back," she'd said as she set down her shovel and gloves and went into the house. With the nice weather she had the storm door and all the windows open. From the kitchen she could still hear their conversation in the front yard.

"Let me ask you something, Scott," she heard Sam say.

"Shoot," he responded.

"Is there really *nothing* happening between you and Jackie?"

Jackie froze in the kitchen, mid-pivot with her hands full of snack bags of chips and a few subs she'd ordered that morning for them all to eat at lunch. She had not given Sam the green light for any sort of conversation like that. Sam was going rogue, and Jackie was simultaneously terrified and thrilled at what may come from it.

Whatever Scott said she couldn't make out. After a few seconds of silence, the next voice she heard was still Sam's. Still loud and clear as though maybe she wanted Jackie to hear her.

"But have you seen the way you both look at each other? The way you make each other laugh so hard you double over and happen to double over so that you're almost on top of each other?"

Jackie put everything on a large plate along with some paper plates and napkins. They planned to eat on the deck since it was a nice day and because they thought they might be a bit too muddy to be on the furniture in Jackie's house. She moved a little closer to the door hoping to hang out for a bit to hear both Sam's and Scott's comments during the conversation.

Undoubtedly, Sam would relay everything back to her later word for word, but there was something to be said about hearing a conversation first person. To be able to catch the subtle nuances, slight pauses, and hesitant voices if there were any.

"No," he said. Jackie could hear him sliding his shovel under another hunk of grass as he said it. Could tell by the way the words left his mouth that he was working while he spoke. "It's complicated," he added.

At this, Jackie literally took her snooping a step further as she stepped towards the front window to what was happening outside as well. The tanks in front of the window did a good job obfuscating her figure while still allowing her a direct visual of Scott.

He carefully lifted the shovel full of grass and dirt and laid it into the wheelbarrow. Muriel had had some concrete removed from her back yard and was in need of grass. Jackie, Sam, and Scott were attempting to create a sort of home-made sod in the way they removed Jackie's grass. None of them knew anything about landscaping or transplanting grass, but it seemed worth a try.

Scott in particular was determined to make it work since he'd become so close to Muriel through all their sessions together. Muriel never could stop talking to or looking at Scott while he filmed, and Scott couldn't bring himself to stop her either. Unlike his sessions with Jackie, Muriel would stop everything she was doing to talk to Scott. Tim went over a few times to act as a buffer, but in the end, Scott went over on his off hours and had Lizzy film them while he helped her set up her decorations even though he hated being in front of the camera.

"Yeah. I get it. I know about complicated," Sam said matter-of-factly. She continued to work as well as they talked.

"I'm sorry to hear that." He laid another shovel of home-made sod into the wheelbarrow. He started to shovel again but stopped. "Do you want to talk about it?"

This intrigued Jackie even more than the conversation about his relationship with her. Two people she knew to be exceptionally private about their lives, who barely knew each other, were going to open up about their love lives?

But Sam just shrugged and drove her shovel back into the patch of grass she was working on. "There's nothing to say, specifically. I'm just saying that I've been with the same man since I was fifteen years old. I understand complicated is all."

He resumed shoveling as well.

"Do *you* want to talk about it?"

Scott chuckled at that. "What you heard from dinner with Babs the other night is the most I've said about any of my relationships in years."

"Fair enough." She plopped another piece of sod in the wheelbarrow and added, "I'm starving. I wonder what's taking Jackie so long."

Maybe it looked a bit too perfectly planned, but seconds later Jackie emerged from the house with the tray of food. Sam and Scott left their shovels and gloves on the ground as they went up to the deck to join her.

"You don't have to feed me every time I'm here, Jackie." Scott ran his hand through his hair and stretched out his muscles a bit as he spoke. Jackie watched him and vowed that she would provide every meal for the rest of his life if it meant he'd stick around.

"I know, I know. You all don't have to help me, either, but you do. The least I can do is feed you."

When everyone was washed up and sitting on the deck with their plates full of food, Sam said, "I remember when I first noticed Jeremy. He was not my type at all. Remember I went through that Leonardo DiCaprio phase, Jackie? Brooding rail-thin guys with hair falling into their eyes?"

"I remember. It was terrible." Jackie treaded lightly as she wasn't sure if Sam's conversation was heading in the direction of a happily ever after with Jeremy, or the direction of where-did-it-all-go-wrong with Jeremy.

"Then there was Jeremy. Kind of a meathead type with his brown hair buzzed close to his head. A bit on the short side with tons of muscles. *So* not my type back then.

"But we got stuck working together on some project or another and I fell. Hard. I couldn't resist him if I tried. And I did try. Because dating in high school was stupid. It led to inevitable heartbreak. Every girl we knew ended up on the bathroom floor of a dance at least once during their high school career in tears or pissed off about some asshole guy."

There was a silence as Sam was clearly lost in the memory of it all, and Jackie and Scott wondered where the hell the memory had come from in the first place.

"Obviously I failed, miserably," she continued. "I avoided him for all of two weeks before he wore me down and I agreed to go on a date with him."

Jackie's chewing slowed as she started making the connection between Sam's previous conversation with Scott and the one she was having, almost with herself, on the porch as they ate.

"This is all just to say, that I can't quite understand how you two are able to -"

"Sam…" Jackie said. But she didn't know what to say after that.

"Act like you don't want to mount each other every second of every day? How are you not dating or at least hooking up?" Sam blurted out.

Scott and Jackie froze, their faces were still looking at Sam, but they were devoid of any emotion since they were caught off guard.

"Not that you owe me any explanation," she was quick to add as she hopped down from the deck. "I'm only throwing it out there because I don't think either of you ever will."

She gathered up what was left of her lunch. "I completely forgot I told Jeremy I would help him with that thing. I gotta run, but you guys talk it over. Or maybe do less talking and more -"

"Bye, Sam," Jackie was quick to interject. With more than a hint of sarcasm she added, "It was so nice to see you today."

"I know," she said with a wink. "Bye, Scott. Have fun!" And then she bounded, yes bounded, down the walkway, put what had become her to-go lunch on the passenger seat, and then she was off down the road before Jackie or Scott could even begin to comprehend what all had happened.

"Always interesting when Sam and Babs are around," Scott said, breaking the ice.

"Always," Jackie agreed.

Jackie struggled to organize her thoughts as all her focus was on the tiny bit of contact between their legs, and on the aching and longing building up *between* her legs. Her mind had been more and more scattered as Scott got more hands-on with the projects. Their fingers overlapped as they held a board in place, he grabbed her waist to help her down from a ladder since her hands were full, and once his entire chest was pressed flush against her back as he helped her get a tote from a high shelf in the garage. She'd had to fight with every ounce of restraint to keep from backing her ass into his hips and rubbing up and down against his...

Nope. Too much. She turned to face Scott as well, and in the process moved back far enough so they were no longer touching. Boundaries.

"You're leaving," she said. A part of her thinking that it was possible he'd respond with, "maybe I will, or maybe won't."

"I have to," he said back with a grimace. "This," he continued with his arm and hand up to motion towards the neighborhood, "it's just not for me."

"And your job...Lana said not to get involved," she added.

"And *you* can't get distracted with your work, either..." he trailed off.

"Right," she said.

"Right," he agreed.

He cleared his throat and broke their contact first by looking back to the unfinished yard, "We should get back to digging."

Scott got up and offered his hand to help Jackie up even

though they were barely off the ground. Against all better judgment, she took it as she hopped off the porch. She foolishly continued to allow herself to believe there was still a possibility for more as their hands lingered a little too long for being only friends.

"But first," Scott said as he walked to the street, "I need to get a picture for Twitter."

"Of this?" She was dubious anyone would want to see the dirt lawn they'd created.

"Wait 'til you see it, Jackie. That mud all over your pants, the shovel, the lighting. It's all perfect. I'm doing a before, middle, and after photo collage. I'll post it once you have the sand down."

Naturally, Jackie was used to being filmed by Scott since she already had dozens of hours of filming under her belt. But being filmed was immensely different from being photographed. Documentary filming required her to move and get lost in her work. The photo he was about to take required her to stand still. Her thoughts had nowhere to go but to him.

"Beautiful," he said as he squatted down to get the picture straight-on rather than at an angle. He stood again and tapped his phone a few times as he walked back towards her.

"Here. Take a look." He extended his hand out to show her the image on the phone. "Remember it's still a bit rough, and I'll make a few minor edits here and there." The image was of her from the knees down and she looked even muddier than she'd realized without the rest of her body in the frame. Her calves and feet were on the right side of the photo with the dirt ground filling most of the middle and left side. One thin section of remaining grass lined the left edge of the photo. He used a black and white filter, so the brown of the mud wasn't as jarring and unsightly.

"You're right. It's a good shot," she agreed, handing his phone back to him.

"I keep proving myself right, and yet you keep doubting me. When will it end, Jackie?" he teased as he pocketed his phone and picked up his shovel again.

"Never."

SCOTT

"**Y**ou're here early? I adore you, Lizzy," Scott said as he beamed at the coworker who was taking over his shift. He'd been filming at the stand Christmas Lights Lane sponsored at the local fall festival. The work itself was fine, but the stand they'd sponsored was with the local blood bank and he was certain they were going to ask him to donate. He'd love to, really, but needles were his Achilles' heel. He'd rather have someone smash his arm with a sledgehammer rather than go anywhere near him with a very small and sharp metal needle.

"I'm here early per Tim's request," Lizzy said. When she caught sight of him packing up, she added, "Don't rush out. Tim needs to see you. He's over at the school board booth schmoozing it up with everyone who walks by."

Damn. He was going to ask Scott to donate, and Scott wouldn't be able to say no to Tim. Very few people could. Not only was Tim surprisingly persuasive, but he was also a genuinely awesome human being who, as far as Scott could tell, had done no wrong. Ever. In his entire life.

Scott's reluctance faded when he almost bumped into

Jackie on his way to the booth to see Tim. Before they could say a word to each other, Tim turned and began to descend upon them.

"Scott, Jackie." His politician tone carried effortlessly through the crowd as he walked towards them. "We have numbers we're trying to hit each hour and we happen to be two down for the five o'clock hour."

"Were you summoned via text, too?" Jackie asked Scott. He hadn't seen her since they'd spoken on her front porch a few days prior. A couple of texts almost made it out of him in the time since then, but he couldn't get the words right and ended up deleting them. Maybe being in a tent with her for the next fifteen minutes or so wouldn't be the worst thing in the world – even if he needed to get jabbed in the process.

"I was working. Just got off my shift." He was able to say before Tim was in between them.

"You two," Tim said, "are the key to us meeting our goal this hour. Are you up to the challenge of saving three lives with your blood donation?" Tim's arms were over their shoulders as he steered them towards the donation tent before even giving them a chance to respond.

"I might not be, Tim."

At Jackie's words Tim stopped in his tracks making them stop as well since he had a solid grip on each of their shoulders.

"The last three times I tried to donate they said my iron was too low."

"Have you tried today yet?"

"No -"

"Then I'm sure you'll be fine. I can feel it, Jackie." Tim's hands dropped from their shoulders as he deposited them at the table outside the blood donation tent. Then Tim was off again already in conversation with a couple that had walked by.

Some of Jackie's neighbors were at the table and tasked with signing up donors and handing out juice boxes, cookies, and t-shirts to anyone who donated blood.

"Hi, Jackie. Hi, Scott" said Jan, the biggest Richard Simmons fan on Christmas Lights Lane. "Are you all here to donate?"

"That's what we've been told," Scott said.

"We heard you all are a little low on donors today," Jackie added.

"We had a steady stream for the first two hours and now nothing but a trickle since then. You're both dolls for coming out to donate."

"Happy to help," Scott said with mild conviction. He was suddenly aware that Jackie was about to see a tiny needle bring him to his knees. They each took a clipboard and filled out the standard information required to donate. Then they handed the clipboards and pens back to Jan.

"Perfect. Just go on through that tent there and they'll get you situated. We'll be here on the other side with all your goodies," the woman said as her pointy, hot pink nails did a sort of jazz hands over the table of food and t-shirts.

Once inside the tent, they sat down to fill out more paperwork and to have their iron levels tested. That Scott could handle. A quick prick to his finger that came right back out again? No problem. Though he could still use a slight distraction. He shamelessly let his gaze fall to Jackie as she had her blood tested. As if he wasn't already crazy about her, he fell a little more watching her subtly cross her fingers and close her eyes, her lips moving slightly in some sort of prayer, as they pricked her finger.

She played it cool when she was cleared to donate, but Scott could see the pure joy in her eyes.

While Jackie had successfully downplayed (to the tent worker at least, not to Scott) her fears about not being able to donate, Scott was going in the opposite direction. He allowed his abject horror at donating dominate his facial expressions once they were inside another section of the tent and in their donation chairs.

The phlebotomist walked into the tent with a flourish and Scott was immediately reminded of a female version of Tim. She was wearing blood red scrubs with a large button off to the side. The button had a Dracula head with a talking bubble that read, "I vant to expertly take your blood for donations!"

"How are we all doing on this fine fall day?" she asked in a sing-song voice.

"Good, thank you," Jackie replied.

Scott couldn't find any words.

"Alright then," she continued. It was clear there was some sort of script she was following and that her same response would have likely followed just about anything they had said.

"I'm Florence and I'll be with you on this journey today. 'What journey is that?' You may be asking yourselves. And I will tell you. It's the journey that starts with you in these comfy chairs here and ends with me collecting enough blood to save the lives of up to three strangers."

There was a pause for effect, though Scott doubted neither he nor Jackie gave her the response or reaction she was looking for as they both stared back at her.

"Alright then," Florence continued. "I'll start left to right which means you are the lucky gent who gets to kick things off for us," she said as she pointed to Scott. "Which arm would you both like to donate from?"

Scott raised his right arm.

"Excellent choice," Florence said.

Something unintelligible escaped his lips as Florence turned away and tended to her tray of tools.

"Are you okay?" Jackie asked.

"I don't like needles," he whispered in her direction. His eyes were glued to the ceiling of the tent, and he couldn't bring himself to look at her.

"Oh, right." A slight pause. "I could try to distract you," she offered.

"Please."

Florence, her tourniquet in hand, said, "Just look at the lovely lady next to you while I get you prepped and stuck. You won't feel a thing." Scott wondered how she slept at night knowing her job included lobbing empty promises at unsuspecting strangers.

Perspiration sprung up along his brow as the tourniquet was placed and he waited for a long needle to settle into his arm for the indefinite future.

"Umm…tell me about swimming with the sharks," Jackie said.

That was all he needed to get his attention from the needle. He turned his head and looked at her, his brow slightly furrowed. "How did you know about that?"

"All set," Florence practically sang. "Just keep squeezing this every few seconds and I'll be back to check on you soon. Okay?" She handed him a foam bar to squeeze and release to help keep the blood pumping. It was working. He could feel the blood draining from his face.

"Yes, thank you," Scott managed. Then his attention was back on Jackie. He kept his eyes glued to hers, which wasn't in itself a difficult task, and willed himself to ignore Florence as she tied up and jabbed Jackie, too.

"It was on Facebook. The sharks in Vegas," she said.

"Yeah, Facebook. I forget I even have it sometimes. Corine posted that. She didn't have an account, so she posted on mine a bit. She was kinda funny like that." He hadn't been hiding his ex-wife from Jackie, or the fact that he'd been married. But he also never spoke about it beyond that it had happened. Well, usually he didn't elaborate. Jackie and Babs had a way of getting things out of him.

"All set on this side, too," Florence said. "Everyone okay?"

They both nodded and gave verbal confirmation that they were fine.

"Fabulous," she sang. "I'll be back in a bit." And then she bounded out of the tent with just as much energy as she'd had when she'd entered it.

Jackie turned back to Scott and back to their conversation. "We don't have to talk about it. I was just trying to distract you." Her face flushed red, and he could tell she was embarrassed to have brought up bad memories.

"No, it's fine. I want to." They were in a tent in the middle of a community event full of people, some of whom they knew, and yet it felt intimate. They were both vulnerable as they laid on the reclined chairs – physically unable to leave.

"Corine was this amazing woman. We met at a bar in Breckenridge, Colorado. I'd never met anyone as outgoing and confident as she was. She intimidated the hell out of me." Scott gave a soft laugh at his admission and Jackie did the same.

"Anyway. We were both on vacation, but we had this connection, so we tried to make it work. I dropped my life in New York, where I was living at the time, and followed her to Vegas."

As he spoke his eyes went back and forth between staring off into the distance somewhere towards the front of the tent and locking eyes with Jackie. While he'd admitted Corine had made him nervous, Corine had nothing on Jackie given how his stomach flipped every time he saw her.

"Vegas sounds fun," Jackie offered. It was clearly an attempt to say something, anything, while avoiding saying the wrong thing during a painful conversation.

"It was an adventure," he agreed. "When I left Milton, I

wanted to see and do everything. I wanted to travel, I wanted to live in different cities. And that's what Corine wanted, too. We were going to see and experience everything we could.

"We did that for a while. Like the part-time job at Mandalay Bay diving in the shark tank. Corine worked there with me."

Just as Scott prepared himself for an emotional purge – the conversation he'd wanted to have with Jackie from the beginning – Florence emerged once again from outside the tent.

"How's everyone doing?" she cheerfully asked as though there was nowhere else in the world she'd rather be.

"Great, thanks," Jackie called out with equal enthusiasm.

"Do you need anything?"

Jackie didn't give Scott a chance to answer. "Nope. We're good. Thanks."

Florence squeezed each of their blood donation bags, and Scott almost vomited in his mouth from the sight of it. Then she was gone, and they were alone in the tent again.

Jackie waited for him to regain his composure before she asked, "So what happened? With you and Corine?"

"I got caught up in the thrill and excitement of it all, and before I knew it, we were getting married at some little white chapel in Vegas. Just us. No family."

"That sounds...nice." It was sweet of Jackie to say, but Scott looked back at those days as some of his darkest. He'd lost himself completely and had tried to find his sense of self and identity again in every city he'd visited since. Had also tried to find it through his marriage to Corine.

"It wasn't. Looking back now I can see it so clearly. My mother and father...they were supportive about the whole thing, but I could tell they were hurt to be left out."

The curtains of the tent fluttered, and Tim appeared in one of the t-shirts they gave out with each donation. Before he could open his mouth to say something, he read the room looking back and forth between Scott and Jackie. He didn't even bother to turn back around. He simply stepped backwards out of the tent and was gone.

"And after the wedding…" Jackie prompted after she'd turned back to Scott.

"We didn't do any of the things we said we would. We rarely left Vegas, which I grew to hate. I met Lana and started working on the documentary with her. That helped. But I was still miserable."

He took a deep breath and continued. "I don't even know how to explain it. Once we were married, it was like everything changed. Or maybe it didn't change. Maybe she was the same person she always was, but I hadn't known her well enough to realize until it was too late."

Scott had to break his eyes away from Jackie's. He was not the first or last person to get divorced, but it was still something that embarrassed him. Even though he had a strong feeling that it shouldn't. They were having blood drawn from different arms leaving their free hands a mere foot apart, Jackie reached across the slight void and grabbed Scott's hand.

He'd had a feeling she would do that at some point in the tent, either to help ease his nerves about needles, or to help ease the pain of talking about his divorce. That was the kind of person she'd always been since the day he'd met her. Scott gratefully accepted and gave her a few quick squeezes to show his appreciation. They stayed that way, her hand in his, until the eager phlebotomist once again returned for their donations and to patch them back up with a square of gauze and a small strip of medical tape.

"Don't forget your juice and cookies on the way out," Florence called as Scott held the tent flap aside for Jackie and they exited.

"Will do," he absently called back. He was just about to ask her if they could grab a bite to eat and talk for a bit when he noticed her start to lean to the right. Her eyes rolled to the back of her head. *Shit, she's going to faint!* he thought as he threw his body behind hers.

JACKIE

*J*ackie came to and was immediately accosted by Jan who shoved the straw of an orange-juice flavored juice box into her mouth. Any other day she would have been mortified to have someone publicly feeding her like that, but after the donation she was incredibly thirsty. Her body was desperate for whatever sugars and vitamins were needed to replenish the blood she'd donated.

After a long pull on the straw she asked, "Where's Scott?" Though she didn't consciously realize she was asking it. It just sort of popped out.

"You're sittin' in his lap, hon," Jan said.

"Right here, Jackie," she heard Scott say from behind her.

As she glanced down, Jackie could see that Scott was indeed right under her. He must have caught her as she fell and then propped her up in his lap so she wasn't lying on the ground. She tried to get up, but her legs were still a bit wobbly, and the attempt made her sight darken again briefly.

"Just sit tight. Sip your drink. You're gonna need a minute or two," Jan said. Then she stood and addressed the crowd that had formed around them. "She's alright. Gonna be just fine. Move along, everyone."

"Scott?" Jackie asked without turning to look at him.

"Yeah, Jackie?" His voice was breathy in her ear and full of concern.

"Thanks for catching me." Her head felt heavy, so she let it fall back onto his shoulder and neck.

His fingertip gently trailed around her ear as he tucked a section of her hair back as if to make sure she heard him. "I wouldn't let you fall, Jackie."

She felt shivers run up and down her body and took a minute to save the memory of what it felt like to be sitting with him. The feel of his strong legs under and around her own and his taut chest against her back. She allowed herself one last deep breath to take in his scent before she forced herself to get up.

Even though Jackie was certain she'd only passed out for a few seconds, Scott insisted on driving her home. She declined once before giving in. They listened to the radio for the short ride back to her house. Milton was a tiny town; most trips were a short way from wherever you started.

"Well, thanks for the ride home," Jackie said as she climbed out of the car.

"Whoa, whoa, whoa," Scott said as he climbed out and rushed around the car in an attempt to help her. "I'm not dropping you on the sidewalk."

"I guess I do feel a little bit wobbly still." She was acting her ass off and hoping he was buying it. Suddenly emboldened by their conversation and time in the tent, she took advantage of the situation and leaned heavily on him as he shut her car door and turned her towards the house.

"Just let me walk you in, please," Scott said in what Jackie swore was a bit of a husky voice. But was his voice off because he was straining to help her inside? "I'd worry the whole way home if I didn't."

Nope. Definitely sexy husky and not huffing and puffing, struggling-to-talk husky. Not to mention the thumb on his hand around her waist that ever so lightly stroked up and down sending chills through her whole body. Her knees really were weakening, and she was grateful he was there. Though in fairness he was the reason for the weakening state to begin with.

Once inside she broke away to get a glass of water per Florence's orders. Her mind went back and forth with what she should do. Offer him a seat on the couch with her to stay for a bit and maybe watch a movie? *No. Inappropriate. He's moving anyway. Let. Him. Go.* She told herself once and for all as she got her water. She reemerged from the kitchen with her drink and said, "Thanks for bringing me home."

Like a mind-reader he was shuffling around building materials and tools to make room for her on the couch.

"Here, have a seat. It's probably too early for bed, but you should still lay down for a bit." He patted the newly cleared spot on the couch and moved the ottoman over so she could stretch her legs out.

"Thanks." She'd been exhausted for the past few weeks and it did feel wonderful to lay down in the middle of the day. "Can you hand me my notebook? I can do some work while I relax."

He gently kicked the black and white composition book towards the other end of the room. "You cannot work while you relax."

"I can't just lay here and not get anything done." She tensed up a bit as she said it. Instead of lounging on the couch she was on the verge of hopping up once again to get her notebook. She wondered if Scott noticed the look of longing on her face as she stared at it adoringly from across the room.

"Okay, I see how this is going to go." Her attention went back to Scott as he grabbed the remote from off the mantle and turned on the tv, settling in next to her on the couch.

"You don't have to babysit me, Scott." Although to be fair, it wasn't terrible having him next to her on the couch. Their arms with matching wounds reminding them of the heart-to-heart they'd had earlier as they'd held hands in the tent. But an even stronger desire was for her to get more work done since she wasn't feeling nearly as woozy as before. The calendar was ticking away days and she had miles and miles to go in the way of her display.

"I do." The tv showed the Netflix opening screen. He left it there and turned to her to talk. "As soon as I leave, you're going to start working yourself to death. Again. It's what you do, Jackie. I know you."

"Sketching designs in a notebook is hardly exhausting work."

"And yet you've been exhausted for weeks."

He'd noticed. Hopefully it wasn't that she looked like shit. She hoped it was based solely on his witnessing her yawning or leaning on him a few too many times.

"Fine. Stay. But we're watching and analyzing docu-mentaries."

"Unbelievable," he said with a smile. Then he broke all of her trust and started scrolling through her recently watched content.

"No!" she called as she tried to grab the remote from his hand.

"What is all of this?" His wide eyes turned to her waiting for a response.

"You don't swipe through other photos when someone hands you their phone, and you don't go through their

Netflix previously watched section when someone hands you the remote. Basic rules of etiquette, Scott." The damage had already been done and so she gave up trying to get the remote back and instead glared at him with her arms crossed.

"You love cheesy Hallmark-style Christmas movies," he accused.

"It was for research." It was also a guilty pleasure, so she added a bit extra to help back up her semi-lie. "Living in Milton on Christmas Lights Lane sometimes feels like I'm in a Hallmark Christmas movie. I'm researching Christmas in small towns. I half expect Candace Cameron Bure to show up during the event with a giant sign that says 'I should never have moved to New York. Forgive me, Gus. I love you.'"

"That was oddly specific."

"Variations of that scenario happen more often than you think. And when it happens to me – highly likely now that I'm living here – I need to be prepared."

"Okay, I'll bite. What happens?"

"I just told you..." Even she was lost after her rambling about Candace Cameron Bure's romantic apology.

"What happens after she holds up the sign?"

"Oh, right. Then Gus, short for Augustus, the hunky and brooding town widower played by some random rugged hot guy, will somehow find it in his heart to forgive her and they'll kiss in front of the crowd, and potentially my house, just as the first snow of the year begins to fall and as they begin their happily ever after in the small, picturesque town."

His eyes narrowed on her. "How many of these have you watched?"

"Oh, bummer. We've run out of down time. Back to work with the documentary analysis." She grabbed the remote from his hand and searched for the Amazing Irish Cooking Show.

"The Amazing Irish Cooking Show? Do you ever watch anything with a rating above PG?" he teased.

"I'll have you know the Christmas movies on Netflix are pretty...graphic in terms of the sex scenes." *Holly Gets Her Halls Decked* for example, which she accidentally watched for the first time with her mother and Tom. Luckily Tom was a cat, but watching the sex scenes next to her mother had been brutal. Babs didn't care, but Jackie did. Her face reddened at the memory and she regretted saying anything to Scott about it.

"Oh, yeah? That's kinda hot. Let's watch one of those."

"No way." She was increasingly close to tearing off his clothes to begin with. Watching something remotely sexy would destroy the last threads of self-control that currently held her back and on her own tiny spot on the couch. "We're watching and analyzing. Remember?"

He gave a loud sigh and settled back into the couch as she queued up the first episode of the latest season. As if they'd settled in on our couch to watch a movie a million times before, his left arm rested on the arm rest and his right slid around her shoulders and she found herself settling in against his chest. Tucked beneath his arm as if that was where she'd belonged all along.

Thirty minutes in and they'd done exactly what she'd wanted them to. She asked various questions about the cameras and how the documentary aspect of it worked, and he'd enlightened her with what he knew or what he guessed was happening behind the scenes.

"See how the background is always showing the side of the tent closest to the person being filmed? They're always pointing the camera from the center of the tent outwards. That way you can have multiple cameras going without accidentally filming the other cameras in the background."

"That's smart. Why don't you guys do that?"

"Our budget is not quite as big as theirs is."

"Oh, right. Good point."

A bit later she asked, "Would you work on the show? If they called you up tomorrow and hired you over the phone, would you do it?"

She couldn't see him since her back was to his chest, but she could feel his body moving and knew his left hand had gone straight to his head. His fingers raked through his hair as he considered his response. "Maybe a season or two. Not sure I could stay in one place and keep documenting the same thing for much longer than that."

There it was again. His unrelenting desire to move from place to place rather than settling somewhere. She went back to technical questions after that.

When the episode ended, Scott reached towards the remote which was sitting on the other side of Jackie. "Seems like a good time to reward all that hard work we just did analyzing the baking show by watching some of those...what did you call them? Graphically sexy holiday movies?"

Instinctively her hand moved the remote to underneath her leg as if that would be an appropriate obstacle for Scott. It was not. His eyebrows arched mischievously as if to say "game on" as he increased his efforts to get it.

Within seconds his right arm, the one that had so tenderly held her against his chest throughout the show, gave a quick movement that sent her rolling over onto his lap while exposing the remote on the couch cushion.

Except that as soon as she was on his lap, the last of her giggles escaped her and neither was interested in the remote anymore.

Scott's smile fell as they locked eyes. Then his eyes traveled down to her lips which were suddenly dangerously close to his own. His hands were on her hips, and she shifted slightly to encourage his hands to move up to her chest or, even better, down her legs where an aching throb had started once again between her thighs. But he resisted and they stayed on her hips while her hands stayed safely on his shoulders.

She was about to give up again when he closed the space between them and gave her the softest kiss of her life. Regardless, her body reacted as though they'd been passionately kissing for the past hour. She had been waiting for his kiss for weeks, months, years even if she counted all the time since their night on the balcony.

The kiss was fleeting, but not quick enough for him to retreat. Without thinking, her hand went to his cheek and jawline, guiding him back to her and returning the kiss with all the intensity of years of pent-up desire rushing through her body. Scott's soft lips on hers, and then his stubble harsh against her skin in a way that made her dizzy with desire. He'd made the first move, but it was hard to say who initiated what afterwards. It was all a blur of lips, tongues, and hands.

She could feel the heat and desire coming from him as his fingers slid up over her thin, unlined bra, and his thumb caressed her hardened nipples through the fabric. His other hand moved to the small of her back and pulled her in closer. Wanting more and needing to eliminate any space between them even though his body was already flush and hot against hers. His touches and kisses no longer gentle as everything turned primal and desperate.

She let her hands make their way up his muscle-ripped chest beneath his shirt. A moan escaped her mid-kiss as he pulled her even tighter to him and she felt his hard length rubbing between her legs through their pants.

She could have stayed that way all night, but her brain caught up with what was happening and protested – insisted on clarifying a few things before they went any further.

"Wait," she said, pulling her face away from his while keeping her hands and arms firmly in place. "What about work?"

Scott leaned in again, this time into her neck, and said in a deep and breathy voice, "Who I'm with is none of Lana's business." His mouth was on her again, but this time on her jawline as his lips trailed from her chin to her ear, and then down her neck. She felt her muscles relaxing like she might pool into him and the couch right then. He gripped her tighter to keep her upright, but it only made her legs and body feel even weaker than before.

"But what about…" Her brain would not concede no matter how much she tried to shut it off.

Scott pulled back and looked at Jackie as he spoke. "The work thing's a bit tricky, but we'll figure it out."

"Okay," she managed before her mind screamed at her, *You could have been doing this weeks ago!*

He pulled away from her and asked, "Is this okay?" with concern lining his face. It was understandable given how many times they'd both hinted at or outright said that dating would be a bad idea for them. It just wasn't a possibility given all the obstacles that stood between them.

"It is. Really." Her hands went to the back of his neck and gently caressed and massaged the skin below his hairline.

He leaned in and made another trail of kisses from her chin to her ear before whispering, "I should have asked you out the night of the first meeting. I'm so sorry I didn't."

She felt a gentle lick and nip on her earlobe. Then her hands were under his shirt again and he moaned into her mouth as her tongue was once again caressing his and begging for more.

When she moved her kisses to trail down his neck he said, "Let me take you out on a date."

There was nowhere they could go in Milton without

risking someone seeing them. She wasn't embarrassed to be seen with Scott (no woman in their right mind would be), but she also wasn't ready for the pressure that would come with making their relationship, or whatever it was they were doing, official town gossip.

"I'd love that," she said between kisses. "But maybe somewhere other than Milton?"

"Right. We don't want Lana or Lizzy to see us out together. Not yet at least."

Jackie felt a slight knot in her stomach. Their relationship already had an expiration date and they both had reasons not to be seen together in Milton. It didn't feel like they were off to a good start. But looking into his eyes she saw nothing but euphoric confidence. Or maybe that look was only a direct result of his current situation where she was straddling him and grinding herself against his cock as they were rounding the different bases. But if he wasn't worried, then she wouldn't be either. As far as she could tell, worrying had solved very little in her lifetime.

As difficult as it was to do, she slid back on his legs a bit so they could talk. "Where should we go?"

His hands moved to her legs and his fingers caressed the muscle groove on her thigh running up and down from her knee to her hip.

"I have somewhere in mind, but I'd like for it to be a surprise."

"I like surprises." She leaned in for another kiss.

"Good. Are you free tomorrow?"

"Yes," she said without hesitation even though she'd already agreed to dinner with Sam and Jeremy who had graciously offered to feed her and help her with one of her decorations. *I'll reschedule*, she thought. *Sam will understand.*

"One more episode of the baking show before I head home?"

"Home? Why not just spend the night? It's getting late." It was a little after seven.

His hand made another sweep on her body as if he was considering her offer.

"That night at the beach is one of my favorite memories. Hands down. But I always regretted that what happened between us was a one-night stand. I have every intention of repeating our beach night – as many times as you'll let me, if I'm honest – but only after we go out on an official date. I want to be a gentleman. You deserve nothing less."

That comment alone made her want to rip his clothes off and do many, many dirty things with him on the couch. But she also loved hearing that it wasn't just sex with him. It never had been.

"One more episode," she agreed. "Bread week is up next." She slid back to her position against his chest with his arm pulling her in tight. His perfectly soft lips gave her a kiss on the top of her head as his fingertips gently caressed the tiny bit of skin peeking out between her pants and her shirt.

JACKIE

*T*he surprise dinner with Scott turned out to be crab picking at one of her favorite restaurants in Ocean City. It was as if they went back and had the date they should have had years ago.

"Are you getting the all-you-can-eat crabs?" Scott asked after the waiter went back to get their drink orders.

"Yes, I'm pretty competitive. But you probably already knew that seeing me in the neighborhood Olympics."

"You do competitive crab picking? You cease to amaze me, Strauss."

"Crab picking is always competitive in the Strauss household. It comes from Dad. He hated crabs – too wet – so he'd always get annoyed at Mom and me when we wanted to get all-you-can-eat crabs. He'd swear we wouldn't eat enough to offset the costs, and we'd stuff our faces trying to prove him wrong. Meanwhile he'd be grossed out the whole time because he hates wet food."

"And did you? Prove him wrong?"

"Never. We're both suckers for the extras they bring out

before the crabs. But I still like the challenge of it all and the memories that come with it."

The waiter reappeared to take their orders then Jackie continued. "I say Dad got mad, but he didn't really. More of a playful annoyance. I don't know that I ever saw him get mad at Mom. That's probably why Mom took his passing so hard and now carts a cat around with her claiming it's Dad."

"I'd been meaning to ask you about that." He took a sip of water as he appeared to carefully choose his next words. "Do I talk to him as if he's your dad? I mean, do you th… Do you know he's your dad?" Scott looked pained as he said it. As if he was sure he was saying the wrong thing which may or may not lead to him getting a drink thrown in his face.

Jackie thought about it for a moment. "I honestly have no idea. In the beginning I played along to placate Mom. But as time passed, I've found myself talking to him even when Mom's not around."

"That sounds…comforting."

"It is," she agreed. "Are you a cat person?"

"Not really. You?"

"Team dog."

The waiter returned again with plates of fried chicken, corn on the cob, hush puppies, and rolls for Jackie, and a tiny cup of cream of crab soup for Scott. While Jackie had zero qualms about stuffing her face in front of him, she did hesitate at the idea of having first-time sex with Scott while feeling bloated from eating excessive amounts of food. And she would count it as the first time again since a decade had passed since. She very much doubted it would be similar to what happened when they were just eighteen with limited experience.

"Just the hush puppies, please," she told the waiter before he was able to unload all of the food onto their table.

"You know you don't have to get the all-you-can-eat

crabs. You can order a dozen and then comfortably eat those twelve without worrying about whether you got your money's worth or not."

"That takes away all the fun." Before she could elaborate on why she couldn't resist eating mass quantities of hush puppies and crabs in one sitting, he was out of his seat with his cup of soup and sliding in next to her at the booth.

"What's with the seat change, Scott?" She was pretty sure he wanted to be closer to her, but she also needed to hear it from him. Their night out, on an official date, was still blowing her mind a bit and she needed occasional confirmation it wasn't all a dream.

"You can probably tell I'm nervous. I practically clipped that truck on our way here."

"I did notice the near fender-bender accident just outside of Milton, yes."

"I figured you might have, what with all the horn blaring and him flipping me the bird." Scott blushed and ran his hand through his hair. They were so close in the booth, and he looked so adorably vulnerable telling her, she couldn't help but to lean over and kiss him. They hadn't kissed when he first picked her up, instead opting for an awkward sort of hug at the door before getting into his car. Almost twenty-four hours had passed since they'd first kissed, and she hadn't been able to think of anything since. Her lips were aching for his. Judging by his kiss back and his move to her side of the table, it felt like a sure bet the feeling was mutual.

"This documentary has been brutal." He had pulled away from their kiss but tilted his forehead down to rest against hers. "I'm always with you, but most of the time there's a camera between us. I'm not actually in your life – I'm an observer. I moved over to this side because I didn't want anything between us tonight."

He gave her a sweet and chaste kiss, and Jackie almost

melted right there. Disregarding the fact that they were in a restaurant, she put her hand up to his jaw and angled down for a deeper kiss. Their nerves and hesitations pushed aside, their tongues were free to –

"Your crabs, ma'am," the waiter said as he placed a large tray of steamed crabs on the table. They pulled away slightly flushed and slightly embarrassed by their public display of affection. "And the rockfish for the gentleman. Can I get you anything else with your meal?"

"No, thank you. Looks delicious," Scott said.

"Enjoy." Then he was off to help another table.

By the time Scott turned back to Jackie, she'd already grabbed one of the crabs and had begun to expertly dissect it over the thick brown paper they laid on top of the table. From the corner of her eye, she noticed he gave her an amused look.

"I love crabs," she said in her defense as she tore off all the legs and cracked the inner shell in half to begin picking at the bits of meat inside. "Did you know that? Is that why you picked Cray Cray for Crabs for dinner?"

"I didn't know that. It wasn't until we pulled up that it even occurred to me you may have some severe allergic reaction to shellfish, and I was potentially driving you to your doom."

"No allergies. We're good." Jackie shoved a large lump of crab meat into her mouth.

"I picked Ocean City because it always makes me think of you and our night together. And I wanted to pick crabs, even though I didn't get any this time, because it takes a while to eat them. I wanted us to have plenty of time to talk during dinner."

"It's the perfect choice. Though I will need a little help from you now and then." She held up her hands already covered in a mixture of crab and Old Bay seasoning. "Can you get my phone out of my purse? It's on the other side of me." Jackie leaned back so he could reach across her to get her purse. "It's in the front pocket. I just need to know if Mom texted me. I worry about her sometimes and I forgot to tell her I'd be out of town tonight."

As if he feared he would tear apart her purse with his Hulk-like bare hands, Scott carefully opened the front pocket and pulled out her phone. He hit the side button to bring it to life and held it up for her to see without looking at it himself. No texts. Babs was fine.

Scott's assistance with the phone check –in particular his body against hers as he reached for her purse – was getting her hot and bothered again. Her gross, spicy hands were the only thing keeping her from accosting him when he leaned back across to replace her purse on the booth seat. His fresh scent overpowered the smell of the restaurant and her crabs, and his thigh against hers was a constant reminder of how much she wanted more.

The rest of the dinner they talked and laughed as they caught up more on the time between high school and their date. Scott's hand often landed and rested on her thigh, and she started to regret her decision to get the messiest dinner ever since she couldn't touch him back when she so desperately wanted to. At one point, she did give in to the urge to playfully bite his shoulder. He returned the favor with a kiss and light lick right beneath her ear that sent a jolt down to her core.

After dinner, they walked down to the boardwalk for a quick stroll even though most everything was closed for the season.

"Who were you filming last Wednesday?" Jackie asked as they walked hand in hand while the ocean crashed in the background. She'd seen his car parked not far from her house on her way to run a few errands that evening. She always noticed his car when it was parked somewhere on her street, and she always felt a slight dull ache in the pit of her stomach thinking about how one day soon he would get into his car and never return. Off to his next adventure.

"Mort with his train display. He insisted I stay for dinner, which your neighbors almost always do now. Either dinner in the evening, or breakfast when I first get there if we're shooting in the morning. They all heard I stayed for dinner that one time with you, and it was all over for me."

"Awe, that's sweet. They're probably lonely and appreciate the company."

"Yeah, half of them tell me as much. I don't think it's me, particularly, they care for. They like the company. It happened a bit in Florida, too, at the retirement home."

She squeezed his hand. "It absolutely *is* you. So handsome and charming…"

"You think Mort likes how handsome I am?"

"*I* like how handsome you are."

They walked for a few blocks on the boardwalk swapping playful banter and checking out the very limited display of Halloween decorations the various hotels, businesses, and condos had up. It had been a nice night when they first left the restaurant, but the temperature began to drop quickly once the sun was out of sight.

A strong cool breeze passed them, and they dropped hands so he could put his arm around her while she tucked her hand in his jacket pocket. He smelled amazing which made her question if she smelled like crabs and Old Bay. Who gets all-you-can-eat crabs on a date? Rookie mistake.

Then his hands slid into the back pockets of her jeans, and he pulled her waist towards his. Even through his thick jeans and hers, she could feel how badly he wanted her. The constant breeze by the ocean along with the cold fall temperatures gave her chills as they walked. But at that moment, standing pressed against him, she was on the verge of over-heating.

They both leaned in at the same time with the same idea. Then his mouth ventured down to her neck, and she moaned softly before she managed to say, "You didn't happen to book us a room, did you?"

"Actually, I did." He turned her towards a hotel just a little ways down the boardwalk. The Sahara hotel in all its glory lit up the sky. She could see the balcony where Scott had hung up towels to shield them from the boardwalk crowds while they had sex all those years ago.

"It's perfect." She gave him a kiss and bit his lower lip as she pulled away. "But we'll sleep in the bed this time, right? It's too fucking cold for another romantic balcony scene."

On the elevator ride up he pushed her up against the back wall, and she groped him through his pants as they rode up to the twelfth floor. The hallway was empty, so they carried on kissing and touching as they looked for their room and let themselves in.

Jackie took a quick glance around the room to confirm it wasn't disgusting – thankfully it wasn't – before she started to pull the different layers of clothing off Scott's toned body. With a little bit of bumping of their limbs, he did the same.

He tossed her bra off to the side, eased her onto the bed, and said, "Absolutely stunning," before he lowered his head to her to gently kiss and lick and tease her nipples with his tongue.

She kissed and licked every inch of his neck and face while he worked her breasts and made her gasp each time he teased her nipples with gentle flicks of his tongue and fingers. She fumbled with the buttons on his pants a bit, but when she got the button undone and freed him from his boxers, it was her turn to hear him gasp from her touch.

It was all too much for her. His mouth and body on hers, the way he sucked in his breath and moaned when she finally grasped his cock and slowly massaged up and down, and the way his musky, masculine scent flooded her sense of smell. Jackie didn't wait for him to take her pants off – she did it for him.

At the time she'd assumed Scott's talents were all in his mouth given how skillfully he'd found and stroked and nibbled every spot she had, but that was nothing compared to what he could do with his hands.

She allowed him a few minutes to caress and explore between her legs before she moaned, "Please," as she arched her hips up towards his body. Then he was gone and back with a condom on. Clearly he did not want to wait another second either.

It was not slow and sensual as Jackie had often imagined it would be. Regardless, it was no less passionate. Jackie pulled Scott onto the bed and then she climbed on top of him and eased him into her. They both gave a gentle moan at the contact. Slight discomfort gave way to waves of pleasure as she straddled and rocked on top of him.

Scott had always appeared to her as nothing less than the perfect gentleman. It was the way he opened and held doors for others, the sweet way he interacted with her neighbors, the way he'd pulled away the night before to ask if she was okay, and the way he'd insisted on taking her out on a date when he could have had her on the couch the night before.

But there was nothing polite about the way he handled her that night and she couldn't get enough of it. His hands went from her breasts to her back and ribs so he could pull her upper body down to him. She moaned into his neck from the sensation of her nipples dragging up and down his chest as she continued to slide up and down his length.

With Scott's hands still on her ribs, he rolled them both so they were in the missionary position with him kneeling and thrusting between her legs while she lay flat on her back on the bed. Since Jackie felt like she had been the one to make the first move that night, she welcomed the change of pace where Scott was taking charge instead. He leaned down to tug and bite her earlobe before he growled, yes growled, and moved his mouth down her neck and back to her nipples again. It was as if Scott was reduced to his most base instincts and Jackie couldn't get enough of it. Who knew missionary could be so hot?

Throughout she whispered or moaned the typical words of "please," "more," "don't stop," and such. It wasn't anything particularly clever or sexy, but that was all her brain would allow.

He flipped her over and pulled her hips up, so she was on her knees in front of him as he entered her from behind. His cock hit just the right spot in the new position and his hand reached around to help coax out her climax as his fingers worked small circles around her clit.

On top of her smutty Christmas movies, she'd read hundreds of steamy romance novels, too, courtesy of Sam. Many described orgasms as mind-blowing with the heroine seeing stars or bursts of light as the most earth-shattering orgasm of her life raked through her body. Through the years she'd wavered between jealously and disbelief as she'd read those unrealistic sex scenes.

And yet there she was, finally experiencing the elusive earth-shattering orgasm herself. With no regard for how thin the hotel walls may be, she let out a loud moan as every nerve in her body lit up with pleasure. There was no blinding light, but her vision felt cloudy as she lost the ability to focus on anything beyond the feeling of pure bliss coursing through her body as Scott's hand and cock worked their magic.

When she came down from her orgasm, she turned her head to look over her shoulder and his mouth moved to hers. Their kiss was sloppy with tongues and nipping of each other's lips along with moans and incoherent sounds occasionally escaping their mouths.

"Jackie..." he'd started to say, but it hung there alone as she felt him lose himself inside of her before collapsing onto her back on the bed in an embrace. His mouth continued to give soft kisses along her upper back and neck.

It would have been nice to look back at their first time as something romantic, slow, and sensual. But neither of them could have done any of that during their first night together. The build-up had been too long coming for their reunion to have happened any other way.

SCOTT

"Good morning, beautiful," Scott whispered as he tucked a section of Jackie's hair behind her ear. He dragged his scruffy jaw along her soft skin as he leaned in to kiss her and rouse her out of her deep sleep. She gave a soft moan as she turned into his kisses and ran her hands over his taut chest. When Scott pulled away, she opened her eyes.

"You are incredibly tempting right now, but we have to get back." If she continued in any way he'd give in and have her again. Waking up next to her naked body turned his semi-morning wood into a raging hard on, but if they didn't leave in a few minutes, they wouldn't make it back in time for his meeting.

"What time is it?"

"Early. Sorry, but I have a morning meeting and breakfast with Mort. He's making sausage gravy biscuits before he decorates his tree. I'm anticipating a day filled with detailed back stories about each ornament." He knew he sounded a bit dorky, but he also knew that if anyone would understand, it was Jackie.

Scott got out of bed, careful to keep his dick out of her view. He didn't want to tempt anything since he had zero self-restraint left. Once he'd found his boxers and covered up, he started to collect their clothes from around the floor of the room. Jackie sat up and unabashedly enjoyed the view of him half-naked walking around and periodically bending to get another article of clothing.

He handed her the neat stack of clothes and gave her a kiss. "Leaving early and putting on the same clothes from last night is not at all ideal, but the Fractured Prune is on our way to the car. You can get a doughnut then sleep the whole way home." He gave her another kiss as if it could somehow ease the negatives he'd just rattled off.

While Jackie had almost immediately fallen into a deep sleep the night before, he'd laid awake for another hour or two trying to figure out what they were doing and how everything would look in the light of day. Scott had watched her sleep for longer than he cared to admit since he worried that it bordered on creepy. But he couldn't keep his eyes off her and he couldn't pass up the opportunity to take in every detail of her. Even though they didn't mention the end date of their relationship, they both knew it was there. The thought weighed on him at all times and wouldn't let him forget that unless he was able to convince her to go with him, he was slowly inching towards the day he would have to say goodbye to her.

If she felt the same burden, she didn't show it. She returned the kiss and smiled. "Fresh doughnuts and a nap in the car? Sounds like a perfect morning to me."

Jackie fell asleep before they even hit the highway. He was worried about her. It was no secret she was putting in twice the hours of everyone else on the street and was probably still behind schedule. For a split second he'd felt guilty about taking her away for an entire night and possibly putting her even farther behind. But everyone needed a break now and then, right?

He left the radio off fearing it would wake her up. Without the music and talking heads to drown it out, he'd been able to hear her cute little snores on and off throughout the ride home. It was a nice distraction from all the worries in his mind about what they were doing and how serious the relationship already was. Even though they'd only recently begun seeing each other, he'd been falling for her since the initial church-basement meeting back in August.

"Hey, we're at your street," he said as he gently caressed her cheek with the back of his hand.

Her eyes fluttered open, and she stretched in the seat. "Thanks for letting me sleep. I feel much better." But the relaxed look swiftly fell from her face when she spotted Mort, who lived across the street from Jackie, outside Jackie's house talking to Babs. Babs juggled her golf ball and Tom made himself comfortable in the newly installed beach as he rolled back and forth in the sand.

"Why is everyone outside your house?" he asked.

Jackie pulled her phone out and he heard her say more to herself than to him, "Shit, I forgot breakfast with Mom."

"Are you late? Will she be upset?" Fuck. He knew he shouldn't have taken her out of town for the entire night. I had been selfish, and Jackie would be the one suffering the consequences.

Jackie shook her head. "No. You know my mom. She's laid back and understanding about this type of thing. And I'm only a few minutes late." After a short pause she added, "Is it just me, or do Mort and Mom look a little too cozy on my porch."

"Yeah, maybe." Scott took another look as they pulled up

to the house. Babs stood in the sand while Tom moved on from rolling around to digging various holes around the beach. Mort was sitting on the porch engaged in an animated conversation with Babs. Mort hadn't said anything to Scott or ever mentioned Babs when they were working together, but at that moment they looked like old friends.

"What are you going to say to them about why I'm dropping you off?" His hand had moved down to her thigh, but he moved it back to the steering wheel. They were back to pretending to be just friends. Even though he knew it was only pretend, it still made his heart feel a bit heavy after the amazing night they'd had.

"We'll wing it," she said with what sounded like wavering confidence.

"Okay, I'll follow your lead." It was her family, so he was happy to let her take control of the situation.

Once they were out of the car, Babs said, "Did you forget about our breakfast date?" She gave Jackie a modicum of time to respond before adding, "Weren't you wearing that yesterday?"

Despite the chilly morning air, Scott felt his palms springing with sweat as Babs called them out within mere seconds of their arrival. Winging it had not been a good idea.

"Um, I don't think so?" Jackie said with a raised tone at the end to make it sound somewhat like a question.

"Morning, Mort. Morning, Babs. Is that a new hairdo? It suits you." It was the oldest trick in the book, but Scott was playing it regardless. He had to do something.

"Why thank you, Scott. It sure is," she said, blushing a bit.

That was all Scott allowed from Babs before he turned to Mort. "Mort, you ready to get breakfast started? You need anything? Want me to pick anything up?" His line of questions to Mort came off as too aggressive. He'd been attempting to load Mort up with questions so that Babs would forget what she and Jackie had been talking about. Instead, it made him look nervous and suspicious. He could tell it only increased Babs's confidence in her initial assessment.

"No, thank you, Scott. I have everything I need," Mort said as he got up from the porch.

Babs caught her golf ball mid-air. "Actually, Scott, we'll be joining you. Mort saw me out early this morning and we got to talking. He invited us over for breakfast, too." Babs turned to Jackie. "Unless you and Scott already had breakfast this morning." Babs let her eyes drag up and down Jackie's outfit from the night before for emphasis. She was no fool. The questions about her clothes and breakfast had been Babs's polite way of saying, "I see you and Scott are sleeping together now."

Scott blushed knowing everyone around him was aware of his sex life with Jackie. Well, everyone except Tom who had been lured away from the conversation by a squirrel.

Scott and Jackie gave each other a questioning look. He shrugged slightly leaving it up to her, and she said, "Would love to join you. Thanks." It worried Scott how relieved he was to hear her say that. A small part of him feared that she might be sick of him already after their night and morning together. It was all too good to be true and he felt the constant, ominous weight of a large shoe about to drop at any minute.

JACKIE

*L*ater that day, Jackie met up with Sam to once again get some help creating her giant, front-yard crab display, and to fill her in on what had happened so far between her and Scott.

"You guys need to have the status talk. Get it out in the open what you're doing and what the end game is," Sam said as she welded together the base of the crab. Jeremy was the professional welder of the two. Sam took it up as a hobby because it looked badass and because they already had all the equipment.

"I disagree," Jackie half grunted as she put another piece into place. "Whatever we're doing, we've only been doing it for a few days. Can't we just enjoy it without labeling it?"

"You almost missed out on what you called, and I quote, 'the most orgasmic breakfast food experience of your adult life' because you weren't sure where you stood."

"It was so good, Sam. Giant chunks of sausage in the creamiest, most flavorful gravy you've ever tasted. And *real* homemade biscuits." Jackie's mouth watered at the memory of Mort's famous sausage gravy and biscuits breakfast.

"You're scared and you're avoiding the subject." Jackie cursed Sam's ability to read her so well. But she did hit the nail on the head so Jackie might as well continue with her avoidance tactic – that was her MO after all.

"I think Mom is sleeping with Mort," Jackie casually threw out. Success. Sam's eyes widened and Babs's love life became the new focus as they continued their work in Sam's garage.

"Seriously? You got that from one breakfast?"

"I know Babs. For one thing, she left Tom at my house when we went over to Mort's, and she touched up her makeup in my bathroom before breakfast."

"Maybe. But also, Tom's been getting ornery lately. She may have just needed a break." Sam moved on from welding to drilling. *Badass indeed,* Jackie thought as she admired her friend's work.

"She was doing this weird laugh during breakfast that I think was supposed to be flirty or something. I don't know. I don't ever remember hearing it before."

"I'm still not convinced."

"Mom's going back to Mort's later tonight to do a private tarot card reading."

"So that's what the kids are calling it these days," Sam joked. "Okay, you may be on to something. You alright with that?" Sam stopped working to give Jackie her undivided attention.

"Mom dating or Mom dating Mort?" There'd been nothing in the way of romance or boyfriends in Babs's life since Tom died. For almost a decade Babs had been alone. It wasn't right. "Actually, no. It doesn't matter. I'm good with my mom dating in general, and I'm good with her and Mort being a thing. He's a good guy."

Sam nodded in agreement and moved back to her work.

The sounds of their efforts filled the room while they fell into a comfortable silence between two old friends.

"Are things between you and Jeremy okay?"

Jackie threw the random question out as they took a break and sat at the table. With the crab nearing completion, they were almost ready to move on to the arduous task of taking it out to the truck.

"Yeah, we're fine," Sam said without looking at Jackie. It hung in the air for only seconds before Sam added, "I mean, things have been a bit different between us for a while, but I don't even know how to start explaining it. I'm not even sure I understand it myself."

"Are you okay?" Not only was Sam being vague about what was going on, but she was looking at the door with a bit of fear in her eyes like Jeremy may come in at any minute and the thought frightened her somehow.

A soft sound of an almost laugh came from Sam as she turned away from the door and looked back at Jackie. For the next thirty minutes Sam told her how she and Jeremy started to have trouble a few years back. They weren't making time for each other and when they were having sex, which wasn't often, it was more routine. Somehow, they'd fallen into a slump and then didn't know how to get out of it.

"He has regrets, Jackie. I know he does," Sam said with a desperation in her voice that begged Jackie to agree with her. She wanted to hear Jackie saw it, too, and that Sam wasn't crazy.

"Regrets? About marriage? Do you think he wants a divorce?" Jackie whispered. It was all so sudden and out of character for both of them. None if it made sense and so she didn't dare say it any louder as if doing so could make it more real.

"I think I do…"

It was more serious than Jackie had realized. In her mind,

people didn't divorce unless there had been years and years of yelling and vicious arguments. But maybe that had been naïve on her part. Can't two people grow apart without tearing each other's throats out? Didn't people sometimes just decide it wasn't working and that was that?

Sam's head fell into her hands and Jackie moved to other side of the table to sit with her and rub her back. Jackie rested her cheek on Sam's shoulder in some sort of sign of solidarity.

"I know that his eyes are roaming lately. I see it." Sam's voice was on the verge of cracking, but she was somehow keeping her shit relatively together even though it sounded to Jackie as if her marriage was on the verge of collapse. *She's not breaking down because she already has, little by little likely, for the past few years it'd been happening,* Jackie reminded herself as she tried to understand how Sam could be so cool and collective as she spoke about her struggles with Jeremy.

"And I can't even blame him because I've been looking elsewhere, too."

"That's natural."

"I'm looking a lot, Jackie. The front desk worker we just hired, the deli guy at the grocery store, a random guy on the street. I keep seeing these other guys and wondering what a life with them would be like. Making up these crazy meet-cutes we would have and adventures we would go on.

"What the fuck were Jeremy and I thinking?"

Stumped at what she should be saying in response and desperate for Sam to continue without her interruption, Jackie merely said, "I don't know. Maybe this is just a rough spot."

Sam shook her head and closed her eyes. "He wants kids."

"What? Since when?"

"He started hinting at it a few years ago when his brothers started having kids."

"Oh, shit. Sam…I'm so sorry." Even though they'd been dating since high school, they'd insisted on waiting until they were twenty-five to get married. Wanted to make sure they were fully formed adults who knew exactly what they wanted from life before they promised their lives to each other. Among other important decisions like where to live and how to save for their retirement, they'd also both confidently said they did not, under any circumstances, want kids.

A shadow passed by the glass window of the garage door and they both jumped.

Sam rolled her eyes. "He's taking more measurements for the backyard. Wants to do some sort of garden bed. Got the idea from Dylan and Brett." Two of Jeremy's brothers. "The more we ignore the divide between us the more he fills it with random projects. Projects that seemingly point to us having kids sometime."

Jackie pictured Jeremy with a few kids maintaining their garden and picking vegetables for their dinner sides that night. It did sound like a lovely future for Jeremy, but she understood how it was his vision, not Sam's. She loved caring for and nurturing animals, but little kids with, as Sam put it, snotty noses, sticky fingers, and poopy butts? Not her scene. Never was, never would be.

Her head went back to her hands, she took a deep breath, and then she was up again. As if she'd hit reset, Sam gathered the hair she'd been raking her fingers through and put it in a ponytail. Then she dragged a few fingers along the skin around her eyes to be sure they were dry and presentable.

"Fuck," she muttered.

"Does Jeremy know how bad things are? How you feel?"

"Kind of. He knows I don't want kids. I've never wavered on that. But he's not directly saying he wants kids now, so no. We haven't had an actual conversation about it."

She turned to Jackie. "Please don't say anything, and you

143

can't treat him any differently." She was ready to protest but Sam added, "I'm serious, Jackie. If you can't, let me know now. I'll make sure you guys aren't in the same room again until you can."

"You have to have the conversation with him. If you're unhappy and don't think it can be worked out, you have to leave. This," Jackie motioned up and down towards Sam, "is not healthy. And it's not fair to either of you."

"I know. I will. I will."

There was nothing else to say about it, so Jackie let it go for the moment. She wasn't ready to offer any sage advice or to hear any more about it until she let it soak in a bit. They'd always been the poster child for marriage; it was a shock to see the one-eighty the couple had taken in the years since they'd said, "I do." Instead of words she leaned forward and gave Sam physical support through a comforting embrace.

They stayed like that, holding onto each other and not saying anything. Simply existing and making it through minute by minute until Jeremy came in to check on them.

"Should I be jealous?" he teased when he finally left his garden and made his way into the garage.

Seeing Sam's reaction to Jeremy made Jackie think that maybe Sam was in the wrong line of work. Clearly she was a natural born thespian with the way she eased out of Jackie's arms, turned to Jeremy, and said, "Never, honey," with a sweet smile and adoring look on her face.

Jackie pretended to check something on her phone to give herself a bit of time to get her own shit together. The last thing Sam needed was Jackie giving any hint that something was amiss. Sam had been working so hard to keep her secret and pretend everything was normal. Jackie didn't agree with her approach, but it wasn't her decision to make. She had to trust Sam's decision.

"It's amazing," he said as he walked over to the crab to

admire their work. "I mean, I'm not surprised because I know you're both awesome, but still. A lot of progress for one afternoon." And then Jackie saw it, too. Everything about their interaction looked like an initial read-through of a play. Everyone knew their lines okay, but they hadn't perfected how to say them or what their character motivation was, so it still came off a bit flat and unconvincing if you looked hard enough.

"Thanks, Jeremy," Jackie managed to say as she busied herself yet again with her phone.

"Thanks, hon. We *did* have to bust our asses to make up for the work we didn't do last night when Jackie blew us off to have sex with Scott. But it all worked out in the end."

Jackie's jaw dropped and she looked up at Sam. "You said you didn't mind and that I should go for it! You literally texted me, *hit that shit*."

"No. Really? Scott?" Jeremy said to Jackie before he turned to Sam. "Why are you supporting this? I thought we agreed Scott's a terrible idea since he's hauling ass out of here at the end of the year."

Jackie was flung into some sort of weird parallel universe where she could feel the conversation and banter coming easily between the three of them, even though the women were only playing a role. Maybe Jeremy was playing a role as well – one that came easily for him after so many years of marriage. Perhaps they were all on autopilot reciting what they knew as the proper actions and responses. It was a comforting and jarring experience all at once, and Jackie couldn't fathom how Sam (and possibly Jeremy) engaged in it day in and day out.

"I only encouraged her to get laid by a hot guy. Nothing more."

"I'm in the room. You don't have to talk about me like I'm not here," Jackie said.

"But you were right, hon," Sam said. "She's already worried he's not in it for anything beyond a quick fling, and she refuses to have the conversation with him."

Jeremy shook his head in disapproval and said to Sam, "As she should be. But I also agree with Jackie that it's too soon to label it with a conversation."

"Thank you!" Jackie said. "It *is* too soon. Even Jeremy agrees."

"Only that it's too soon to label it," Jeremy said to Jackie as he finally acknowledged her presence in the room. "I still say this is a terrible idea. We're too old for flings that don't mean anything. You should have let me set you up with Norm from accounting."

"Norm? Really?" Sam asked, her voice dripping with disgust. She turned back to Jackie. "He got smashed at the office party and peed in Jeremy's trash can."

"It was one time."

"One time too many, hon."

"Enough. Both of you. It's fine. We're fine. We'll figure it out," Jackie said. Her tone was too harsh for their playful conversation, but she didn't care. In the corner of her eye, she saw Jeremy give Sam a what's-wrong-with-her look. Still the old married couple, she silently responded with some sort of look that he understood and accepted.

"Okay," Sam gently said with her hands up in defense mode as if Jackie was a wild dog about to attack her. "We'll drop it and trust that you'll work it out in your own time. Right, Jeremy?" He nodded his reluctant agreement to butt out of Jackie's sex life. Then something, some kind of communication that's only possible after years and years of marriage, went between the two and the room literally felt a few degrees colder. Jackie couldn't have described what it was if her life depended on it, but it was there regardless.

With a fake smile plastered back on her face Sam said,

"Moving on to another subject, what are you up to for Halloween tonight? Want to order in some take out and watch scary movies while we hand out candy to trick-or-treaters?"

The excess of lying through omission in the garage was eating away at her soul. There was no way in hell she was going to stay any longer. Luckily, she already had plans for the night with Scott. Though she did feel a pang of guilt wondering if Sam wanted her there with her for some sort of moral support.

"I would, but Scott already asked me to do the same thing with him. We've been texting all day." Each text exchange had left her with the goofy grin of a love-struck teenager. But saying it aloud to Jeremy and Sam she could muster only a small smile. Mostly she was assessing Sam's reaction to see if she was okay having yet another night alone with her some-what-absent husband.

But Sam seemed genuinely happy to hear about her date with Scott. And it didn't hurt that Jeremy, who disliked her involvement with Scott for some unknown reason she couldn't understand, would be annoyed to hear about it, so Jackie elaborated a bit more.

"He got us matching costumes to wear tonight. Turns out my street goes all out for *all* holidays. Tim already politely warned me that if I don't have full-sized candy bars, or something similarly impressive in size and deliciousness, the older kids will egg and toilet paper my house."

"Scott wants you guys to wear matching costumes to hand out candy?" Sam asked. "Sounds very coupley. Wouldn't you agree, Jeremy?"

"No," Jeremy said. "It's temporary. He can do and say everything perfectly from here until December 31st. But that doesn't change the fact that he's going to hop on a plane and leave you alone and crying in the BWI airport lobby."

That explained his annoyance at her relationship with Scott. And despite how upset she was with Jeremy at the moment, she understood the feeling. They'd known each other so long and in only a platonic way, that she and Jeremy really did feel like siblings. There was bickering and disagreements, but they still cared deeply.

"What are the costumes?" Sam asked.

"Richard Simmons," Jackie admitted.

Jeremy busted out laughing. "See? Not a couple. That's not a couple costume. Also, I have to see pictures of you as Richard Simmons. What is *that* all about?"

"It's for the neighbors. They all adore Richard Simmons. There's even a small group of them who meet a few times a week in one of their basements to do his workout videos. And it's kind of an inside joke between Scott and me so it *is* a couple's costume," she countered. "Besides, everyone in the neighborhood is strongly encouraged – quotes around encouraged because ringleader Tim runs that street like a mafia boss, and I am very uneasy about disobeying him – to dress up as something that is family-friendly. Richard Simmons, with Bob Ross and Fred Rogers tied as a close second, is the epitome of wholesomeness."

"No slutty nurses?" Sam asked, genuinely confused by the lack of adult, scantily clad costumes on Halloween.

"None."

"No slutty elves? Or maybe a Mrs. Clause as a hoe, hoe, hoe?"

Jackie laughed at the thought of Tim finding Margaret or one of the other neighbors dressed as a slutty Mrs. Clause. "I really hope not."

"That's boring," Sam said. "Come on, hon, let's help Jackie get this beast of a crab into the truck. We'll help you get it set up and then we'll leave you to your special date with Richard Simmons tonight."

JACKIE

*T*hat evening, Jackie was putting some finishing touches on her new Santa Claws crab when Scott pulled up. She'd braced herself for a ridiculous Richard Simmons costume that may even result in her libido plummeting for at least the night, but she was very pleasantly surprised when he got out of the car

Scott wore white sneakers with tube socks pulled halfway up his calves. *Meh,* she thought. That's not so bad. He had great calves so he could almost pull that part off. His red and white striped mini shorts were impressively high (he must have been wearing something underneath to keep his well-endowed manhood from tumbling out for the world to see) and his thigh muscles were impeccably toned. Not too muscley and zero flab.

The further up her eyes went the more she had to remind herself that they were supposed to be playing it cool and keeping their relationship low key. No jumping Scott and dry humping on the hood of his car in public.

His tank top was solid red with a holiday scene bedazzled to the front of it. She could see his arm muscles perfectly, and when he moved just the right way, she could catch glimpses of his sculpted chest beneath his shirt. The final piece of the costume was a brown wig to match Simmons's famous hairdo.

"Hey, that crab looks awesome. Did you make it?" he asked as he made his way over to her house from his car.

"I helped. This one is mostly Sam's creation. See how she made it so that the top of his Santa hat will move back and forth along with each of the giant claws?" With her hand Jackie gently made the hat move since it wasn't plugged in at the moment.

"I see that. She heals animals and – that's welded right? – she welds and does electrical on the side?"

"Yup. She's fabulous," Jackie agreed. "Speaking of fabulous…" she said, lowering her voice. "How the hell do you look so good dressed up as Richard Simmons?"

"You like my top? Margaret decorated it for me yesterday while we had tea." Scott got a cocky smile on his face and in an equally lowered voice said, "I have no doubt you will look just as stunning in your costume, Mrs. Simmons."

He looked up the street and waved to one of the neighbors Jackie recognized but hadn't gotten to know yet. "Unfortunately for me, Lana got word of the delightful costumes on your street so I'm on duty in a few minutes with Mac and then for the first thirty minutes or so filming trick-or-treating around this end of the street. That should be plenty of time for me to get some good shots in. Lizzy's working the other half of the block."

"What are other people doing that has Lana all hot and bothered? Is Simmons enough for me?" It was the first meeting of the lights event and the Olympic games all over again as Jackie felt woefully unprepared in comparison to her seasoned neighbors. Would she ever shake that feeling of being the fish-out-of-water new person?

Living on Christmas Lights Lane had become a bit of culture shock since the event planning started. People didn't simply live there, it was its own society with the many special events, rules, and traditions that filled her calendar September to January, not to mention the few spring and summer events sprinkled in as well.

"Relax, we're crushing it. Remember Kathleen and Edward? They were the ones who brought up the jazzercise documentary during the first meeting. They're psyched and can't wait to see our costumes." Scott paused before he added, "I may have also promised a squat-off at the end of the night."

"This isn't exactly us keeping it low-key. We're both wearing the same costume and you're going to hand out candy at my house. And a squat-off? Seriously?"

"It's fine. They all think I'm just helping you out since you're extra busy redoing your holiday house theme."

"Okay. Maybe you're right. Is that my costume?" she asked, pointing to the bag in Scott's hand.

"Sure is."

"Can you set it inside for me?"

"Absolutely. Then I need to get over to Mac's house to do a short bit of filming."

Jackie, still on the beach next to the porch stairs, stayed put and nonchalantly craned her neck to see Scott going up the porch steps. Then she took a quick look around to see if anyone was out before she dashed up the steps after him.

She almost plowed into Scott as he turned to make his way back out of the house. He opened his mouth to say something, but she covered it with her own as her hands reached up his shirt desperate to feel the hot, tight skin and muscles beneath the bedazzled top.

"Don't judge me," she said in a deep, husky voice as her mouth moved to his ear and down his neck, "for wanting to fuck you while you're Richard Simmons." Her hands moved down his chest, over the six pack, and were pulling at the waistband of his teeny tiny shorts when he caught her wrists and backed away from her panting.

"Wait," he breathed. "We can't. I'm supposed to be at Mac's in a few minutes." Scott's hooded eyes looked her up and down once more before he turned away and let go of her hands.

"Okay," Jackie agreed in between her own deep breaths.

"But I'll see you tonight." He adjusted himself and kissed her on the forehead before heading out the door.

She chuckled to herself as she looked out the window and caught a glimpse of Richard Simmons's tight ass jogging away with his camera case.

That evening, Jackie's doorbell rang and she opened the door with her cauldron of king-sized Snickers bars only to find Richard standing on her porch surrounded by mini pirates, vampires, princesses, and superheroes.

"Trick or treat!" they all shouted. As the kids accepted their candy bars with varying degrees of polite replies, Jackie felt a firm hand on her waist and a quick caress of Scott's thumb on her hip under her shirt as he squeezed past her into the house. Goosebumps covered her body and her core lit up again.

"Thank you," she said to the kids, "I mean, you're welcome. You're welcome. Happy Halloween."

She closed the door and turned to see Scott laughing at her. He stopped when she pushed him back onto the couch and straddled him. This time their thin shorts and position allowed her to feel everything happening below his shorty shorts waistband.

Before she could move her hands to relieve him of his shorts the doorbell rang again.

"Shit," she breathed into his neck. "I honestly completely forgot we have another hour of this." She peeled herself off Scott and adjusted her clothing and wig. "Be right back," she said with a wink before she bent over to get the bowl from the floor without bending her knees. She felt a slight pain in her right leg (she wasn't twenty anymore, that was for sure) but it was totally worth it to hear Scott give a quick whistle of approval from the couch.

When she returned from her duties, she found Scott coming out of her bathroom.

"We can't keep starting and stopping. It will kill me."

"Me, too," Scott said as he adjusted his shorts again.

"Then we're in agreement we won't kiss or even touch until this thing ends at seven thirty?"

"Agreed."

"Wait. Is there really a squat-off afterwards?"

"Yes. And there's a pool going. You know how your neighbors get." Jackie's shoulders slumped. "But after I had to jog to Mac's with a raging hard-on, I already canceled for both of us. I told them you were having some issues with your pipes, and I needed to snake them."

Jackie's jaw dropped. "Tell me you did *not* use a euphemism for sex when we will actually be having sex."

"They don't pick up on that sort of thing. Their older minds aren't nearly as dirty as ours," Scott reasoned as he took a seat on the couch.

Jackie sat on the other side of the couch, careful to keep her distance from him.

"Were they upset that we bailed?" She was torn about the whole thing. She hated the idea of not attending a neighborhood event, but she'd also devoted most of her life the past few months to it. At some point she had to draw the line to keep her own mental and emotional well-being intact. Becoming Tim was a very real fear for her.

Scott shrugged. "A little. But they're having the squat-off anyway without us. Jan's favored to win three to one if you want to place a bet with Tim. He relieved me of my booking duties for the time being."

Throughout trick-or-treating they mostly kept their distance from each other while handing out candy to the kids. Towards the end, Jackie traded a goblin an extra candy bar for a lollipop from his candy collection. She licked and sucked the cherry ball of sugar in a way that made Scott's dick visibly twitch beneath the thin fabric of his costume.

"Where did that come from?" he balked. "Does your costume have pockets?"

"Don't worry about it," she said between licks. When the doorbell rang again, she got up to hand out the candy since Scott probably shouldn't be around children with his small shorts and in his excited state. Afterwards, she closed the door and found Scott practicing his lunges in front of the couch.

"Think I'll get a few squats in since I'm already in these fancy workout clothes." He went into a perfect squat with his back straight and his leg muscles popping from the effort.

Jackie laughed. "Is that your comeback from my sexy lollipop sucking? You're going to seduce me *as* Richard?"

"The key is to squeeze your buns," he said as he went down for another squat.

"Nope, it's not working." Jackie twirled her lollipop on her tongue and thought, *is there anything hotter than a man with a sense of humor?*

"Whew," Scott said at the end of a short rep. "I feel a little hot from that. You feeling hot? Your face looks a little flush, Strauss. You okay?"

"There's the bell again. I gotta go. You just keep going with your leg day, Dick. I'll be back."

"How'd you know people call me Dick?"

Jackie turned back to him. "Shhhh, not in front of the kids."

Mid handing out candy, a bull horn sounded from somewhere on her street – probably Tim's house – signaling the end of trick-or-treating.

She turned back to Scott after she shut the door and found him right behind her. His wig was off. He quickly rid her of hers as well and relieved her of the cauldron of candy. She was about to tease him more when he pinned her body between his own and the door and grabbed her wrists so they were up against the door as well on either side of her head. Her core ached as she felt his hard cock pressed against her body.

SCOTT

"*I*s this okay?" he breathed into that soft spot between her neck and her collar bone. His tongue gave a few playful licks before he kissed and gently sucked at the base of her neck. She let out a moan as he continued to work her neck and slowly grind himself against her.

"Yes," she finally managed.

He'd been somewhat embarrassed by his behavior the night before, the way he'd attacked her like a piece of meat. Not that she'd complained or seemed in any way against their epic romp in the sack, but that wasn't how he'd wanted their second first time to be.

And yet she brought out that savage part of him every time. He made his way up to her face and ran his tongue over her lower lip before sealing his mouth over her own.

"Mmm, you taste like cherries," he moaned when he came up for a breath. As soon as his hands released her wrists, she tugged his shorts down while he worked her shirt and bra off. She pushed back off the door and they stumbled backwards toward the couch.

Without breaking contact, Scott turned her as if they were in the middle of a dance and Jackie ended up on the couch with him kneeling in front of her. As his hands roamed up her impossibly soft and smooth legs, he leaned forward to capture one her nipples with his mouth. Jackie had perfect tits and he couldn't get enough of them.

As she leaned back into the couch to enjoy his mouth on her chest, his hands gradually worked their way down her stomach. They grabbed the elastic top of her shorts and she lifted her hips so she could ease them off. Her hands went to the back of his head with her nails lightly scratching and massaging his scalp as he moved closer to her legs.

"Mmmmm, Scott," she moaned as she let her head fall back onto the couch and widened her legs to give him more access.

The night before had been a flurry of discarded clothes around the hotel room with bumping and fumbling limbs as they each tried to explore every inch of each other with their hands and lips and tongues. They'd completely skipped over oral sex in their haste to come together as one.

This was it. His big redemption. Because eighteen-year-old Scott hadn't exactly known what he was doing the last time he found himself lucky enough to be going down on Jackie Strauss. He'd earned an A for effort, for sure, but he'd since learned a thing or two about pleasing a woman and he was painfully aware of his previous missteps.

He wrapped each arm around her thigh and kissed his way towards her center starting at her knee. Scott could feel her legs trying to move under his grip as she bucked in an effort to get him to his destination faster. But he held tight and made her wait the few remaining seconds for his lips and tongue to reach the smooth wet folds between her legs.

She pushed her hips forward to grind against his mouth and he wanted to come right then. Some women were shy when a guy had his tongue between her legs, Jackie was not some woman. She knew what she wanted, and she wasn't afraid to ask for it.

"Yes, right there. That's perfect."

Before he had a chance to do it himself, she took one of his hands and put her lips around two of his fingers before putting them on her wet pussy. His cock ached thinking about how she'd lick and suck it just like she'd licked and sucked his fingers.

He slipped his fingers into her and massaged her G-spot while his thumb worked the area just around her clit in firm, circular motions. Jackie's fingernails worked the back of his head, and she gave encouraging moans and whimpers. He could tell she was close when her thighs squeezed together, and her hands pulled at his hair giving him a bit of pain and pleasure all at once.

She continued to rub against his mouth and tongue as her breath quickened. Then her muscles tensed around his fingers before her entire body relaxed into him and the couch.

"That was amazing." Her eyes told him that he had in fact redeemed himself. She laid down on the couch and went to pull him up and on top of her.

"Not here." He got back to his feet in front of her. He pulled her up from the couch and into his arms for a kiss. They hadn't discussed what they were doing regarding how serious it was between them. Not surprising given how recent their first kiss was, but it left him feeling uneasy. Like maybe she was getting the wrong idea about what he wanted from her.

Earlier in the night he'd watched her at the door with a set of trick-or-treaters and a feeling of awe had settled over him. The way she interacted with the kids, her sense of humor about the costume he'd picked out for them, the evidence of her skill and talent all over the house. It hit him all at once that he could easily fall in love with Jackie Strauss, and she needed to know that.

He couldn't tell her verbally given his fear that it would freak her out to hear it so early in the relationship. Was it even a relationship? He also wasn't one hundred percent sold that she felt the same way about him. So no, he couldn't say aloud he was falling in love with her. Scott wasn't ready for the potential rejection just yet. He also hadn't fully thought out what that could even mean. Would he get married again? Could he do that? He didn't know.

But he could at least hint at his serious feelings towards her by slowing down and worshiping her body with his mouth and hands.

With her still in his arms, he set the new pace with soft, gentle caresses of his tongue on hers. His hands weren't frantically up and down her back; they were in one spot on her lower back as he put all his focus into their kiss.

Then he moved his hands below her ass to hoist her up to his hips as her legs instinctively locked around his waist. He turned to walk her back to the bedroom.

"Last night was amazing and perfect, but let's slow it down tonight."

"Hmm, I like that idea."

The romantic mood he was setting dulled only slightly when he bumped her into a wall and the bedroom doorway on their brief walk to the room, but she only laughed it off and they went back to kissing each time. Damn movies making it look like carrying a person back to the bedroom while kissing them wouldn't result in injuries.

Mostly intact, he laid her down on the bed and eased off what little remained of her clothing before he continued to slowly caress, lick, and suck every inch of her body.

JACKIE

For the next two weeks Jackie spent her weekdays at work, her evenings working on her displays with Sam or Babs, and her nights in bed with Scott. It was exhausting and exhilarating all at once.

To keep their relationship a secret, Scott had started to park a few blocks away and enter Jackie's house through the back alleyway which was mostly uninhabited and deserted. They would have slept at his place, but he was only in town temporarily and staying with his parents. They hadn't broached the subject yet, but Jackie got the impression he did not want her to meet his parents, and she certainly didn't want to meet them, as she was coming and going late at night or early in the morning.

All in all, Jackie was fine with it. Sometimes it felt silly or deceitful, but mostly she didn't care what other people (mainly Sam and Jeremy) thought about it. For Jackie and Scott, it was working out just fine. They were still getting to know each other anyway – why rock the boat with questions about how serious it was and what would happen when the documentary was over? Why risk the current work dynamic between Scott and Lana if it might not even work out anyway?

That was what she kept telling herself over the past few weeks, though some days it was harder to believe than others. Especially once Jackie started to explore her potential future at Preserve the Bay. Jackie had reached out to Stephanie, the contact Jeremy had given her, and Stephanie gave Jackie a chance to shadow her at their current office to get a feel for what the organization did and what they were trying to do in the future. By the end of the day Jackie was in love with her potential future career. And yet she wasn't as excited about the future as she should have been because Scott wasn't going to be a part of it. He didn't want to stay in Milton, and she wouldn't let him if he tried to stay just to be with him. He'd stayed in Vegas with his wife, and he'd felt miserable and stuck. She couldn't allow herself to be involved in a similar situation with him. It would break both of their hearts.

Late November Sam and Jeremy were at Jackie's again putting final touches on the tank displays while Jackie sorted out her final ideas for stringing up the blue lights on the outside of her house to create the illusion of waves gently moving over the siding. She had a quickly approaching deadline for her final light count so she needed to get it all sorted as soon as possible. Scott was at Muriel's house shooting Muriel and a few neighbors stringing up her outside lights.

Most of Jackie's conversation with Sam and Jeremy during lunch and while they worked had been about her new potential career, but they inevitably transitioned to Scott from there.

"What does Scott think about the new job?" Jeremy asked in a tone that said he highly doubted Scott knew about it.

Sam and Jeremy were each on a ladder with their hands in the top tank arranging the tiny houses they'd helped to create and paint while Jackie sat on the couch sketching out different light patterns and designs in her trusty old-school composition notebook.

Jackie's pencil slipped on the paper resulting in a large dark gray line across her previously tidy sketch of the house and light display plans.

"I mentioned it in passing not long after you first mentioned it to me. We haven't discussed it since then," she said as if it were some minor topic and not a potential life-changing career move. "The conversation happened a while back, before we were together."

Sam and Jeremy both began speaking at once. They talked over one another with their strong opinions on how they expected Scott to react and why Jackie hadn't thoroughly broached the subject with him yet.

"You just went on and on about how excited you were about the job. Do you really not discuss it with him at all?" Sam asked.

"It's because you know he's going to panic when you start discussing anything serious or long-term," Jeremy insisted.

In a strong, commanding voice – potentially her future presenting voice when the students get a little too rowdy during assemblies – she spoke up over them both and said, "I haven't told *anyone* else about it yet or discussed it at length with anyone else because it's not official. There's a lot more that goes into a decision like this. I need to figure out a lot of logistics with it." That silenced Sam and Jeremy, making the house a bit too quiet. In a softer voice Jackie added, "I don't even know if I'm going to stay in Milton beyond the lights event…"

Jackie couldn't look at Sam when she said it. When they'd parted after high school for college, they hadn't realized how much they would drift away from each other. This departure would be different. She would be walking away from Milton knowing she was leaving a bit of their friendship behind. She'd leave knowing that Sam was in a bad place and that she was abandoning her. But just like she couldn't let Scott stay because she needed or wanted him to, she couldn't stay in Milton only because Sam might need her for support.

"Right," Sam said. Her voice apathetic. "Why stay here where you have family and friends, a house even, when you could follow Scott to who the hell knows where." Jackie wanted to say something about how Sam didn't understand, but Sam did understand.

The room fell quiet, and everyone allowed it. The light rumbling of the miniature houses jostling about the small pebbles in the bottom of the tank along with the scratching of her pencil on paper served only to highlight the lack of conversation in the room.

At least thirty minutes passed this way. Jackie pretended not to notice their silent conversations as she tried to focus on her work. She couldn't figure the two out. There were days, like this one, where they seemed like their perfect married selves. Jeremy wasn't on his phone at all. Jackie wasn't even sure if he had it on him or not. And Sam seemed genuinely happy versus the fake, 1950s-looking happy housewife she sometimes portrayed. They were playful and appeared loving towards each other.

"Do you want to do Thanksgiving with us?" Sam offered as if there hadn't been an awkward half hour of silence. "Jeremy's brothers and kids will be there, too, and a few of my cousins and their kids. But there's always room for a few more. Babs, too, if she's interested."

"Thanks, guys. I appreciate the offer. But Mom's hosted Thanksgiving at her house all my life. She won't want to go anywhere else. Besides, she feels bad leaving Tom behind and she feels bad bringing a cat to someone else's house aside from mine."

"Okay. But the offer stands if anything changes," Sam said.

"Will Scott be joining your family for this major holiday?" Jeremy asked.

Sam shot him a warning look but didn't say anything. Apparently, she wanted to know as well.

"We haven't discussed Thanksgiving yet..." Jackie rolled her eyes in anticipation of the lecture she was about to get from both of them.

"Seriously?" Sam asked. "This is getting a little out of hand, Jackie. I know you guys are playing it cool or whatever, but you're not teenagers anymore. You can drop the games and stop playing coy."

Jeremy didn't say anything, but his smug expression said plenty. Jackie tried not to take it personally. She reminded herself that Jeremy wasn't a dick, per se, he was just too competitive for his own good. His determination to be right about Scott made him overlook how Jackie fit into it all. At least she assumed that was what was happening with him. Ever since Sam told her about what was happening between them, she wasn't sure what to make of Jeremy. He didn't seem to be the man she'd remembered him to be.

"It's not playing games, Sam. We're just two people who are having a good time together without stressing about the future."

"Thanksgiving's next week. That's not the future," Jeremy said as he reached into the tank to rearrange mini-Margaret's house which had slumped into mini-Mort's house.

"Fine. I'll text Mom now to make sure she doesn't mind, then I'll invite Scott to Thanksgiving dinner." She got up from the couch, expertly maneuvered through the tangle of blue lights on the floor and grabbed her phone. "It's not like he hasn't already met Babs and Tom. This will be fine," she said more to herself than to anyone else.

A few seconds later her phone buzzed with a response.

"Well?" Jeremy and Sam asked at the same time.

"She's having Thanksgiving at Mort's with a bunch of the neighbors," Jackie said in disbelief.

"Your mother and Mort," Jeremy said, "are the perfect example of a committed relationship."

"Enough, hon," Sam said with a flick of water towards her husband. "We get it."

Jackie typed away at her phone with a few questions for Babs before sitting back down on the couch. The composition notebook lay neglected beside her.

"The tank looks pretty good, Jackie," Sam said. "I think we might head out while you finish up here and get Thanksgiving sorted out."

"You don't have to leave -" Jackie started to say before she was cut off by the doorbell.

Jeremy, who was still at the bay window with his hand in the upper tank, had a perfect view of her front door. "It's your mom. And she doesn't have Tom with her."

"We're going to go. Right, hon?"

"Yup, look at that time." Jeremy toweled off his arms and hands. "Thanks for the late lunch, Jackie."

"Text me later," Sam said as she and Jeremy made their way to the front door. "Hi, Babs," she greeted. "Unfortunately, Jeremy has a thing, and we have to run."

"A thing," Babs said. "Sounds very urgent indeed. Good luck with that," she humored.

They all said their goodbyes and then it was just Jackie and Babs in the organized chaos of Jackie's living room. "Have a seat, sweetie. We should talk."

SCOTT

"Tom's gone?" Scott asked as he unpacked the dinner he'd picked up for them. Any conversation that included Tom made him nervous. Since Jackie was still unsure of how to act around him – sometimes she called him Tom and sometimes she called him Dad – he really wasn't sure how to act around the cat either.

"According to Mom, yes. My father's spirit is gone and all that's left now is a cat who I guess we'll continue to call Tom." She picked up a fork and poked around a bit at the garlic chicken dish he'd placed in front of her.

"It's a long story...Mom, Thanksgiving, Mort, Tom...I don't want to talk about it."

He hated to see her so stressed about it. It was already a difficult time with the event going on, the upcoming holidays, and even with their sneaking around all the time. This on top of it all was too much. He could see it in her face that she was close to breaking down from exhaustion.

Scott stopped organizing food and moved around the table to Jackie. "Hey," he said as he reached for her hand. "Are you okay? Come here." He pulled her into a hug and gently rubbed her back as he felt her relax into him.

"I'm fine," she eventually said as she pulled away and they both sat back down at the table. "I guess I got used to having at least some version of my father I could talk to even if he couldn't talk back. In a tiny way it's like losing him all over again – even if I didn't actually believe it to begin with."

"I can see how that would be comforting."

Although Jackie said she didn't want to talk about it, he got the feeling it meant she did want to talk about it but only on her own terms and when she was ready. He'd wait it out until she offered more information.

She picked up her fork again and took a bite of chicken and rice. "You did not have to go all the way to Shipley to get Chinese food. There are at least three other restaurants right here in Milton."

"Yes, I did," he said as he loaded up his own plate with chicken and an egg roll. "You sounded sad on the phone, and you've mentioned at least a half-dozen times how they're your favorite." To him it felt like it was the least he could do. There was no manual on how to help a girlfriend whose spiritual dad left the cat body he'd been inhabiting. Not a single card at Hallmark even came close to what he needed.

He reached out for a packet of soy sauce when she caught his hand and gave it a squeeze. "Really, thank you for this."

He squeezed back, kissed her hand. "My pleasure."

As they ate, they talked about how their days had gone. Scott had been working all day with Jan and Mac, while Jackie had Sam and Jeremy helping her with the fish tanks. Scott had a few stories about his day, mostly consisting of all the crazy antics involving Jackie's neighbors, but Jackie didn't say much about her time with Sam and Jeremy. Normally he'd asked her questions to try to engage in more conversation, but he was having trouble reading her that night. She'd say a few things in a flurry of rambling sentences, then shut down again and not want to talk about it.

Scott wondered if Jackie's distance during their dinner had anything to do with how tired she was of whatever they were doing. Of the sneaking around. Then he remembered she was already stressed with the event and upset about the second loss of her father, so he immediately felt like a dick for making it all about him in his mind. He was better than that.

Jackie insisted on cleaning up after dinner, mostly throwing away the paper plates and empty cartons of food, since Scott had driven to pick it up. Even though he'd just vowed to do better, given how upset she'd been earlier, he didn't argue with her about it. Personally, he liked cleaning whenever he was stressed out. Going through his apartment and creating order where before there had been chaos was immensely soothing to him. As an added bonus, not only was he left with a clean apartment, but he was often able to work through whatever was bothering him as he'd cleaned. If she needed to busy herself or tidy-up to feel better, he wouldn't take that from her.

As Jackie gathered their plates she said, "I texted Mom about Thanksgiving and then suddenly she's at my door – because she must have been with Mort, again – telling me that she's doing Thanksgiving and Christmas with Mort and some of my neighbors." She dropped the trash into the trash can. "We've never done Thanksgiving anywhere but my house."

Had she not mentioned that part of her day sooner because she didn't want to get into the whole holiday conversation with him?

Scott nodded as he took a swig of beer. "Yeah, Mort was telling me about an annual Thanksgiving block party at his house. Said since everyone is so busy with the unveiling the next day, Thanksgiving became too difficult with family or friends who weren't part of the event."

"Well, Mom's part of it now, too. That was when she started getting into the whole thing about how Tom's been acting funny this past week or so. Wasn't himself: devoured all his wet food, started rubbing up on anyone who got near him, and scratched Mom when she put on his leash for a walk."

Jackie's pace quickened as she talked as if she were upset or nervous. Even though they'd been spending a lot of time together recently, it became glaringly obvious there was still so much he didn't know about her. When she was upset like she was at that moment, should he jump in and try to help her, or let her work through it by trying to do everything herself so she could take her mind off it?

"That's why Babs thinks he moved on?" he asked. He wasn't sure what the right way to respond was, so he went with his gut. When she went to gather up the discarded duck sauce packs Scott's hand took hers again and gently massaged with his thumb.

She sat back down and placed her other hand on top of his. "That, and she's always said she's tuned in to people's spirits and auras. It's how she's able to give tarot readings. Tom's aura changed around the same time he started acting weird."

"Is this because she's been spending so much time with Mort?" Most of their relationship so far had been light and full of lustful sex. They hadn't tackled any problems together aside from logistical ones with her displays. He tried to tread lightly on the subject of her family while still helping her work through it.

"They're not just spending time together. My mom is

dating Mort." Jackie absently grabbed a handful of crunchy noodles in a pack still left on the table to munch on.

"Mort's a good guy."

"Yeah, he is. And I want my mom to be happy." She paused to munch on a few more noodles. "I don't know what I'm feeling right now. Please don't feel obligated to stay here tonight. I can't guarantee I'll be good company."

The normal routine they'd fallen into since they first started seeing each other had been for Scott to go over Jackie's around dinner time (on the days he wasn't working in the evenings) and they'd eat together, have epic sex, and then fall asleep before they'd even finished one episode of The Amazing Irish Baking Show. There were variations, of course, like the time Scott had to run through a rainstorm and showed up dripping wet. He'd felt bad about the mess he'd made when he'd flooded the kitchen floor where Jackie's back door was, but she couldn't have cared less as she eyed him up like a piece of meat. Jackie helped him remove his wet clothing and then helped into a nice hot shower. That evening dinner had waited until after the epic sex.

"Do you want to be alone?" Scott offered. He wanted to stay. He'd always want to stay, but it wasn't about him that night.

"No."

"Then I'll stay."

"Okay."

"Okay," he repeated. Upstairs, Scott took advantage of his few minutes alone to run her a bubble bath while she finished up some last-minute notes about what she needed to get completed in the upcoming week.

"I didn't know you like bubble baths," she said as she stepped into the bathroom, gave him a quick kiss, and then started to brush her teeth.

"I don't. It's for you."

"For me?" she asked in a muffled voice as she brushed. Her face scrunched up as though she had never encountered a tub full of water and bubbles and didn't quite know how to proceed.

"Yeah. You seemed like you needed to relax a little tonight." He ran his hand through his hair, a nervous tick he was very aware of but had little control over.

Jackie finished brushing and spit into the sink. "That's really sweet of you, but I don't like taking baths."

"Really? I thought all women liked baths."

Jackie shrugged her shoulders and replaced her toothbrush on the sink.

"And you have a giant thing of bubbles on the side of your tub."

"Aroma therapy bubbles. Mom insists on getting me that stuff each year. I put it out to make her happy, but I never use it."

"That would explain why I had to open it," he said, looking mildly sheepish.

"Sorry..."

"You have nothing to be sorry for." Scott turned to let the water out of the tub. She left the bathroom, and he could hear her collapse onto the bed in the other room with a loud sigh and rustling of the sheets.

"I do. You're going out of your way – literally with the Shipley Chinese food run – to do sweet things for me and I'm a miserable lump unworthy of any of it."

When he walked back into the bedroom to talk to her, his eyes immediately fell to Jackie, laying on the bed with her knees bent. Aside from her gorgeous legs which were perfectly angled to accentuate that line on her outer thigh that inexplicably drove him wild, the bottoms of her skimpy shorts had dropped towards the bed revealing a peek at her panties beneath.

They'd been having sex regularly for almost a month, and yet his cock jerked at the sight as if it hadn't been attended to in years. Jackie was a mess of emotions on the bed and all he could think about was all the other times he'd seen her on that same bed and in that same position but with much, much less clothing on.

He strategically laid down next to her on the bed and was careful to embrace her without letting the bulge in his pants rub up against her like a dog in heat. That was the last thing she needed.

"It's not your job to entertain me or to be on when we're together." When she didn't immediately respond beyond settling into his embrace he said, "You do know that, right?" There was a slight panic in his voice, but he didn't care. The idea that she thought he only wanted a good time when it came to her made his heart heavy.

"I know that."

It would have to be enough for the time being since harping on the topic would likely only do more harm than good given the circumstances of the night. He gave her a gentle squeeze before he released her and stood to make his way to the bathroom to get ready for bed.

"You're doing Thanksgiving with your mom and Mort then?" he said as he started to brush his teeth. She had brought up Thanksgiving but then they'd moved onto another topic before he was able to firm up any plans with her. He hoped it was okay to bring up again and not something that was going to upset her.

"Looks like it." Her voice sounded clear and unbothered by the topic, so he pressed on.

"Should be pretty good food though. Mort's quite the cook."

"I don't doubt that. I'm already planning on fasting the

whole day to make sure I have enough room to try everything."

He finished brushing and took an extra moment or two in the bathroom looking at himself in the mirror. He'd brought up the whole Thanksgiving topic again hoping that they would end up making plans to spend it together. But the more the conversation dragged on and the more he tried to hint at an invite, the more rejected he felt when it didn't come.

"What about you?" she asked as he climbed back into bed with her.

"No plans. My parents are snowbirds. They just left for the Keys and they won't be back until May." Not that he minded their absence. With his extended family around there had been some explosive holiday disasters in his family's past – hence his parents' tendency to keep all conversations to the bare minimum of pre-approved topics. It was probably for the best that they were a few states south for Thanksgiving, freeing him from feeling obligated to attend whoever else in his family would be hosting that year.

"Do you want to come with me to Mort's?"

Scott turned to look at her and found her looking adorably nervous. "Mom and Mort already know we're together – or whatever this is." Scott opened his mouth but before he could say anything she continued, "But everyone else will probably just assume Mort invited you since you've been spending so much time with him the past month or so."

He waited a few beats in case she wanted to add anything else before he said, "You sure you wouldn't mind?" She'd just offered, but it sounded a bit like she was just trying to be nice. The last thing he wanted was for her to feel like she had to invite him.

"Not at all," she said as a smile drew across her face. "I

think it would be nice to do Thanksgiving together." Her hand found his and she intertwined her fingers with his.

"Me, too." He leaned in to give her a quick kiss goodnight.

They hadn't simply slept together yet. There was always sex before. It had felt more like a fling that way. While Scott highly doubted it, he sometimes wondered if that's what they were doing, some sort of intense fling. Like when she'd said he didn't have to stay because she wouldn't be any "fun." He worried she meant he didn't need to stay since they weren't going to have sex. The idea that they had to have sex or it wouldn't be worth it for him to spend the night weighed heavily on his mind.

Because of that, he was extra careful that night to make sure he didn't do anything to make her feel like he expected to get laid. But when he leaned in for his quick kiss goodnight, before he could pull away, she reached a hand behind his neck to keep him close. She opened her mouth and without even thinking about it he found his tongue suddenly and deliciously intertwined with hers. In the weeks since their *fling* had started, they'd shared many hurried and heated kisses. Kisses where there was too much pent-up sexual tension and the need for relief drove them to more than just kissing.

This kiss was different. It was lazy and unexpected. They took their time exploring each other and savoring every caress of their tongue, each soft moan they couldn't hold back, and the overall feeling of having nowhere else to be and nothing else to do.

Even though they were passionately kissing, in bed, Scott still made no move to take it further. He was only there to please her and so he decided he would sit back while she took control. When she trailed her hand from his neck down his back, he kept his at her waist.

She pulled away and asked, "Is something wrong?"

Ugh. He couldn't get anything right. While he'd been trying to be the gentlemanly boyfriend who respected his girlfriend and wanted to give her space to grieve, instead he came off as the boyfriend who was uninterested in what she was offering.

"Nothing. This is amazing," he murmured before he rolled on top of her. "But we don't have to do this if you're not up for it."

She tilted her head up to once again find his mouth with hers. He loved the way she tasted like peppermint from her toothpaste, the feel of her nails raking up and down his back, her silky soft legs wrapping around his waist, and the way her teeth tugged at his lower lip as if she couldn't completely suppress her animalistic urges when she was around him.

"I want to. I need you," she breathed back between kisses

JACKIE

*F*our days before Thanksgiving she was in the living room after work going over her event calendar and various upcoming deadlines when she got a text from Tim.

I need to go over a few things with you. Is now a good time?

Sorry. I'm about to head out, she wrote in an effort to politely tell him no, it was not a good time.

Only take a few minutes. Promise. On my way with Lizzy. Please put your mic on.

She could tell it wouldn't be a good meeting. The tone of his text was completely out of character. It sounded more like Lana than Tim. *Oh god, please don't show up with Lana.* There was something about her no-nonsense attitude that intimidated Jackie. She didn't care what Scott said he saw the other night. There was no way Lana, the automaton, had ever smiled, joked, flirted, or had sex at any point in her life.

Luckily, Lana was nowhere to be seen when Tim showed up at her door with Lizzy in tow. The red dot on the camera blazed brightly showing Jackie that even though she'd just answered the door, it was already go time.

"What's up, Tim?"

"Can I come in? I'd like to go over a few things."

"Sure," Jackie said as she stepped aside to let them in.

Tim went straight for the fish tanks at the bay window. "That is...wow. With the tiny white fish like a snowstorm around the mockups of all the houses. Genius."

"Thanks," she said, waiting for him to get to the real reason for his unplanned visit. Tim did not drop by anywhere just to shoot the shit. Not during the Christmas season, he didn't. Too much to do and not enough time to do it. And the fact that he'd brought the camera with him was downright ominous. Ever the professional, Lizzy remained stoic behind the camera and revealed nothing.

"And your Santa Claws crab? Unbelievable. It will be a hit, undoubtedly. One of the must-sees of the neighborhood." Tim made himself comfortable on the couch and so she sat down as well on the other side of the coffee table facing him.

"I had a lot of help with that one, from friends. But thank you. I'll send along your compliments."

"It's great. Really." He paused to consider his wording. "But I get the feeling that it could be even better. From my point of view, I'm getting about 85% from you right now." Tim sat back slightly as if waiting for a lengthy response or rebuttal from her.

She almost looked from Tim to Lizzy to gauge her reaction, but she kept her icy stare on Tim. He'd accused her of being less than committed, so it wouldn't have been a good look to immediately break the documentary rules by acknowledging Lizzy to ask if she agreed with Tim's assessment.

After what felt like an eternity, she finally managed to ask, "Are you serious?" She didn't wait for an answer. "I am giving *everything* I have. I have no social life and I work the least number of hours possible without getting fired. Half the time I'm still doing event stuff while I'm at work."

He nodded along with what she said, but Jackie could tell he didn't agree with her.

"Then your best is not cutting it."

Her body flamed up with heat from the embarrassment of being called out for mediocre work. It was bad enough as it was, but the fact that it was being done on camera made it exponentially worse. She couldn't even fathom how many future nights she would lay awake reliving that particular moment and reliving the embarrassment that accompanied it.

How was it possible that Tim, Tiny Tim, mister bright and bubbly over Christmas cheer, was in her living room telling her she wasn't good enough? How bad did it have to be to get a one-on-one surprise visit from him? Was the whole neighborhood talking about how she wasn't pulling her weight? This was not good. Also, this was not going to be the quick conversation he had promised.

"I don't understand..." Jackie began to say even though she had a slight idea about what he may be referring to. She'd been hiding it from herself for a while and making excuses, but in the back of her mind she'd had similar concerns herself.

"You missed your light count last week and left us in a tight spot with the website and social media reveal. People like that trivial information like how many lights each house has and how many there will be total. Rather than guess at your actual number, we had to put off our big reveal."

"You could have guessed."

"And jeopardize the integrity of the entire event? No, that was never an option. And the fact that you'd suggest it shows your lack of understanding about what we're trying to do here."

Jackie took a deep breath. There was no argument against what Tim said. It was true. She'd marked the light count due date on her calendar, but she'd still missed the deadline. And while she would have loved to have a long-winded story about a series of unfortunate events that kept her from meeting her deadline, there was none. She simply had forgotten. Unheard of for her, and yet it had happened.

She also couldn't argue that Tim and the rest of the neighborhood's attention to detail and their overall integrity was part of what drove the national attention they'd received. It wasn't a hobby for the people involved; it was a lifestyle. Their stunning end-result each holiday season was evidence of that. She knew there was no room for, "I forgot."

"I apologized for that, Tim," she said. "I hadn't realized what a difficult job determining my final light count would be. It feels like everyone else has an advantage since they're only making minor changes to their houses each year and only need to adjust their final counts based on those changes." She could feel her body language matching her defensive tone as she crossed her arms and tensed up. "I'm starting from scratch. I would appreciate a little more leeway."

"You *requested* to start from scratch. You could have easily kept Ollie's theme for your first year to get your feet wet before reinventing the wheel." It seemed Tim was not one to back off when it came to holding someone accountable for the event. Usually she would admire it, but being on the other side of the critique made her uneasy. Especially when it was being filmed.

"You have, on average, one third the number of reflections as everyone else." She could read it in his face that this was the part of his position he hated. His eyes were searching for some sort of understanding from her that he didn't want excuses. He wanted better results from her in the future.

Unfortunately for him, Jackie was standing firm with her defense that she wasn't distracted, and she still had an excuse or two left to play whether he wanted to hear it or not.

"Yes, I can do better with those. I just keep pushing it off until later in the day, and then I guess I forget to do them." Jackie's conscience allowed the half-truth since it was better than the whole truth (Scott's presence made her forget each night) and better than flat-out lying. On the days Scott showed up earlier than she'd expected, she couldn't bring herself to leave him to do her reflections. It was silly and stupid, but she was in deep, and she had trouble giving up any of her precious time alone with him.

The thought reminded her they were getting dangerously close to the time she was expecting Scott to show up. She pulled her phone out of her pocket and said, "Excuse me. Just a minute, please," as she typed out a quick text to Scott.

ABORT! Tim here with Lizzy!

The eternal optimist in Tim returned as he watched Jackie text and said, "Yes, put reminders in your phone. That's a good idea. You should be doing at least three reflections a week if not more. I'm up to five a week myself though I could be suffering from a bit of overkill. I admit."

"Yup. Putting this into my calendar now, so I should be good going forward." She put the phone on the coffee table and looked back at Tim. "Do you have any other concerns?"

She said it as a formality and as a gentle nudge for him to conclude the conversation and get going. She'd heard him loud and clear and would do better going forward. No need to drag it out any further.

"Yes," he said as though it should be obvious their conversation would need to continue. "We're down to the final week before the reveal and I see you're still missing most of the lights on your house."

"That's correct." *Ugh, will he never leave?* "But in fairness

I've been helping Mort put most of his final lights and decorations up, and he's promised to do the same for me." Tim's face was unreadable, so she added, "In the next two days, Tim. Promise."

His eyes narrowed. "Is Mort dating your mom?"

Jackie looked down at her phone, but Scott hadn't messaged back. "It appears that way, though I don't see how that's any of your business." Her patience was officially depleted. Tim had worn out his welcome and now he was getting into her mother's personal life?

Tim had the decency to shift a little in his seat to show that he too acknowledged his over-step with the question and resulting conversation. "Mort is a little behind this year as well. Not behind on any of his due dates, but everything he'd done prior to this year had been completed well in advance of the given due dates. This year everything's been right on time which is highly unlike him."

"Babs is a free spirit; her lax attitude trickles down to those around her."

Tim sighed as if to say he didn't give a flying fuck as to why it was happening, he just wanted it to stop. "We have a chance to keep expanding and growing what we've carefully cultivated here, or we can get lax and mediocre about it."

"I understand, Tim. I am picking up what you're laying down." Her phone remained black with no notifications or messages. *Damnit, Scott. Look at your phone!* her mind screamed as she calmly nodded in agreement with Tim. She needed to end the conversation with him and get him and Lizzy out of her house.

"Good. I don't mean to come off as too gruff, but I'm in charge of monitoring the integrity of the event and it's a job I take very seriously." He was still lounging on the couch as if he were there for tea and didn't have anywhere else in the world to be.

"I get it. I'm going to get back to work right now," she said as she stood up hoping to encourage him to follow her lead.

Mercifully, Tim rose as well, and Jackie's tense muscles finally released in the knowledge that he would be out of her house in the next minute or two. But even that short amount of time was too long. As they made their way to the front door, Scott came in through the back.

A while back she'd ruined a decoration by stopping to let him in one night, so she had a spare key made for him. It took a few visits, but he eventually came to feel comfortable letting himself in and making himself at home. So comfortable, in fact, that on this occasion as soon as he was in the house, he was stripping off his clothes as he shouted, "Hey, babe. I need to take a quick shower and then I'll be right back down."

Scott was shirtless and had his pants undone by the time he got to the main hallway and saw Tim, Lizzy, and Jackie in the living room.

"Hey, Tim." Scott held his shirt in front of his bare chest to hide his nipples and turned bright red. "I didn't know you were stopping by today." His eyes went to Jackie in search of some sort of explanation.

"I texted you," Jackie said through clenched teeth. Aside from the occasional picture and Twitter post, Scott was not one to be attached to his phone. It was pure bliss that she never had to compete for his attention, and yet infuriating when he missed calls and texts from her for hours and hours at a time on the days he left his phone on silent.

Tim's face showed no reaction to the half-naked documentary cameraman in Jackie's house. "I stopped by to talk to Jackie about her performance and progress with the light event," he said to Scott. "I told her I was concerned that she was losing focus and falling behind. She assured me she was not, but I think I may have found her distraction."

Scott looked to Jackie for some sort of hint as to how she wanted him to play this, but she was at a loss. Sneaking around the neighborhood had been fun and somewhat sexy. She hadn't thought too much about any actual consequences that could come from their relationship or from them keeping that relationship a secret.

"It's my fault," Scott said. "I'm the one who crossed the line."

"No, I'm just as responsible as you are, Scott." There was no way she was going to let him take the fall for something they were equally guilty of.

Tim ignored Jackie and continued to stare down Scott. "Does Lana know?"

"I don't talk to Lana about my relationships." He let his shirt drop in some sort of defiant move towards Tim.

Tim shook his head in disbelief before addressing both Scott and Jackie again. "This isn't a game. Lana's pouring her heart and soul into this documentary, and the entire neighborhood has paused their lives for the success of this event."

"So are we," Scott countered.

"No," Tim practically shouted. "You're distracted by whatever this is. And if you can't see that, you're not being honest with yourself."

No one said anything. Scott stood shirtless with his pants unbuckled, daring anyone to question him. Tim rubbed his temples, and Jackie searched her brain for possible arguments against everything Tim had said. She had trouble coming up with anything.

Tim finally turned back to her. "That's why Scott's sneaking in the back door. Because you know I'm right."

"What about you? Your and Lana's relationship isn't affecting your work?" Scott challenged Tim.

"We have a professional working relationship. That's it."

"Oh, please. Don't give me that shit," Scott shot back. "You guys were all over each other the first night we set up the reflection room."

Once the accusations turned to Tim, it was obvious he regretted having Lizzy present. His hands balled into fists at his sides in frustration and maybe a bit from embarrassment, too. "Yes, we were. And we both agreed it wasn't appropriate." His voice was much softer when he continued. "I get it, guys. I do. But your actions affect the larger group whether you believe that or not."

Again, Jackie and Scott had nothing to say in response. "I'm sorry" felt too small, too insincere, too inadequate. But was silence better?

"I have a meeting with Lana tomorrow at noon. If you don't tell her by then, I will," Tim said more to Scott than to Jackie. That made sense given Lana was Scott's actual boss. Tim and Jackie were only neighbors when it came down to it.

After Tim left, Jackie unmic'd and turned around to find Scott fully dressed. He looked miserable.

"I should go," he said.

"No, don't." She took a few tentative steps towards him, but while he didn't step away from her, he also didn't look as welcoming as he usually did. "Tim already knows, and Lana will tomorrow. You might as well stay now."

"He's right, Jackie," Scott said in a barely audible voice.

"So, we'll put more time into our work."

"I was with Margaret today getting footage of her granddaughters helping to put lights up." He'd been looking at the floor, but he looked up and met her eyes. "I kept looking at my watch waiting for it to be six so I could come see you."

Jackie smiled as she imagined this amazing man checking his watch and counting down the minutes to see her.

"I didn't notice one of the younger ones off to the side playing with a string of lights until a parent said something."

His eyes left hers again and it felt like each time it happened *he* was leaving her. "By then the kid had moved on to something else. It was the perfect shot and I missed it because I was distracted, like Tim said. The lighting, the movement. The perfect candid shot. And I missed it."

"That's one time. You could just as easily have been checking the time in general -"

"No." He shook his head and his voice raised. "It's not the first time. And who knows what I've missed and didn't even realize I'd missed it." He ran a hand through his hair before both hands landed on his hips.

"Okay," Jackie said only because she felt she needed to say something. She didn't want to undermine his concerns by saying it wasn't his fault or that it wasn't a big deal. It was. Tentatively she said, "So…" but she couldn't finish it because she didn't want to even guess how her sentence would end.

"So I need to have some time tonight to think." His eyes were back on the floor, and she hated that he couldn't look at her as he said it.

"Okay," she said again. As if their relationship were on a thin wire high above the ground and all that it could handle was a word or two. Anything more would send them both plummeting to the hard, unforgiving surface below.

"I'll call you tomorrow."

She had the chance at that point to go to him. To say more, to kiss him, to comfort him. But in the scenario of fight, flight, or freeze, it turned out she was a freeze kind of person. She hadn't realized that about herself.

"Okay."

SCOTT

*F*uck. Lana had practically saved him in Vegas. On the verge of divorce and with the looming dread of being able to make rent, solo, at a new apartment, Lana had taken a chance on him and hired him as a cameraman on her documentary crew.

It had been a miracle. He'd been desperate to show her what he could do and devoted his life to that project even though it was immensely dull work. But it was all worth it when midway through that project Lana offered a position on her next one. An opportunity to get out of Vegas.

Lana deserved better than what he was giving her in Milton. On top of that, she deserved honesty about his involvement with Jackie. It wasn't an option for him to allow Tim to tell her about his relationship.

Sitting in his car in his secret parking spot away from the neighborhood, he couldn't help but wonder what the hell he was doing.

"Fuuuuuuck!" He yelled into his steering wheel. He looked at his phone to confirm that there were no messages from Jackie. Did he want her to message him? He didn't know what he wanted. He said he needed time to think so it made sense she wouldn't immediately be sending him messages. Why had he said that?

He tried to prioritize. First things first, he needed to reach out to Lana. Once he talked to her, he'd have a better idea of what his next move with Jackie would be.

Can we talk? he texted.

He figured she was in the neighborhood somewhere given how close they were to the big reveal event, so he waited in the dark in the car for her to respond.

Text? Phone? In person? she'd replied.

In person

At my apartment. We can meet here.

The whole way over to her apartment, all of seven and a half minutes thanks to how tiny Milton was, Scott tried to plan out how he would approach the subject with Lana. He couldn't help but smile when he found himself going with Jackie's favorite method of winging it when it comes to outing a relationship. That hadn't worked too well for them in the past, but maybe it was worth it to give it another try.

"What's wrong?" Lana asked as she opened the door and stepped aside for Scott to enter.

"Can I come in?" he asked as he walked by her. He'd been there a few times before for work-related issues, so he felt comfortable walking in and sitting at the small table between the kitchen and the living room.

She cocked an eyebrow at him. "Should I invite Jose to join us?"

Jose Cuervo had become a running joke with them after their first day at the retirement home in Florida. It had been a hell of a day full of randy retirement home residents who were either at each other's throats or shoving their tongues down each other's throats. Scott and Lana, with still at least six months of filming ahead of them, found themselves drinking heavily that first night to numb the horror of it all.

"Yeah," he said. "That's a good idea." He thought it might remind her of that night they were both human and friends. Scott had never seen Lana cut lose like that before. So much so that within a few months of the infamous Jose Cuervo night he'd almost convinced himself he'd imagined it. The next day, Lana had effortlessly reverted to her stoic, workaholic self.

Lana grabbed the bottle and two double shot glasses and sat down at the table with him. Without another word she poured two full-to-the-brim shots. They tapped glasses, tapped the table, then downed the shots.

It was no way to take shots of tequila, but it was their tradition. Their first night with Jose, they didn't have salt or limes. Even though this time around Lana may have had both in her kitchenette, she wasn't offering them, or she was a softy for tradition and favored replicating their previous night together as closely as she could. Even if that meant taking double shots of tequila without a chaser or anything else to help wash it down.

Fucking robotic Lana, he thought. Because of the situation he didn't want to put her out any more than he already was by asking for anything beyond the booze. She poured another round, and they downed the shots again. Her face looked as though she'd just had a sip of water while he was sure he looked like he'd just ingested rancid meat.

As he waited for the warmth to continue coursing through his body, Lana moved over to the balcony and opened the door. She took a cigarette from a pack laying on a side table and lit up in the living room as she attempted to blow the smoke out of the apartment via the balcony screen door. It wasn't working.

After the first drag he could see her loosening up as her

head dropped forward a bit. While it was slightly alarming to see her in her unnatural and slouched state, it was also a sign she was going to let her guard down for a bit. A rarity indeed. He'd seen it happen only a few times in the years he'd known her.

She smiled as she asked, "Do you remember our first day at Shady Maple?"

Flashes of that day went through his mind and that, along with the booze that was working its way through his system, allowed him to relax a bit, too.

"I will *never* forget our first day at Shady Maple."

A smile spread across his face, too. They had been working on a documentary at a retirement home about elder financial abuse. At the time he thought it would be a very difficult and somewhat depressing few months working in the home due to the topic of the film, but that quickly changed their first day filming.

"Marge swatting down Mabel's garden gnome and shout-ing, 'No one wants your snatch, hussy,' is my got-to memory whenever life gets too shitty," Lana said with her voice changing to create an impeccable imitation of Marge's voice.

That was all it took. Scott clearly saw it all happening again in his mind and it was just as glorious in his head as it had been in person. Marge, a force to be reckoned with in her motorized wheelchair, had been having a lovely conver-sation with Lana as Scott filmed them walking down the hallway. Without any warning, Marge reached a hand out at Mabel's door to knock her garden gnome from off her welcome mat. Garden gnomes, it turned out, were a signal to the gentlemen of the retirement home that she was single and available for sexy time. As she'd swatted at the gnome, she'd also yelled a few colorful expletives at Mabel's door during the oh-so-slow motorized wheelchair drive-by.

That was just the beginning of their initiation into the

seedy sexual underbelly of Shady Maple Retirement Homes. Their last day of filming, Lana and Scott again got drunk on tequila to celebrate the end of that portion of their assignment, and to rehash all their favorite retirement memories. That was the same night Lana had been looking over his shoulder while he quickly scrolled through Twitter and saw the pictures from Milton's Christmas lights event and got the idea in her head that their next project should be in Milton, Maryland.

The Vegas documentary had him bored out of his mind and questioning his career choice, but the retirement home job with Lana had convinced him to give it another chance. He was glad he did since it brought him back to Milton and back to Jackie Strauss.

After they'd reminisced about their favorite retirement home stories and the laughter died down, Lana said, "I'm tired, Scott." Her hand lazily waved through the smokey air before she gave up and stepped out onto the balcony. She left the sliding door open so she could continue to talk to him from outside as she lit another cigarette.

"I've been spending every waking hour that I'm not filming going through what we have so far."

Scott wasn't sure what to say in response. He had not been spending every waking hour he wasn't filming working on some other aspect of the documentary. In fairness he also wasn't expected to, but it made him feel guilty regardless knowing how much time he'd been spending with Jackie. While Lana was working herself to death, Scott had stepped down on his work efforts and had focused more on his new relationship. He should have known better than to accuse Tim of having a relationship with Lana. Lana would never allow something like that to compromise her work.

Lana continued to smoke as she looked off into the night

somewhere, so Scott filled the silence and asked, "Are we behind? Is that why you're working so many hours?"

"According to my original plans, we're slightly ahead of schedule now since I've already outlined a few episodes and tagged the clips I want to use."

"Then you should take some time off," he offered even though she certainly didn't need his approval to do so. "Maybe even go out sometime...on a date. Remember those?"

A slight flicker went through her eyes, and he wondered if she was thinking about some past romance – perhaps even Tim.

"No time." She turned back to him. "I found our next project." She stubbed out her cigarette, walked back into the apartment, and closed the sliding door behind her.

Scott let out a sigh of relief. Milton had been his third project with Lana, and he wasn't sure if she'd keep him on with her or not for her next one. A small part of him worried he was only in Milton because he grew up in the area and Lana wanted to leverage that knowledge. Not that he'd given her any reason *not* to want him on her team. But so far, he was the only camera person to work on multiple projects with Lana and it wasn't clear to him if that was by choice or not.

He shook his head as if to say she was hopeless. "Already onto the next one. Sounds about right. What'll it be this time?"

"Australia," she proudly announced.

"The British convicts in New South Wales?" In the early days of their Vegas documentary, Lana had taken on uncovering her family tree as a bit of a hobby. She didn't have much extra time, but the few minutes she'd had were always spent researching or browsing websites dedicated to helping its customers discover their long-gone, ancient relatives.

Going all the way back to the late eighteenth century,

Lana discovered her father was one of the ill-fated convicts taken to Australia, then New South Wales, to work in a labor camp. She'd been fascinated about Australia's history ever since. Getting to film a documentary about the subject was a dream come true for her.

"It's finally happening, Scott. I just got the okay a few days ago."

She refilled their shot glasses, and they repeated the tap of shot glasses, the tap on the table, and the downing of their shots. It was clear to Scott that Jose had appeared due to the fact that she wanted to share her news and excitement with someone rather than her concern over whatever had been bothering him.

"The okay from whom?" Vegas tourism had funded their first documentary, a hard-won grant had funded their Florida documentary, and Lana was putting her own money out for the Milton documentary since it was a bit of a passion project for her. She hoped that she'd be able to pitch it to DocMe, the up-and-coming streaming service that showed only documentaries. But who in their right mind was going to pay them to go to Australia?

"DocMe." Lana was downright giddy at that point. And rightfully so. Everything she'd ever wanted was within her reach. "I sent them a pitch for Christmas Lights Lane along with your Twitter handle, and a few clips I've strung together."

Scott failed miserably at hiding his skepticism. "And they bought it, just like that? Before the actual unveiling of the event?"

Her smile faltered ever so slightly. "Yes, though I'm sure it didn't hurt that Tim's old college roommate runs the marketing department at DocMe. I got our work in front of someone because of Tim's connection. I got the greenlight for Australia based on what they saw."

Scott cocked an eyebrow at her. "They just started streaming three months ago. They're desperate for new material, aren't they?"

"I have no idea," she said, dodging the question. "What *I* really want to know is, are you coming with me, or do I need to start searching for a replacement? As long as I can keep splicing and editing footage every waking moment I'm not filming, we're leaving as soon as we finish here."

"I'm all in," he said without hesitating. Australia. Exploring the world for a job that he (mostly) loved.

"Even if it means leaving Jackie behind?"

"She'll come with me," Scott said with equal confidence. The only reason Jackie was even Milton again was because she inherited a house and wanted to be a part of the lights event. Once the event was over, she'd be ready to move on to whatever was next while she waited for the documentary to finally air – likely a year, possibly two, into the future. He hadn't heard another word about the non-profit position, so he was sure that wasn't a factor either.

He narrowed eyes at Lana, sitting across from him at the table and refilling their shot glasses. "Did Tim tell you about Jackie?" he asked.

Lana's eyebrows raised dangerously close to her hairline. "Tim knows? I bet he lost his shit about it…" she said with an undeniable fondness in her voice.

"He and Lizzy caught me half-naked in Jackie's house tonight. I came over here to tell you myself."

Lana's head flew back with laughter, and she almost spilled the shot she'd been about to take. "I'm picturing it now," she said between guffaws, "and it's all so glorious." More laughter. "Oh, man. I can't wait to see that footage."

Scott wasn't sure if Lana really didn't care since everything with her career was falling into place regardless, or if she was just too tipsy to remember she'd previously forbid it. He wondered if she'd had a few shots before he arrived.

"You said no fraternizing with anyone involved in the documentary. Why the sudden change?" he asked before throwing back the shot. Likely a mistake but he'd been making a lot of those lately. What was one more?

Lana's laughter tampered enough for her to take her shot as well. Finally, like any other human being he'd ever met, her face scrunched in disgust as she downed the amber liquid.

She exhaled, placed the glass back onto the table, and said, "We have work to do. There's no time for the other stuff." Her hand waved about the air as if love was some trivial thing that only a small percentage of people even bothered with.

"And yet," she continued, "I could see it between you and her from that first meeting. Did you think it was luck or coincidence you were assigned to her section of the neighborhood?" She lit another cigarette, not bothering to open the door this time. "It was me, Scott. I was your matchmaker. I couldn't guess how far you guys would take it, but I was there gathering footage just in case. Ring cameras, plenty of footage from Lizzy, your footage...I saw it all. I watched you fall in love. Hell, I practically dove into some bushes one night while I was smoking a cigarette out back at Tim's house at some ungodly hour trying to avoid you seeing me when you were sneaking across the back field and into Jackie's back door."

He sat up in his chair as what Lana was saying started to sink in. "No, no...I never wanted to be in these things, Lana. I'm okay with sitting and listening to Muriel, but not this..."

It occurred to him at that point that maybe he should have eaten something prior to having the shots. He'd had lunch hours ago and it was doing little to soak up the alcohol running through his system and fogging up his brain.

"Jackie's been busting her ass trying to make a name for herself with this documentary. Putting any focus on our relationship is going to take away from that."

Even with the booze loosening her up, Lana's face turned serious. "We all know the odds of Jackie getting some sort of show or actual traction from this documentary are slim at best."

He was ready to put her in her place at that comment, but Lana beat him to it. "She's talented, Scott. I know. I get it. But she doesn't have *it*. Few people do. Her only chance at getting extra exposure on this documentary is for us to push the romance subplot of your relationship."

"She's talented enough to make her more of a focus based solely on her work," he argued.

"It's a documentary about the entire neighborhood, the culture of the neighborhood. You don't even know all the different story lines we have going on here. You're filming less than half of the neighborhood. You're seeing less than half the story."

It was a valid point. He purposely kept himself at a distance from the bulk of what else was happening with the documentary outside of his own role with it. For one thing, the business and marketing aspect of documentaries bored him. For another, it sometimes distracted him from his work. It was best for him to focus only on what he was responsible for.

He looked down at his hands for a moment as he wrapped his mind around what Lana was saying, and as he tried to clear his increasingly muddled mind. He was too old for consecutive double shots of tequila. The tolerance he'd once had back in college was long gone.

Still looking down into his closed hands between his

knees, he said, "It sounds like you're giving Jackie a choice. As to whether or not she's...*our* relationship is part of the documentary."

She tilted her head side-to-side as if debating her response. "Never. I will do whatever I think is best for the documentary." She took another drag of her cigarette and blew the smoke off to the side even though it permeated throughout the small apartment regardless of where she turned her head when she exhaled.

"But in this instance," she said, "I do feel a bit dirty about it for lack of a better term. So yes, I am offering an out."

Scott wondered if she had felt this way from the beginning, or if she was only saying it in his presence and with the presence of alcohol in her system. Would she change her mind in the light of day?

"Dirty sounds a lot like the right term to use." He was no longer looking down at his hands. His eyes were trained on hers and didn't leave. Lana was more relaxed than she normally was, so she was allowing reactions and emotions to come across her face. It was essential for him to be able to pick up on what she was feeling since she would rarely offer that information up herself. Drunk or not.

She pursed her lips slightly as if to bite back something critical or argumentative. She was holding something back. Scott pushed further to see if he could get her to spill whatever it was she was hiding.

"You had Tim show up with Lizzy tonight, didn't you? You staged him catching us." It was intended to be a false accusation, just strong enough and outrageous enough to get her to say whatever the real truth was. He never expected that that *was* the real truth. Never expected Lana to stage anything when it came to her documentaries.

"Tim didn't know the extent of it. I knew you were sneaking in late in the evenings, so when he voiced concerns about Jackie's work," she said as she shrugged like it was business as usual, "I suggested he confront her about it in the evening. Around six or so. Said he should take Lizzy since he and Lizzy had been working so closely together this past week."

Scott sat in stunned silence. He watched as she nonchalantly smoked her cigarette. Not a care in the world even though she just admitted her documentary was slipping into reality television territory under her direction.

"I had the chat with Tim a week ago. I figured nothing came of it since I hadn't heard anything since then. Took him long enough to get the nerve to confront Jackie." Her last comment sounded more like Lana. Whatever ease and comradery they'd enjoyed earlier in the night was gone. That was his cue to leave.

"Thanks for the drinks, Lana. But I should get going."

The act of standing and starting to walk again made the booze hit him even harder. The room moved slightly and he had trouble texting Jackie for a ride home. Before he could shut the door behind him he heard one last comment from Lana

"Sure, sure. But, Scott, do yourself a favor and check the comments on your Twitter posts."

JACKIE

*J*ust two hours after he'd left her house, Scott texted and asked for a ride from Lana's house back to hers. She breathed a sigh of relief as she pocketed her phone and raced out the door to get him. She was eager to hear how his conversation with Lana went, though she assumed if he was texting and asking to see her again, it was good news.

As soon as Jackie pulled into the lot, she could tell Scott was more than a little tipsy by the way he gently swayed out front of the building. But he made his way into the car without incident and greeted her with a sweet kiss that had a kick of tequila.

"You okay?" she asked when he pulled away and rested his head back in the seat.

"Mmmm," he responded with his eyes closed. When he opened them to look at her, he added, "It's all such a mess, babe." Those tipsy eyes looked so morose as he said it, even though he looked at her with nothing but admiration and possibly even love.

"We'll figure it out. Together." She stroked his stubbly

cheek with the back of her hand. He pulled it to his lips for a quick kiss before dropping both of their hands down to his lap. Good thing she didn't drive stick.

"Let's get us home, first. Then we can talk."

They were about to pull out of the apartment parking lot when she noticed the passenger of another car pulling in. It was Jeremy, and the driver was some woman she didn't recognize.

That son of a bitch, she thought as she turned right only to do a U-turn a block away and pull back into the lot.

"I don't want to talk to Lana any more tonight," Scott said, assuming that was what Jackie had in mind.

"We're not. I just need to see something really quick." She pulled her hand back from Scott's, turned down the radio even though it was already off, and then parked in the first available spot.

Jackie had seen enough romantic comedy movies to know that this could all be explained away. If she jumped out and started to make accusations, it would turn out that the woman was Jeremy's cousin or something along those lines. To prevent any misunderstandings, she let the car idle as she watched Jeremy and the woman get out.

It was only when the woman leaned into Jeremy as they walked up to the building, that she finally made a move to get out of the car. Scott likely realized what was happening but must have figured it wasn't his place. He remained watching from the passenger seat.

"What the fuck, Jeremy?" Jackie called as soon as her foot hit the asphalt. The two continued to cling to one another as they turned to see who was yelling at them from the parking lot. Just as Jackie expected, they both gave a look of surprise and innocence as she approached them. As if they had no idea why someone may be upset that some strange woman was clinging to Jeremy, a married man.

"Jackie? What's wrong?" Jeremy asked. His voice was full of concern for her, not himself, even though she'd just caught him red-handed.

"Oh, let me guess. She's your cousin, right? All one big misunderstanding," Jackie said sarcastically.

He looked her up and down like he was trying to assess her state of mind before he said, "This *is* my cousin. You remember Chastity?"

Once her adrenaline slowed and her heart stopped pounding quite so loudly in her chest, Jackie took a moment to really take in the woman with Jeremy. She wasn't affectionately leaning into him; she was using him for support. Her brown hair was a mess and covered most of her face. She looked smashed.

"Just picked her up from The Cut and Run. Her shitty friends left her drunk and in the bathroom."

Still unable to accept that this woman was indeed Jeremy's cousin and not a mistress, Jackie reached out to tuck a bit of hair behind Chastity's ear to get a clearer view of her face. They'd met a few times before when Chastity was a child. It was more difficult to recognize her dressed for a night out and intoxicated, so it was hard to tell for sure if this mess of hair was really her.

Bleh! Chastity wretched right as Jackie's hand was by her face. She jumped back instinctively though nothing came out of Chastity's mouth.

"Ugh, been puking so much she doesn't have anything left," Jeremy said as he shifted her a bit to get a better grip on her. "I'm staying the night with her to make sure she's okay." He appraised Jackie again. "Are you okay? Is everything alright? Is Sam okay?"

"Yeah, no. Everything's fine. I...I didn't realize it was Chastity."

She didn't outright say that she assumed he was walking

with another woman back to her apartment. She didn't have to. As his facial expression darkened, she could see him putting two and two together.

"Really?"

Jackie opened her mouth to defend herself though she had no idea what she could possibly say to save herself.

"I don't have time for this," he said, turning himself and Chastity back towards the house.

Jackie looked back to Scott in the car and found him looking back at them with a quizzical look in his flushed, also hammered, face. What was it with everyone getting smashed on a Monday night, and why hadn't she thought to do the same?

Jackie noticed he was eating a granola bar he must have found in her glove box. After a silent prayer that he wouldn't yak her granola bar in her car, she held up a finger for him to wait and then she caught up with Jeremy and Chastity to help them both into the apartment building.

SCOTT

*J*ackie looked almost unsteady herself as she walked back to the car and climbed in some time after she'd disappeared into the apartment with them.

"I'm a little drunk right now," Scott admitted, "but that was Jeremy with some other woman. Wasn't it." He stated it more than asked it, because aside from his mild mental impairment, he could mostly see just fine. The granola bar had helped, too. Adorable Jackie had snacks hidden all over her car as if she could be stranded in a blizzard at any moment and needed to be prepared.

"His cousin. She called him to help her home since she was too drunk to function, let alone drive."

"Are you sure? Guys sometimes say that sort of thing. The whole it's-my-cousin excuse when it's really another woman."

Scott never had, but he'd had a few friends in the past who would lie to their wives or girlfriends right in front of him. The worst was a night in Vegas when one of his guy friends, Burk, used him as an alibi while he was out with another girl. The girlfriend called Scott, who was alone in bed at the time, looking for Burk and he'd lied and said Burk was passed out in his living and couldn't talk. The girlfriend thanked Scott for being such a good friend looking after Burk like that. Scott spent the rest of the night awake and feeling like shit. He'd since broken off all ties with Burk and any other friends he'd had like that.

Turning back in her seat and starting the car up, Jackie said, "I know. I had my suspicions. But I've met her before. They're cousins. Sam and I used to help Jeremy babysit her."

"Is everything okay?"

"They're fine. She doesn't have anything left to throw up and he's crashing there with her. He'll take her to get her car in the morning."

Scott had seen Sam and Jeremy together a few times while filming. There hadn't been much interaction between himself and Jeremy, but he'd seen him with Sam and with everyone in general and he seemed like a good guy. If he was honest, he was a little jealous that Jeremy and Sam had such a strong marriage and had found each other so young.

Jackie took a deep breath. "I can't not talk about this anymore. The only reason I thought Jeremy might be cheating is because Sam said she's seen his eyes wandering and that they're not happy anymore." She had been looking straight ahead but turned to see what Scott's reaction was.

His alcohol-swamped brain took a bit to process it all. He also needed a second to think about if he wanted to know any more about it or not. Almost immediately he decided he did not. He'd been through one downfall himself and it felt like a bit of PTSD was settling over him hearing about Sam and Jeremy's troubles. The tightness in his chest made it feel like something was around him constricting his airways. Not to mention the lurching of his stomach which may have been the alcohol, the news, the stale granola bar, or Jackie's jerky driving. Maybe a combination of it all was what threatened to send him retching forward and dousing Jackie's pristine floorboards with regurgitated granola and tequila.

Jackie, distracted by her conversation with Scott, didn't see the stop sign ahead and had to slam on her breaks. His head dipped forward with the sudden stop, and he closed his eyes to prevent himself from feeling sicker than he already felt.

"I know," she said, hitting the gas again and making her way back to her house, "I'm sick to my stomach over it, too."

He didn't want to hear about it. The less he knew, the better. The car ride was getting to him, so he opened his eyes again to try to focus on something and steady his mind and stomach. For the final few minutes home, he stared at the dashboard in front of him as Jackie went into detail about what Sam had said and what she herself had seen happening between them.

"I'm sorry I'm dumping all of this on you. I know you don't want to hear about it, but Sam hasn't brought it up since and I can't bring myself to talk about it with her if she doesn't want to talk about it." Another deep breath. "And now I'm rambling."

She was rambling. He'd seen her do it before and it was usually endearing to watch as she tried to organize all her thoughts in her head by prattling them out to anyone who may be around to hear it. In the car talking about Sam and Jeremy's marriage, it was only making him anxious and concerned about their own relationship.

Back at her house they quietly and mechanically got ready for bed, too lost in their own thoughts to have much conversation beyond asking for the toothpaste or if an alarm was set for the next morning. She made sure he drank two large glasses of water before bed.

. . .

They got up early the next day since they both had to work. Scott tried to clearly remember how Jackie had reacted when Tim first found them together. What she had said to Scott after Tim and Lizzy had left. It all happened so quickly that it was a bit of a blur to him the next day. Had he imagined that she'd been as upset and concerned as he had been?

After a bit of thought, he realized the answer to both of those questions was yes. It was *his* career that had been on the line, and she blew it off. Had practically said, "Lana will know anyway tomorrow, so just stay tonight." Doubts about their relationship started creeping in once again.

It was on the car ride back to the apartments to pick up his car that Jackie finally asked about what Lana had said the night before.

"Lana said she'd had a feeling there was something going on between us…" he said, letting his voice trail off at the end. Initially he had planned to follow that up with how Lana wanted to make it a feature in the documentary, but was miraculously leaving that decision up to them. Except when it came time for him to say it, the words wouldn't come out.

They didn't even know what they were doing, so how could they make a decision like that about their relationship? *She has too much on her plate now as it is*, he thought as he tried to reason with himself about why he shouldn't discuss his full conversation with Lana with her.

"She already knew?" Jackie asked.

"Yeah."

"That's a good thing, then. Right? Why aren't you happier about this?" she asked cautiously.

"Tim just told you your work is slipping. I *know* mine has been."

She took a deep breath like she was trying to suppress her frustration. "True. But that's already in the past now. Going forward, we'll do better. Manage our time better."

When they arrived at his car, Jeremy was nowhere in sight. He leaned over the center console to give her a quick kiss, but her hand went around his neck bringing him closer. There was some sort of desperation and urgency in her kiss, and he felt guilty that she could feel him pulling away before he even got up the nerve to say it out loud.

"Have a great day," she said with what sounded like forced enthusiasm once she finally released her grip from his neck.

"Yeah, you too."

That morning he was tasked with getting more creative and artistic shots for the documentary. Most neighbors already had their lights up and ready to go, so there wasn't nearly as much to film in regard to preparation for the event. But again, he couldn't focus on his work the way that he should be. Everything about the last twelve hours was not sitting well with him. Tim's accurate criticism that he and Jackie were not performing at their optimal levels, Lana's admission that she'd begun staging aspects of her documentaries, and Jeremy and Sam's deteriorating marriage.

What he really needed was a week without the distractions so he could focus again. He needed one week without Jackie.

JACKIE

She couldn't focus at work. It wasn't a complete tragedy given how slow the marina was in late November, but it very well could be if it boiled over into her event planning and event work.

The holiday event *should* be her top priority since it was likely to be her best chance to achieve her ultimate career goals – her dreams, really. When else was she ever going to get the opportunity to be part of a documentary that showcased her do-it-yourself skills and design talents? Sure, the documentary could flop with nothing ever coming from it. But based on the reception of Scott's initial social media images, it was going to be a hit. She could feel it.

But she couldn't ignore what was happening with Scott. And whether she liked it or not, that was taking priority over her event planning. Things had been off between them since Tim called them out. And even though he had nothing to do with the whole Jeremy and Sam situation, for some reason that was having a negative impact on their already tenuous relationship as well.

It shouldn't have been a surprise when Scott called Jackie

at work and suggested they take the rest of the week off to think things over, get their priorities straight, and catch up on their work. On the phone Jackie was cool and collected. "Yeah, I think you're right," she heard herself say. But as soon as the call ended, she was a teary mess at the front desk. Good thing they hadn't had a customer come in for over a month.

As much as her heart ached knowing she was going home to an empty bed that smelled of Scott's scent, she knew he was right. That first day she'd been so determined and focused to make the event her only priority. How quickly that had faded away once she and Scott became an item. And then what? After the documentary was over, he was leaving. She'd be left single and mourning her lost opportunity.

Unacceptable. This was her shot; it was meant to be. As her mother's daughter she couldn't help but feel like inheriting the house the same year a documentary was filming the event was not coincidental. There were no coincidences, after all.

She allowed herself a long, solid cry at the front desk, then she made her game plan going forward. She needed to get her lights up that week and she needed to ignore Scott while she did it.

"I can do this," she said to the empty room where she worked. "I am a strong, independent, driven woman. I am a fucking rock star. I can ignore Scott and get my shit together." It felt good to say it out loud. "I don't need him or any other man; I have a vibrator." Okay, that one felt a little weird to declare at work. But still, things were looking up.

By Thanksgiving, she had done the impossible by finishing all but the minor details of her decorating plans. The next evening, Black Friday, she would be ready for opening day and the big unveiling of Christmas Lights Lane.

Scott and Jackie had been successfully co-existing for the past few days as coworkers and nothing more. He had set the tone the first day with minimal formalities and she followed his lead. It was awkward, at first, to greet with a simple "Hello" and to end it with a "Goodbye" with no plans of seeing each other later. That was it. Maybe it was stubborn of her, but she never allowed herself to text him or call him to talk about it further. He'd wanted space; she'd given it to him.

That evening everyone was in high spirits around the Thanksgiving table at Mort's house. Babs no longer felt the need to cart her cat around with her everywhere, so he was at home while she acted as co-host with Mort. A dozen or so neighbors were there along with a few of Mort's cousins.

In a turn of events that Jackie should have seen coming, Scott was there to film some of the dinner before he joined them at the table.

Even though neither had talked about Thanksgiving since her initial invite, Jackie had assumed Scott would not be joining her. But Mort and her mother wouldn't hear of it. As Scott packed up his camera, they, along with the rest of the table, insisted Scott stay for the actual meal. Muriel slid over a seat so that Scott could sit between her and Margaret.

After the first bottle of wine was quickly kicked, Scott offered to get another, and Jackie jumped at the opportunity to speak to him alone for a few minutes. Even though it had been just under a week, it was time to figure things out once and for all.

Mort's kitchen was usually filled with generic cow décor, but he'd switched it over to Christmas cow décor early (surprise, surprise in this neighborhood) so they were surrounded by cows adorned with holiday flair. Jersey cows in Santa outfits, a calf unwrapping Christmas presents, and a myriad of cows singing carols. Jackie's personal favorite was a large cow magnet that covered the front of the refrigerator. The beast was dressed head-to-toe in a Christmas onesie, with an udder cutout, and was covered in a fancy font that read, "You're udderly fabulous and you deserve to eat ALL the Christmas cookies!"

In short, it was a less than ideal location for their talk, especially with her mother and a large number of neighbors on the other side of the wall.

"Hey," she said once they were in the kitchen.

"Hey," he said back looking over his shoulder as he pulled another bottle of red from the cabinet. He was wearing a red and black flannel shirt and he let his scruff grow a little longer than usual. Instead of looking unkempt, it only heightened his good looks and casual attitude about his appearance. He gave her one of his easy smiles and her heart did that thing where it started to beat so hard she swore it was obvious even under her thick sweater.

"Can we talk about everything?" Jackie took another step towards him – the pull to be near him and touch him wouldn't ease up regardless of their less than sexy surroundings. Dressed as Richard Simmons, surrounded by festive cows? It didn't matter.

"I'd rather not talk about it here." His expression showed genuine remorse that their conversation would have to wait a bit longer while they navigated the rest of the holiday in limbo. Scott popped the cork to a bottle of white. "After dinner?"

After dinner? Scott was planning to see her alone, after dinner? Her typical optimistic personality, and the generous glass of wine she'd already downed, took that as him practically proposing later in the night.

"Sure," she said. "That works."

The conversation in the kitchen made dinner much more bearable. She'd mentioned to her mother and to Mort that she and Scott wanted to keep their relationship quiet – not a secret – while they were still figuring everything out. Mort and Babs didn't hear about the Tim debacle or their "break" for the past few days. As far as Babs could tell, Scott's cool attitude towards Jackie was a part of their charade to keep their relationship private.

Hell, she probably thought she was doing Jackie a favor by insisting Scott stay for dinner when Jackie herself wouldn't for fear of the neighbors catching wind of their relationship. In Babs and Mort's minds, they were covertly saving the day.

Throughout dinner she snuck glances at Scott and thought she caught him doing the same. It was hard to tell. She was back where she was in August wondering if her feelings for him were one-sided or if he was throwing down subtle hints that she may or may not be seeing. To distract herself she stayed engaged in conversations at her end of the table asking Mort about his latest train garden display in the basement, Lillian about her granddaughter's latest steps towards becoming an official chess master, and Evelyn about the candy food truck she'd managed to convince Tim to allow for the lights event that year.

Before she knew it, she was more than a little tipsy from the flowing wine. *Shit, these septuagenarians can really hold their booze*, she thought when she realized she'd been going glass for glass with her seatmates, and they still seemed perfectly fine while she was felt all warm and tingly inside.

"Have you seen my Precious Moments collection?" Muriel asked her.

"I have not, Muriel. You haven't invited me over yet." That last comment sent every red to Jackie's brain. She was officially drunk.

"You'll love it, dear. You have to stop by for tea and coffee one day. I'll make you my oatmeal cookies and we can go through them one by one. Though I'm sure Scott's already told you all about them."

"Yes, that would be lovely." *Lovely?* she thought. *I'm becoming one of them...* The idea would have terrified her back in Philadelphia. But after she'd spent a few months in Milton, she found it soothing and comforting. The neighborhood had become an extended family of sorts. She'd fallen in love with the small-town life of Milton where everyone was Kevin Bacon, and you never even needed all six degrees to connect any two people in the town.

"By the way," Muriel continued in a lowered voice. She leaned in, too, and Jackie could smell her thick floral perfume and the wine on her breath. "How are things going with Scott?"

"What's that?" Jackie leaned in even closer, sure she hadn't heard her correctly.

"You and Scott? How are things going?"

"Oh, no. We're just friends."

Muriel laughed. "No need to play coy with me. He and I spend a lot of time together and I can't tell you how often I caught him sneaking a peek at his phone. He thinks I can't see because I asked him to read something for me once. But really, I didn't have my contacts in that day. Ever since then he's openly been reading text messages and responding in front of me while I pretend I can't read them. But I can."

Muriel almost laughed her way out of her seat at her little prank on Scott. So much so that Jackie couldn't help but to laugh along with her. Booze had a way of making her extra friendly and extra giggly.

"Oh, my," Muriel said when she could speak again. "I saw a few messages between you two. You should have seen the love-struck look on his face whenever he'd read your messages. I asked him once who he was texting, but he wouldn't say. Just asked me more questions to get me to stop asking him questions."

"Really?" Her eyes found Scott again at the other end of the table and her heart hurt a bit. What she wouldn't give to go back to that time when there was only possibility, to the time before everything got so messy.

"I don't think so..." Jackie said. If she remembered correctly, and it was certainly possible she did not given the wine she'd drunk that night, she and Scott were still down-playing everything and denying to the death if anyone assumed otherwise.

"I know what I saw," Muriel insisted. "I also know I saw some risqué texts from the both of you. I have kids and grandkids; I know what those emojis mean."

Jackie's eyes widened thinking of the sexting she and Scott occasionally engaged in and how Muriel had seen it all. Mid-sip her wine went down her windpipe and she began to cough uncontrollably as she tried to clear it out.

All conversation around the table stopped and everyone turned to see if she was okay. Jackie's face turned red from embarrassment though it probably looked as though it were red from choking.

"You're okay," Muriel said with a few hits to her back. "I think she was choking on a bit of the roasted eggplant, but she's fine now."

Jackie, suffering now from a new cough brought on by Muriel's reference to the eggplant emoji, could barely make out the words, "I'm fine; I'm fine," before she excused herself to recoup in the bathroom.

"Jackie, dear, maybe you should head home," Babs said with a quick squeeze to her arm. When Jackie looked around the table, she noticed half of the guests, including Scott, had already left.

"Oh. Right. Yes," she said as she carefully lifted herself out of her seat and made her way to the door. Luckily, while her mind felt a little hazy, her coordination was still intact. "Thank you, Mort, for having me tonight. Everything was delicious. It always is when you're cooking."

"My pleasure dear," Mort said with a hug. "Honey, will you walk out Jackie while I start rounding up the troops here?"

"Sure thing, hon." She put her arm around Jackie and walked her out to the front porch.

Jackie glanced around for Scott, but she didn't see him or his car anywhere.

"What happened between you and Scott?" Babs asked.

Damn intuition and aura reading. Jackie knew better than to lie to her mother. It wasn't necessarily a respect thing but more of a logical thing. Babs always knew. It wasn't worth the hassle to even attempt to lie.

"It's complicated."

"Yes, sometimes these things get complicated," Babs empathized.

"No, I mean it's really complicated this time."

"My husband was reincarnated as a cat for almost a decade. His soul was only freed when he knew I found Mort and had someone to look out for me."

Jackie reverted to her teenage self (probably because of the booze) and rolled her eyes at her mother.

"You win," she said sarcastically to Babs.

"I'm just saying there's too much involved with love for it not to be complicated."

Jackie nodded. "I'm pretty beat. I'm going to go home now."

Babs leaned in for a big squeeze. "I'm proud of you,

honey. You were lost for a while there, but I see it in your eyes and in your aura. You're home now; you're happy now."

Jackie, in complete misery at Scott abandoning her, cocked an eyebrow at her mother. "This is me happy?"

"This particular moment is not a good look on you, no. But these past few months I've never seen you happier. I think that's another reason why Tom left. He knew both of his girls were going to be okay."

Jackie said nothing. She'd deal with everything her mother was saying in the morning when she could think a bit clearer about it all.

As if Babs could read her mind she said, "You should probably go sleep it off. We can talk more tomorrow."

"Thanks, Mom."

"Love you, sweetie."

"Love you, too."

Her mother waited until she was inside the house before Babs went back into Mort's house. Jackie smiled to herself thinking of how overprotective her mother could be. As if something would happen to her just crossing the street to her house.

She turned the lights on in the living room and nearly screamed when she found Scott sitting on her couch.

JACKIE

"*H*oly crap. You scared me," she said as she clutched one hand to her chest.

Scott was on his feet and walking towards her. "I'm sorry. I didn't mean to. Then when you walked in, I didn't know how to say anything without scaring you, but maybe staying quiet was worse." His face, full of concern, was a few feet from hers. "Are you okay?"

He didn't reach out to her, and she couldn't help but notice and overanalyze all of it. What did it mean that they barely spoke the past few days, they didn't really talk during dinner at all, and there he was in her living room but still keeping his distance? Still treating her like a friend again.

"It's fine. I'm fine." She dropped her hand back down to her side and waited for him to make the next move. *He* was the one who randomly appeared on *her* couch after all.

"I thought you went home," she said. So much for letting him make the next move. But she couldn't help it. She was starting to get a bit pissed at how everything was going down on his terms. She'd allowed it at first and followed his lead, but tipsy her, standing in the living room still coming down from the adrenaline of finding him on her couch in the dark, was losing patience.

"Can we sit?" he asked. He didn't make his way over to the couch and just assumed that she would follow. He stood, waiting for her confirmation that she would indeed like to sit down. She really liked that about him, so she sat to hear what he had to say. He sat a comfortable distance away from her. Somewhere between where Tim would sit (practically in her lap) and where Mort would sit (at least one entire cushion away so as not to give any discomfort). It was too ambiguous to make anything concrete of it, but she was certain she'd overanalyze that little detail on top of everything else once she had the chance.

"Lizzy and I have been meeting with Tim and Lana almost daily the past two weeks. Since you and I decided to take a break, Tim and Lana both made multiple comments about how you've been crushing it."

Work talk? She finally had Scott, on her couch, at night, and he wanted to talk about work. After they'd already spent most of Thanksgiving dinner talking about the event?

"That's great," she said because Scott stopped talking and she felt like she needed to respond in some way.

He gave her a confused look in response. "Don't you remember telling me how this was the most important thing in your life right now? I wasn't sure when you'd first mentioned it to me if you had a shot or could even pull off half of the crazy ideas you had for your house. But you did it. Better than I could even imagine it."

"I never doubted myself, but good to know you did." *Stand down!* her mind screamed at her. It was crazy how confrontational she could become when Scott was involved. He was such a good guy, and yet when she felt hurt by him, she resorted to caustic remarks rather than rational conversation.

He dropped his head in frustration and then picked it up again. "I hadn't seen you since you were a teenager, Jackie. I had no idea the person you'd become."

Oh, god. No. This sounds like a period conversation now where I've become a woman before his eyes. "Great. I'm glad I turned into something worthy of your temporary attention and affection."

She hadn't meant to sound so harsh, but she needed answers. Each evening she'd been on a ladder or in her yard hanging lights preparing for the event. Once she'd gotten into a rhythm, autopilot had kicked in with her movements, so her mind was freed to be preoccupied with taking a fine-toothed comb through every conversation and interaction she'd had with Scott. No gesture, tone, look, or touch, had been spared. Sam would be pleased to hear her drop all of the games and get right to the point. Not that Sam was above games herself, it seemed. But still.

"I get that you didn't want to stop whatever this is," he said as he gestured between them, "but it was the right thing to do."

"Fine. You were right." Fuck. Again, she sounded much more flippant and bitchier than she'd meant to. A few days of pent-up anger and frustration was mixing with the booze, and she wasn't liking the end result of it all. But then she also couldn't bring herself to stop or to apologize for it.

"I'm not looking for validation..." he said before he gave her another quizzical look. "Are you drunk?"

Busted. "Kind of? Yes? But everyone at dinner was..."

"I don't think so. No."

Jackie thought about it. "Really? Because I was keeping pace with everyone else."

"No. Though you did move about the table a bit. Maybe you got confused about who was drinking what?" he offered.

Jackie leaned back on the sofa to try to gather her

thoughts. She hadn't eaten much of anything earlier in the day so she could binge on all of Mort's amazing dishes. But once Scott mentioned it, she did remember seat hopping with some of the other neighbors after the meal as everyone was mingling more than eating.

"Crap. I think you're right."

Scott took a deep breath and leaned back into the couch, too. "Maybe we should just talk tomorrow."

"No, please. I can't do another night like this. Unsure about what's happening between us." Jackie sat back up again and moved a little closer to Scott as if proximity could help her win her flimsy argument.

"Okay," he turned on the couch to properly face her and put his hand on her leg, which he could reach since she'd moved closer. Maybe the proximity part had helped. His thumb gently rubbed her leg as he spoke. It made her wonder if he was soothing a future heartbreak or mindlessly caressing his lover's leg.

"The night after Tim saw me at your house, I did a lot of thinking." Another pause and his hand moved off her leg as he draped his arm on the back of the couch. "I can't be the reason you don't get your show – which, having filmed your work for the past few months, I know is a real possibility. You're so talented: the creativity, the design, the execution – even your presence is flawless."

"You're not getting in the way -"

Scott's don't-bull-shit-me look made her stop mid-sentence.

"Much," she finally ended. "I mean, everything worked out okay. I finished everything I needed to."

"Barely."

"Then we can get back to us." She leaned in to close the space between them and kissed him. Jackie had to. Each time she put on her mic she could almost feel his fingers grazing her skin. Everything about her work for the event reminded her of Scott, and event work had been her main focus for the past week. She'd had to ignore him as she worked her ass off and he did the same behind his camera – always the professional without any hint that they'd ever been more than coworkers.

She felt his soft lips moving with her own and his hands on the small of her back and behind her neck. Muscles she hadn't even realized were tensed up relaxed under his familiar touch and scent.

Jackie leaned back on the couch and Scott followed, pulling her shirt off as he went. His mouth worked its way down her body as he said, "I have to work all day tomorrow, morning to night."

"Sleep here tonight." She fumbled with his shirt buttons as she spoke. "You'll get to bed faster than if you drive home." That was a lie so long as they continued down the path they were going.

"You're right. I don't feel like walking back to my car anyway."

JACKIE

The morning after their amazing make-up sex, reality hit again. Scott's alarm went off at six. The jarring melody of beeps roused both of them from a deep and much-needed sleep.

Jackie's head had a dull ache as her body worked to get rid of all the toxins from the wine she'd poured into it the night before. She lay there with her eyes still closed until she heard the shower. Then one eye shot open, and she found herself alone in bed. No kiss good morning. Her head fell back onto her pillow, and she worried that maybe Scott had regrets about the night before. Maybe she had regrets.

She propped up on her elbows in bed. The sheets conveniently slid down to her waist leaving her exposed breasts to catch Scott's eye as he re-emerged from the bathroom with nothing but a towel around his waist. Jackie bit her lower lip at the sight of his chiseled torso speckled here and there with drops of water. His hair a perfect and glistening wet mess. Not to mention the small patch of wet, matted hair that disappeared under the towel.

Sure, he was incredibly sexy and in general she'd always

been attracted to him. But that morning in bed, a strong part of her desire to feel his arms around her and feel him buried deep within her came more from insecurity than any sexual desires. They'd solved nothing the night before; the problems between them were still present whether they acknowledged them or not.

"I have to get to Lillian's house in ten minutes. Tim and Lana will be there, too. I can't be late," he said more to her tits than to her as his eyes were locked on her exposed breasts.

He's pulling away again, Jackie thought. She didn't have anything pressing to do at that moment, so she slid back down under the covers and watched him get dressed. He still had a few shirts and pairs of pants left at her house. Not his own drawer or anything official like that, but a stack of clothes that sat on an old chair in the corner of the room.

As he buckled his belt, he looked over at her. "Hey, are you okay?" Scott sat on the edge of the bed, careful not to disturb her too much under the covers. "You're looking a little rough this morning." The back of his hand was to her forehead, and then his lips replaced his hand.

"I have a little bit of a headache." She breathed him in. Even though he'd used her soap, he still had some sort of lemony smell to him, or maybe it was his clothes. Regardless, it was intoxicating because it was thoroughly ingrained in her mind as his smell.

His hand moved from her forehead to cup her jaw and stroked her cheek. "I have a few more minutes before I need to head out. Can I get you anything? Tylenol?"

"No, I'm fine."

Scott kissed her forehead then got up to continue getting dressed. "If you're feeling better later, maybe we can get lunch together?"

"Do you have time?"

"Lana's pretty tight with the schedule lately, but even she knows people have to eat. We're all taking a quick break at noon and going to The Cut and Run. You can get that sushi you love."

"Cute. But I think I'll sit out lunch with Tim and Lana." No way could she bring herself to sit down to a meal with those two. She was still mortified every time she had to meet with Tim. He was professional and didn't bring it up again beyond that evening he caught them, but it still ate away at her regardless.

"Oh, okay." He looked disappointed by her absence at lunch later, and it gave her hope.

"What *exactly* did she say, anyway?"

"Who?"

"Lana, when you talked to her after Tim…"

Fully clothed and angling towards the door, Scott said, "She said she could tell something was up between us. But she didn't say one way or another if it was a problem." He shrugged his shoulders. She couldn't tell if he *wanted* to say more, but she knew there was more to it based on the way his eyes looked off towards the door.

"Gotta run." He went back to the bed and gave another quick kiss to her forehead while she'd expected a kiss on the lips. So she kissed the empty space in front of her where his lips should have been. "See ya," he said as he practically ran out the door.

"See ya, pal," she repeated once he'd already left.

"Where's Scott?" Sam asked. She was there without Jeremy and without any explanation as to why he wasn't there. Or rather, without any explanation beyond, "He had a thing."

"I thought he'd be here now, too," Babs said as she

grabbed her ball mid juggle and turned her attention to Jackie.

"Scott's not here," Jackie said in a way that made it sound like Scott was supposed to be there but wasn't. As if he had abandoned her. In reality he wasn't scheduled to shoot her house until after lunch, but she didn't elaborate. She didn't want to talk about Scott anymore, and in a way, she did feel abandoned whether she was justified in those feelings or not.

Sam's attention turned from her inspection of Santa Claws's moving hat to Jackie. "What's happening?" she whispered. "I thought you guys worked it out last night. You know." Sam made an obscene gesture with her hands which Babs thankfully didn't notice since she was staring expectantly down the road looking for Scott.

"I don't want to talk about it. Aren't you supposed to be at work or something?" Jackie accused before she started up the ladder. Tom hissed at her from below in response.

"Our offices are closed today, and Dad's on emergency duty," Sam said, but Jackie wasn't listening.

"And what is Tom still doing here?" Jackie said loud enough for Babs to hear. She wasn't in the mood for any of the nonsense from her family, friends, or pseudo pets.

Babs scoffed, "We're not calling him Tom anymore. He's more of a Frank maybe...We don't know just yet. But his aura now is just the worst." She waved her hands towards the cat as if she could disperse his bad vibes. Babs looked up at Jackie. "His aura matches yours today." As an aside to Sam she said, "She drank too much wine at dinner last night. Probably a bit hungover. You'd have thought she'd have grown out of that by now."

Sam's eyes went back and forth between Babs and Jackie as she sized up the escalating situation between mother and daughter.

"My aura's off, Mom?" Jackie challenged as she made her

way back down the ladder. "Not enough sunshine and rainbows for you?"

They were face to face when Sam came forward to step between them. "Let's focus on the event -"

"I'm trying," Jackie said. "That's *all* I want to do right now."

"Great, then let's -" Sam started to say before she was cut off, again.

"You can't, sweetie," Babs said with an apologetic smile. "Look." She pointed up at the spot where Jackie had just been working. "You adjusted that wave three times and it's still off. You're not focused."

"Okay, let's hear it, Mom." Jackie's hands went up. "Tell me all the ways I'm fucking up. Please, I'd love to hear about it from you."

"Jackie, you should probably -"

"Nope. Not you too, Sam." Jackie snapped. She and Babs continued their stare down – a stare down for Jackie, really, since Babs was merely looking at Jackie. Then she jerked her head towards Sam.

"I don't want to hear your advice about *anything* right now, but mostly I don't want to hear *relationship* advice from you." A few weeks ago, she would have added, "Someone who's been dating their soulmate since high school." Things had certainly changed since then, but the urge to ignore any and all relationship advice from Sam still stood. Sam couldn't work out her own issues or even have the courage to talk about it with Jeremy, so she lost privileges to give Jackie any advice.

Hurt settled into Sam's face as they both took in the enormity of what was just said. She turned and walked back to her car. "Text me later when you're ready to apologize," Sam called out the window. After a slight hesitation she added, "Or if you need me to weld anything, but I'll be pissed the entire time."

She probably would have preferred to speed away, but the posted speed limit was 15 miles per hour and Sam was a rule follower when it came to driving.

"Sweetie, I'm worried about you," Babs said when it was just the two of them and the cat.

"I'm fine, Mom," Jackie gritted as she climbed back up the ladder. She wouldn't verbally admit it, but her mother was right about the wave being off and she needed to fix it.

"While you're up there, you should double-check the sea turtle, too."

"It's fine, Mom." Jackie discreetly glanced over at the turtle to see if she believed what she'd just said to her mother.

"It's not. There's -"

"Enough, Mom. It's fine. Whatever is wrong with it, it's fine. At this point it needs to be good enough. I have nothing left to give." Jackie gave a final tug on the string of lights for the few extra inches of chord she needed to raise the crest of the wave up just a smidge higher. But the wire had been caught on one of the hooks holding up her turtle, so the final pull yanked the turtle off the house and sent it plunging towards the unnamed cat below.

In a desperate attempt to save the turtle, Jackie's first instinct had been to lunge for it. As if she could have caught the massive steel decoration in her hands while she was outstretched on the ladder. She missed the turtle, kicked the ladder out from under her, and grabbed onto one of the industrial hooks that used to hold some of Aunt Ollie's larger Christmas displays.

The ladder and turtle crashed to the ground below with the cat meowing as it bobbed and weaved like Indiana Jones through a gap in the ladder. The ladder hit the ground, and the cat narrowly missed the turtle fin that had been heading straight for him.

Babs screamed and her hands covered her mouth. "Oh, thank God," she muttered once she saw Jackie would not be joining the ladder and holiday décor in a heap on the beach below. "Mort! Mort!" she called.

"Shit," Jackie muttered to herself as her feet gently swayed a few stories above the ground. If she fell at this point the sand would be soft, but she'd mangle her legs hitting the metal turtle and ladder below her.

"This is fine…"

She heard a commotion around her, but she couldn't tear her eyes away from the section of house directly in front of her. The previous look down to watch everything crash to the ground had been a mistake and she didn't dare look again.

"I'm here! I gotcha!" Scott called up to her. She felt the ladder slam into her right leg. Ignoring the pain, she felt around with her foot until she found the steps. White knuckles slid down the sides of the ladder as she made her way back down.

"Sorry," he said as she descended. "I was trying to get the ladder up to you as soon as I could. I didn't mean to hit you with it. Are you okay?"

Once on the ground she turned and pulled him in for a hug. "Thank you," she exhaled into his shoulder and neck.

"I wouldn't let you fall, Jackie," he whispered into her ear.

There was a small crowd of neighbors around them, but Jackie was only mildly aware of their existence. The adrenaline rushing through her coupled with Scott's muscular arms around her, tore down any hesitation she had from that morning. Without even realizing what she was doing, she kissed him. Jackie was reminded of where she was only when the crowd of neighbors surrounding them gave an unrehearsed and yet strangely coordinated, "Awwwwww," at their very public display of affection.

Mort led her mother and the rest of the neighbors away, encouraging them to go back to their houses and own displays. "I'm going to help Mort, Sweetie," Babs called back to her.

"Wait, Mom," Jackie started to say.

Babs shook her head with a smile and said, "We'll talk later. Come on, Harold," she called to the cat. Harold trotted off after them as Mort and Babs walked hand in hand back to Mort's.

Scott pulled her back into the moment by cupping her chin and turning her back to face him. "Hey, are you okay? You look a little pale."

Maybe it was the near-death(ish) experience or the stress of the event officially beginning later that night, but Jackie cracked under the question. She had tried to convince herself it wasn't a good idea for them to date, she'd pretended it was fine that it was just a fling in case it didn't go anywhere, and that morning she'd pretended she was fine with him leaving even though nothing had been resolved. It was a pattern that looked eerily similar to what Sam was doing and she refused to follow that path.

"I'm not okay," she whispered.

SCOTT

*S*cott looked around, held up a finger to signal to someone down the road to give him a minute, then he placed a hand on the small of her back as he guided her into her house.

"Is this about us?" His stomach knotted thinking that he was the cause of the tears brimming her eyes.

"I don't know," she said as she paced the tiny foyer. "Ah, fuck. No, that's a lie. I do know."

His palms started to sweat, and a feeling of impending doom went up and down his body. He'd noticed that morning she didn't look well, but he'd hoped (selfishly) that it was due to Mort's heavy wine pour the night before and not to her hesitation about him. He'd been trying to ignore it all morning, the way she'd turned down lunch with him even though they hadn't really seen each other in a week and would both be incredibly busy all day.

"Then tell me," he said in a voice just above a whisper. If she was going to take off the bandage, the least she could do was rip off in one painful yank rather than drag it out.

"I love this." Her hand went to his face to feel the slight

scruff that covered his chin. Her fingers reached to the back of his head to slide through his hair in a way that drove him crazy. Her lips met his and he obliged when her tongue sought out his. How could he not?

"Me, too," he said when she pulled away again. Relief washed over him knowing that they were headed in the right direction, even after he almost blew it with his request to take a brief hiatus. He felt guilty that he'd ever doubted Jackie's commitment to her own work or felt that she didn't respect his work. Looking at her house so close to completion it was obvious that she had been right. They could have reprioritized and made it work for the past week.

Jackie bit her lip. "This past week was hell for me."

He kissed her again, briefly. "Me, too," he admitted as he nuzzled his face into her neck and hair. He took in her scent and felt himself relax into her.

She found his mouth again with hers and they kissed before she pulled away and whispered, "I can't go through that again."

"You don't have to."

"But I do."

At that he pulled away from her to get a proper look at her eyes. His hands had been freely roaming her neck, back, and hips, but now they found hers and his thumbs rubbed a gentle massage into her palms.

"Are we...breaking up?"

The hurt in her eyes broke his heart more than the words.

"You're just going to leave me when this is all over. Her voice was steady and confident, as if she'd given it all the thought she needed.

He furrowed his brows in confusion and his thumbs stilled on her hands. It had been stupid to keep his next project from her, to let her believe that he didn't want her to go with him. Maybe it was too soon for them to be making such commitments to each other, but he had to try.

"I hadn't gotten around to asking you yet – too scared of your answer, I guess – but I'd hoped you'd maybe consider going with me for my next job?" His dark eyes searched for a reaction from her.

"Move to LA with you?"

"No, not LA. Australia. Specifically, Sydney, but we'll probably travel to at least three or four other destinations along the way."

Her eyes were still registering confusion rather than excitement and he could feel the sweat forming again on his palms as the panic set in.

"Don't give me an answer yet. Think about it." His hands squeezed hers and he gave her a quick kiss before he let go. Scott had to get out of there before Jackie said something they both regretted. This sort of decision wasn't to be made lightly or on the spot. He needed to give her some time to think it over properly and to dream about how in a few short weeks she could be on a plane with him. Taking off from soon-to-be snowy Baltimore Washington International Airport, and landing in sunny and summery Sydney.

"I have to get back to work. I'll see you at noon when I'm back here to get shots of your end of the neighborhood." She opened her mouth to say something, but nothing came out. He took that as a good sign. It wasn't an immediate no, and at the time that was the best he could hope for. He caressed her cheek with the back of his hand and said, "We'll talk later tonight, okay?" She gave a slight nod and then he was out the door again.

He was scheduled to get final shots of Mac, Otto, and Lillian before lunch. And while he still had another hour to go, he didn't think he needed that much more footage. When he first got there, he found plenty of drama and mishaps to film, but that had since been resolved. He had all the footage he needed and was mostly playing around with some artistic shots of the displays while the neighbors stood around gossiping and teasing him about his newly uncovered and no-longer-secret romance with Jackie.

It felt good to finally talk about it in the open, though the neighbors did revel in their ability to make him blush on more than one occasion. He told them about his plans to go to Sydney for his next documentary and how he'd asked her to go with him.

"We knew all along," Muriel said. She wasn't part of the section of houses he was filming at the moment, but she tended to gravitate to wherever he was when he was working. "I'm not sure who you all thought you were fooling or why you even needed to."

He had his tripod out since he was shooting stationary objects rather than people at this point, and he kept his eyes on the adjustments he was making to the camera as he talked to them.

"It's...complicated."

"Maybe it *was* complicated when you were sneaking around and busy with work. But the cat's out of the bag now and the hardest part for the event, the set-up, is over. It's easy sailing now," Mac said.

Otto nodded beside him. "We don't even need to turn anything on or off anymore. It's all on timers now." He rubbed at his stubbly chin and turned to the women. "Technology. Who knows what they'll come up with next?"

They nodded in agreement that technology was indeed a magical thing.

"When are you all leaving for Australia?" Muriel asked. Scott knew she really enjoyed having the documentary crew there the past few months and would miss the company. Not Lana, of course. No one missed Lana's company. But Lizzy had started to bond with her as well since she had to be there filming Muriel's conversations with Scott.

"I think right after New Year's." He stepped back from his camera and gave Muriel his full attention for the conversation. It was the least he could do. "But Jackie and I both still have family here, so we'll be back to visit. Often," he added when he saw his words did little to comfort them.

They'd all become a bit of a family that fall, more than he'd ever experienced in his previous jobs either with documentaries or any other career path he'd dabbled in prior. It finally dawned on him that maybe Jackie felt the same way. Her response to him asking her to move may not have been solely based on the assumed LA destination. It may have been due to him asking her to go anywhere with him. She may not want to leave, even if her staying meant the end of their relationship.

As if reading his mind, Mac asked, "Is Jackie excited about Australia? I've never been myself – never even left Maryland if I'm honest – but I've heard lovely things about it. Nicole Kidman is from there."

"And Hugh Jackman," Muriel added with an extra sparkle in her eye thinking about the leading man.

Scott chuckled at Muriel's comment. "Indeed he is, Muriel. But Australia's a big country. Not sure we'll be seeing that many movie stars while we're there working."

She gave a sad nod in agreement. Scott promised himself that if he did happen to see Hugh there, he wouldn't hesitate to make an ass out of himself to get an autograph, photograph, or anything else he could get to send back to Muriel. She was like a grandmother to him at that point.

"I'm sure Jackie will be excited once she wraps her mind around it all. I only told Jackie about it just now. I told her not to give me an answer until she's had time to think about it."

The neighbors' jaws dropped open in unison and they spoke over each other as they either criticized his approach or asked questions about when he expected to hear back from her and what he would do if she didn't want to leave.

Scott immediately regretted saying anything to the neighbors and was reminded once again why he and Jackie had not wanted their relationship to be public. At least not while they were knee-deep in the lighting event.

He put his hands up defensively. "I know, I know. I should have handled everything better than I have. I know." Hands back down his sides he added, "I need to get a few more shots in, guys."

Muriel, Otto, Lillian, and Mac finally took the hint that he did not want to discuss it with them anymore. He ducked down behind the camera again to line up his next shot, his hands moving over the various buttons on the equipment until he had everything just right. As he was about to move the camera in a large arch to mimic the path someone's eyes would take when looking at the display in-person, Mac piped up again. He clearly didn't lay it on thick enough with how annoyed he'd become with their conversation about his relationship.

"What city are you and...are you going to?" he asked. His mid-sentence correction informed him how little Mac believed Jackie would join him. He glanced at his watch. Only twenty more minutes until he had lunch. Afterwards, he would be in Jackie's part of the neighborhood again and would see for himself, based on her mood and body language, what she thought of his invitation.

"Sydney," he answered as he swept the camera up to the top of the house and then inched back down again in a slow and lazy zig-zag motion.

"That sounds lovely. Though we sure will miss you here, Scott," Lillian said. The others nodded and murmured their agreement.

His shot finished, Scott turned to face them again. "I'm not going anywhere just yet. We won't be leaving until January second at the earliest."

JACKIE

"You do this a lot. You know that, right?" Sam asked Jackie as the two unloaded the turtle decoration from Sam's truck and carried it into Jeremy's workspace in the back of their garage.

"I drop large nautical-themed metal decorations and then ask you to help me fix them?"

Sam stopped a few feet short of the garage and Jackie nearly barreled into her. "Ouch. What the hell, Sam?"

"You know what I'm talking about."

"I already said I was sorry about earlier today. What else can I do?"

Just as abruptly Sam began walking again and Jackie was tugged along by the death grip they both had on opposite sides of the turtle's shell.

They carefully made their way to the back of the garage to where Jeremy stored all his welding and metal fabrication equipment. Sam was well versed in all of it since she and Jeremy had once been one of those disgusting couples who did everything together. If needed, Sam could assist Jeremy with his welding, and Jeremy could probably help Sam deliver a cow. Luckily for Jeremy, it hadn't come to that yet.

Once the turtle was secure, Sam pointed at Jackie while she told her all about herself. "You do this thing where you pile everything onto your plate and then strain your muscles trying to carry it all day in and day out. It's impressive how long you hold onto it and everything you've piled on top – but it can't hold forever. And then, you don't just lose an item or two at a time. It's like you spread your hands and just let all the shit fall to the floor as you unleash your nasty, anxiety-riddled attitude onto everyone around you."

Jackie was about to argue, but her hands were coincidentally (symbolically maybe?) full of her most recent outrageous project and she did happen to lash out at Sam just an hour or two prior. It was best for her to simply accept her friend's thorough and accurate analysis of her self-destructive behavior.

"Looking cool as a cucumber on the outside," Sam continued, on a roll by that point, "even though your plate is stacked a mile high. But on the inside, you're swelling up with anxiety that threatens to burst at unexpected times, spewing nastiness from your mouth towards any poor soul who happens to be near you."

"I did that today. Yes, and I apologized. Twice now." She pulled the bag from off her shoulder to produce the large hooks that attached to her house and held, unsuccessfully, the turtle. After the turtle fell, she'd called Sam to help her fix it. They were both terrified the thing would fall again and smash some unsuspecting tourist admiring the lights, so they decided that while they were touching up the turtle, they'd also better weld the thing to the hooks rather than to have it sit loosely upon them.

"No," Sam said as she too set down the turtle before

rooting through the garage for the various tools she needed. "It happens a lot."

"I disagree."

"Fine. We'll agree to disagree in that regard, and I'll keep my examples strictly to current events."

"Can we not do this right now? I can't even begin to tell you how much stress I'm under right now. You yourself just said I'm about to crack – and you're right. I agree. I'm cracking. Happy?"

Jackie assumed victory when Sam turned away, found the welding rods she'd been looking for, and then pulled down her mask before starting up her welding torch. Even though at the moment Jackie was annoyed with Sam, she was also in awe of her. All around the shop were mock-ups and miniature models of Sam's different welding projects and sculptures. When they were growing up, Sam had been the one in awe of Jackie's crafty talents and eye for design. But clearly as the time passed, Sam grew into her own and found her own art and beauty in the metal she manipulated and bent to her will.

Once the turtle was fixed, adding the hooks was a minor task that did not take long to weld. Sam took off her helmet and apron, and stepped away from the project and towards Jackie.

"Hey," she said as she reached out to rub a comforting hand up and down Jackie's arm. "You kick ass and take names on the daily. And now, since you've been home, I've gotten to see it over and over again."

Jackie couldn't accept the compliment. She was too busy wondering what other words Sam had for her. She looked at her phone to check the time. Scott would be working his way towards her house soon and she needed to get back.

"Thank you, and I promise that I'll work on that other stuff. But can we start to head back now?" She made a circular motion with her finger to drive home the point that they needed to wrap up their conversation.

Sam didn't budge. "Are you serious right now? I'm trying to tell you that I'm worried about you. Look at you."

It sounded rhetorical and yet Sam paused as if Jackie would take her up on her offer to take a quick inventory of herself.

"You look like shit."

Jackie's head fell back with the blow to her ego. How many people that day were going to tell her she looked terrible and had a personality that matched her appearance?

"Sorry, but you do. You got zero sleep all this past week trying to give Scott space because that's what you thought he wanted from you. And this morning you're all pissy because he left things ambiguous when he ran out."

"He didn't leave things ambiguous." Jackie hadn't intended to tell Sam about Scott's offer for her to join him on his next job until later that night when the reveal was over. But she couldn't stand to hear the things Sam was saying about her and Scott and the desire to set the record straight was too strong to ignore.

"Scott wants me to go with him to his next job. Out in Australia." It felt so good to say out loud. In her mind she'd gone back and forth as to whether or not it was an actual possibility, but in the garage with Sam, she said it as if it were a done deal.

Sam huffed back, "*Scott* wants you to go to Australia with him. Do *you* want to go?"

Damn, she'd turned that on Jackie so quickly. Rather than accept that both Jackie and Sam were probably not in the best head space to be giving each other any relationship advice, Jackie decided to double-down and throw some harsh truth back to Sam.

"Your marriage is crumbling, Sam – whether the two of you acknowledge it or not, it is."

Sam flinched only slightly. "Then you know I know what I'm talking about."

Jackie softened at the realization of what was being said between them. "Shit. I can't believe I just said that, Sam. I didn't...That's not fair of me."

"It's cool enough to take now," Sam said, referring to the turtle and officially ending the relationship conversation. They both reached for the newly welded hooks and carried the turtle back to the truck.

They rode in silence for a few minutes, and then just as Jackie was about to apologize for her heartless comments, Sam said, "Jeremy and I are separating." Jackie let her mouth drop open for a second before lunging over the center console to smoother Sam in a bear hug.

"Fuck...Are you okay? Whose decision was it?" When the traffic light they were at turned green Jackie let Sam go so she could continue to drive. Instead, she kept a hand on Sam's thigh as a way to still comfort her. Maybe it was awkward, but she needed to do something.

"I said it first. Thanksgiving was bad, Jackie. For the first time I really took in the way Jeremy is with our nieces and nephews. In general, we've been drifting apart lately, and I see now that's at the heart of it all. Us wanting different things in life and turning into different people."

Jackie's inability to notice the breakdown of Sam and Jeremy's marriage sooner was on her. Up in Philadelphia, not even that far away, Jackie had fallen into a bit of a slump. She'd stopped going out, stopped calling friends back. It was so much easier to escape into a book in the safety of her apartment. She'd often promised herself she'd call friends back later. In the moment it seemed as though nothing was too pressing, and that time would stretch on forever. There was always time the next day or the next week to make a call or make a drive down to visit.

"I…" Jackie started to say. But everything that came to her mind sounded cliché and thoughtless. Too generic for actual friends to say to each other.

"I was in denial for a long time. Every time I thought about saying something to you, Jeremy and I would have a good day again, and I'd tell myself it was all in my head. Not to mention that everyone we know keeps making these comments about how fucking happy and perfect Jeremy and I are. I didn't even know how to start a conversation about it. I've tried a few times with my mom and other friends, and every time they would say something along the lines of, 'You two will work it out. You're perfect for each other.'"

Sam didn't explicitly call Jackie out for being one of the ones to comment on the perfectly happy marriage, but she knew she was culpable as well.

"I'm so sorry, Sam."

Sam rolled her eyes and gave a light laugh. "You're way too critical of yourself. Do not turn this into something you're going to beat yourself up over. You didn't know. Like everyone else you probably thought it was a compliment, something nice to say."

"But still, I'm sorry." Jackie couldn't help but feel a tightness in her chest at the thought of how her words had been hurtful – intentional or not. Beating herself up over both major and minor slip-ups and mistakes was an artform Jackie had perfected at an early age. Regardless of Sam's assurances, Jackie knew she'd lose a bit of sleep over it in her near and distant future. And rightfully so as far as she was concerned.

"You can stay with me, you know. Until you get things sorted out."

Sam gave a weak smile. "We never did get a chance to be roommates."

As small kids they'd fantasized about getting an apartment together in New York City where they were both wildly successful businesswomen who didn't need anyone else for anything. The fantasies stopped once it was clear Jeremy and Sam were going to the same college, and it was no longer just Jackie and Sam, best friends forever.

Silence filled the truck as they pulled up to her house and parked. Feeling defeated and exhausted from the tumultuous morning, Jackie slowly got out and followed Sam to the back of the truck to unload the turtle.

"If you want some help, I can stick around and give you a hand," Sam said as she closed the tailgate.

"I love you, Sam."

"Yeah, I know. I love you, too. Together forever, right?"

As they worked, Sam told her how her rift with Jeremy had formed right under her nose without her even noticing. While Sam had been happy and comfortable with their marriage and life together, he'd started to feel like he was in a rut and trapped. Had started to want something different from life.

"I got this feeling Jeremy was there, but not really. I could tell he was just going through the motions." The two had already re-hung the turtle and had moved on to placing large seashells on the sandy beach. "He'd have this blank look on his face or a staged smile on our date nights sometimes."

Jackie interjected occasionally with a few words here and there or a question, but mostly she let Sam talk.

"Except every time I brought it up, he'd swear nothing was wrong. He'd get annoyed at me like I was nagging him which…it hurt, Jackie."

It seemed like Sam was about to break down and cry. Instead, she lifted her shoulders higher and with a slight shake of her head she continued.

"I haven't told anyone this...but I finally got him to break down and talk to me one night after I threatened to leave him."

Jackie stopped to give Sam her full attention.

"I had an overnight bag packed and everything." Sam gave a small laugh and said, "Was even going to show up at your apartment in Philly if I'd gone through with it. Be roomies for a bit while we got it all sorted."

Jackie went to sit on the front porch and Sam followed. During the brief lull in conversation Jackie stole a quick glance at her watch. Ten more minutes before Scott was due to start filming.

"That finally got a reaction from him. We talked all night about everything. So many tears, Jackie. So many. He said he was thinking about maybe wanting kids but that he knew I didn't want them. He said we weren't compatible anymore. Eventually, it came down to if we still loved each other or not. We both said that we did and couldn't picture life without each other."

Jackie's arm went around Sam, and she leaned into it as their legs dangled below them.

"I took the comment about not having common interests to heart and I took on welding as a way to get closer to him. But then he pulled away even more. A few months later I finally got it out of him that he felt even more smothered. He said he'd liked how independent I *was*. He didn't see that in me anymore. He said I started taking on his interests as my own."

Jackie mostly listened with the occasional agreement with Sam or choice word against Jeremy. She grimaced as a stream of consciousness flooded through her mind carrying all the self-centered and trivial conversations she'd initiated with Sam those past few months while Sam was struggling alone with such a heavy burden. She grabbed Sam's hand into both of hers.

"I'm so sorry, Sam. For not being there. For not…knowing. I should have noticed and known something was wrong even if you didn't say anything."

Sam squeezed her hands. "It's fine."

It wasn't. But as the spokesperson for people who say, "It's fine," when it wasn't, she wouldn't call her out on it. Jackie understood that sometimes people needed to tell themselves it was fine to survive the day, sometimes even to survive the minute. Of course she'd give Sam the rest of the day to pretend it was okay. It was the least she could do.

"When are you going to tell him?"

"Tonight. I had a feeling it would be soon. I didn't want to do it right before Thanksgiving, but I also can't wait until after Christmas. I'll do it tonight."

SCOTT

*L*izzy, Tim, Lana, and Scott grabbed a high top in the bar area for a quick lunch. So quick that Lana ordered cheeseburgers, fries, and sodas for everyone ahead of time so that it would be ready when they'd arrived.

"Thanks, Bruno," Lana said to the bartender who brought out their food. "Now, let's discuss our next move. Tim and I have been talking about where we're going from here and how much there is to film after the big reveal." She motioned for Tim to take over as she took a bite of her burger.

Unaware he was about to be on the spot like that, he swallowed the giant bite he'd taken and practically choked. Lana looked on expectantly.

"I'd hate to say the event peaks today, but in a way it does. The set-up is the most difficult part and gives the best opportunity for…entertainment, for lack of a better term."

Lana's face displayed her displeasure at Tim's use of the word "entertainment."

"It's mostly tourists coming and going for the next month

with very little to be done by the neighborhood," he added to appease her.

Mission accomplished. "Yes," Lana agreed, "which means we will no longer be staying through the new year. Or rather you and I won't be staying," she said, referring to Scott. She turned to Lizzy. "You'll stay with Tim and work closely together throughout the event to capture anything that might come up, but there's no need for everyone to remain."

Lizzy nodded her head in agreement. "That works for me." As if she had much of a choice in the decision.

"That should be fine. The drama and excitement are minimum from here out," Tim agreed, taking yet another giant bite of his burger.

"That doesn't work for me," Scott said in a loud voice that caused Lana to stop sipping her soda and turn her full attention to him.

"We can't just pack up and leave." He was referring not only to himself but also Jackie who had to stay and finish out the season.

"So you'll leave ahead of her and Jackie will catch up when she's finished here," Lana said matter-of-factly as if Scott were an idiot not to put together that solution himself.

"I only asked her to come with me a few hours ago. We haven't had time to discuss Australia. We also haven't talked about if we want our relationship to be part of the documentary."

Lana's face remained even. "Then you should have talked about it sooner. And the relationship will be part of the documentary regardless."

As much as they needed to get in and out of The Cut and Run so they could get back to work, suddenly Lana was the only one eating.

"What the fuck, Lana," Scott said in pure frustration. Bruno paused his glass polishing and eyed up Scott.

"I said from the beginning not to get involved with anyone in the documentary, and I even gave you an out earlier which you didn't take or follow up on. So the most recent clips and outlines I've sent to DocMe include your relationship. It's too late."

Lana took a sip of her drink as Scott sat wide-eyed across from her at the table unable to move. "Australia Day is January 26th. Leaving now gives us an extra month of footage and on-site research leading up to the main event."

Lizzy and Tim busied themselves with dipping fries, working the stubborn ketchup bottle, and twisting the straws of their drinks as if it were the most fascinating thing they'd ever seen. Scott remained silent.

"I've been working towards this for years; I will not give when it comes to this project. And if this means things have changed and you're not going with me, I need to know. Now."

Her nail hit the table with a loud tap that normally would have been drowned out by the cacophony of sounds moving about the restaurant. But it resounded loudly in the empty restaurant at half-past eleven on the Friday morning after Thanksgiving.

The sound snapped him out of his shocked silence. "I'm in. I'm coming."

Her face remained the same showing she didn't have doubts about his commitment to the project. He was the good soldier she'd molded him to be.

"Good. We need to hit this thing running as soon as we get there. I plan to edit both documentaries once we're done filming in Australia, but I need to get in as much filming as I can before Australia Day."

Scott nodded in agreement.

"I want your conversation with Jackie on film. Be sure to let Lizzy know when you're going to talk to her."

Defeated, Scott merely nodded in agreement. The others ate and idly chatted about the event: who was filming what, must-have shots, and tentative plans to film over the weekend before they were down to just one camera person. If they noticed him pushing his food around his plate but not eating, they didn't say anything.

Judging by the way Jackie and Sam were sitting on the deck together, Jackie's arm around Sam's slumped shoulders while Sam's head was supported on Jackie's shoulder, Scott could tell something had happened since he'd last seen Jackie just a few hours before.

Cautiously he approached. "Ladies, is now a good time? Should I come back?"

"Now's good," Sam jumped up and said before Jackie could say otherwise. He set up his tripod at the end of the lawn and pretended to tend to it to give them a bit more time to adjust themselves. From the corner of his eye he saw them wipe away tears and help each other touch up their hair. He didn't think they needed it, but he understood being up against something daunting and having the desire to fix anything that could be fixed, no matter how small.

The shots were mainly of the house and the decorations. Jackie and Sam helped to adjust a string of lights or bits of holiday flare here and there, but mostly they were off to the side having hushed conversations as Scott worked.

As is custom with the neighbors on Christmas Lights Lane, other homeowners couldn't help but venture out of their houses to join them in Jackie's yard. It was a sweet community of people who often acted like a family with their lack of boundaries with one another. Scott felt a bit of sadness wash over him as he moved from shot to shot knowing he would be leaving within a few days.

He set the tripod off to the side and put the camera on his shoulder for his final few shots of the house. Then he turned to Jackie and said, "Can you turn on Santa Claws for me? I'd like to get a shot of him in motion."

"Lights too?" she asked as she walked towards him.

"No, thanks. We'll save all the lights for when I come around again this evening to film everything fully lit."

Jackie didn't turn to make her way into the house. Instead, she kept walking towards Scott and hooked her hand in his elbow, and then led them both into the house.

"Sam's leaving Jeremy. Tonight."

"Is she okay?" Scott was momentarily transported back to Vegas in his tiny apartment bathroom with Corine. They'd been fighting all night and she'd followed him in there yelling at him, even reaching out to smack him upside the head at one point. It was there where he'd first said the words aloud that he was leaving her and that he wanted a divorce. As soon as the words were out, he felt the impossible feeling of an immense burden rising off him while simultaneously feeling a void opening in his gut. It stayed with him for months, maybe even a year. The unmistakable emptiness that accompanied him at all times as he navigated life solo once again.

The visceral memory sent his hand to his head as if to sooth the ancient slap from Corine, and it caused his stomach to clench as he briefly relived every detail of that moment in Vegas.

"No, she's not. But she's good at hiding it." Jackie shifted her weight from one foot to the next as she fiddled with a small section of her curly hair. "She's also terrible at asking for help, so I'm forcing it on her and insisting she move in with me for a bit while she gets everything figured out." Her hand let go of her hair to flick her wrist and move her hand about in order to demonstrate the "everything" she was referring to.

"That's good. She'll need you," Scott agreed. He knew only a portion of what Sam was feeling given that his marriage lasted only a portion of the time that hers had, but he wouldn't wish that abject misery on anyone. So even though it meant he would leave for Australia without Jackie, he knew it was the only option they had.

She looked down at the floor. "I don't think I can go with you."

He reached out to tilt her chin up to him and found her eyes brimming with tears.

"I know. At lunch Lana gave us an updated itinerary. We're flying out Monday now. Leaving Lizzy behind to film the rest of the event solo." He wiped a tear from her cheek with a swipe of his thumb. "I know you can't leave."

And he did know it. Deep down he'd watched her fall more and more in love with living in Milton on this crazy street. Noticed how bit by bit she'd made her mark in her new house: the teal and purple throw rug that should look hideous but somehow pulled the whole room together; the pictures with Sam, her parents, and even a recent one of her with Scott lined the mantle; the books about chemical oceanography on her coffee table and nightstand.

She wasn't leaving Milton and her decision had been made weeks ago. Before he'd gotten up the nerve to ask her and before Sam decided to end things with Jeremy. Jackie's decision had been made based solely on what was right for her, so he didn't dare try to change her mind.

"But you'll wait for me?" He asked the question even though he wasn't convinced he had any right to ask her, to put the burden of a long-distance relationship on her when she had so much else going on already.

"You're coming back here after Australia?" There was hope in her voice and he clung to it as well.

"The minute we stop filming I'm coming back. I'll have at least a few weeks off work while Lana locks herself up somewhere to edit."

He took her hands in his and he was massaging the area between her thumb and her pointer finger. Similar to that first night at The Cut and Run where everything had begun.

"I…" Her eyes were searching his for some sort of answer she couldn't find. "You're just going to leave again after that." For a beat they both looked at each other as if some possible answer they'd not yet considered would magically appear if they were patient and wanted it bad enough. It didn't. "You don't know how long you'll be gone, and you don't know how long we'll have together when you're done with that job before you leave for the next one. Or where that next job will be."

He opened his mouth to give a rebuttal, then closed it when he realized he had none. Her phone buzzed and it pulled her attention from him for only a second, but it sent a chill of panic through him. He was losing her, and he hadn't even gotten the part about their relationship being featured in the documentary.

He let out a deep breath. "We'll talk more about it later. But for now, there's one more thing." He braced himself for the next moment where it all may slip even farther out from his reach once again. Possibly for the last time because for whatever reason, nothing seemed to come easy when it came to their relationship, and he couldn't blame her if it became too much and she decided she did want to call it quits after all.

"Lana has footage of us…together."

Her phone went back into her pocket as she leaned back

and narrowed her eyes in anger while her mouth formed a stern thin line.

"How the fuck did she do that? Is that even legal?" Her eyes went wide and her head jerked around the room as she looked for hidden cameras before she turned back to Scott. She eyed him up suspiciously as though maybe he had a hidden camera on him at that moment.

"No, I mean footage of us in public. Ring cams and Lizzy when we weren't paying attention."

The anger faded as she processed what that would mean. "She wants us, this, to be part of the documentary?"

"It *will* be part of the documentary."

Her shoulders slumped. Then he saw something pass through her mind, some realization or resolution – he couldn't be sure which – but whatever it was it took over. Jackie's height increased an extra two inches as she straightened up.

"That's fine. Really, I'm okay with it." There was a pause as if her brain were confirming with itself that it did indeed not care. Once it had confirmation she moved on to Scott's reaction. "Are you okay with it? You hate being filmed."

He ran a hand through his hair and leaned back against the back of the couch. "It came up at lunch and Lizzy mentioned to me that my Twitter comments are full of people asking about the two of us already."

"Really?"

Scott was just as surprised. He never read social media comments. For every dozen or so that lifted you up there were at least one or two scathing comments that would tear you down much further below where you'd even started.

"Lana saw the traction my Twitter posts got and tasked Lana with posting photos of her own. I tagged her Twitter handle a few times in mine to get her followers going, but that was all I've had time for. I didn't see that she was posting photos of us. Together."

The right corner of Jackie's mouth hitched up at the idea of candid photos of them. Her expression softened.

"I'll have to take a look at them. And you say the comments are...not horrible?"

"Christmas people are a lot nicer than the usual social media trolls," he guessed.

She nodded, took her phone out again to check it, then slipped it back into her pocket. "It's one. What time do you need to go?"

"Now," he sighed. He'd made it through being pulled into so many different directions the last few weeks by telling himself that it was almost over. That the lead up was much more stressful than the filming after the first night of the event. In December they'd have all the time in the world to go out to eat, drive around town looking at the decorations as they went Christmas shopping, and relax in the evenings with, as Jackie calls them, graphically sexy holiday movies before they themselves create some steam scenes of their own. But that wasn't happening anymore. He'd be gone in a few days. He'd be halfway around the world working his ass off all day and then falling into a cold, empty bed at night.

Sensing his stress, she reached out to run her fingers through his scruffy jawline before moving them back to his head where she ran her nails gently up and down. Scratching and massaging some of the tension out of him. If she wasn't worried about it, maybe he shouldn't be either. They still had a few more days together.

He gave her one last long kiss, then he was off yet again.

The rest of the afternoon went by quickly. Not only was he getting his last-minute shots leading up to the official lighting of the displays, but he was also posting to Twitter a few times each hour to help build up some excitement over the big reveal. He doubted most of his followers were even in a position to travel to Milton to see the event in person, but his real purpose was to generate excitement. He hoped that when their limited series did finally air, there would be enough hype surrounding the series already that it would debut with an audience of at least thousands, if not tens or hundreds of thousands.

He was aware he may be getting ahead of himself. But he knew what he was capable of, and he'd seen some of Lizzy's work from meetings with Lizzy and Lana. They made a solid team, and it wasn't as if it were unbelievably happening overnight. At least not for Scott and Lana. They'd already been working towards their goal for years.

For the opening of the event, Lana gave Lizzy free reign to pick which house in her section she would film first. Lana herself would be filming somewhere in the middle of the street, and she stationed Scott to start with Jackie's house. Surprise, surprise given what he knew about Lana's ulterior motives of having he and Jackie's relationship featured as a subplot of sorts in the documentary.

The temperature had peaked that day at fifty-four degrees, but once the sun went down it would start to work its way to just above freezing. A slight wind and not a cloud in sight. A bit of snow would have been the perfect weather for their opening night, but the weather they currently had was in a near second place in terms of ideal conditions.

Each year Tim would begin his official introduction to the event starting at the beginning of the sunrise, and he would continue his speech through the end of twilight which was approximately thirty minutes later.

Lana filmed Tim's speech out front of the church where they'd had their first meeting. It was at the end of the street so immediately afterwards people would begin their walk down the neighborhood to see the displays before looping back around to the church parking lot where they'd parked.

The rest of the neighbors stayed at their houses on the off-chance that something may go wrong, a mis-set timer or an unexpected faulty bulb, when the event officially began at 5:11 that evening. Tim wanted them at their homes to make sure everything went off without a hitch. Going forward people would come and go since the event was every night from Black Friday to New Year's Day. The neighbors couldn't be on lockdown in their homes all that time. By the end of the first weekend, when everyone was sure all the timers were running well and things were secure and reliable, they'd start to get back to their normal evening activities while their houses ran on autopilot.

After getting final shots of Muriel's and Mort's houses, he made his way back to Jackie's and started to set up in the living room. When he heard her footsteps coming down the steps – unmistakably hers in sound and rhythm, yet another thing he'd miss – he set the camera on the floor and stood, turning to see her. She looked stunning in a red coat and dark, almost black jeans. Earlier that day she'd broken down and lost it in the same living room – just hours before. But minutes away from the big reveal she radiated confidence and was glowing.

He ran his knuckles over her cheek and tucked a small section of hair behind her ear. "You ready?" He took her hands in his and his thumbs absently massaged circles as his eyes stayed locked on hers. Never in his life had he met someone with hands as soft as hers. All her skin, really.

Whatever she was doing in the way of skin care, it was working for her. He couldn't resist touching her when she was near.

"I'm absolutely ready to kick some major holiday-decorating ass," she answered before leaning in for a quick kiss.

Her confidence was part of what got him every time. She was adorable when her face was all scrunched up in thought and concentration and when she was nervous and fumbling with her words. But when her big brown eyes lit up with that patented Jackie Strauss assurance, he fell a little harder for her every fucking time.

He picked up his camera and they both went out to the front yard to get set up. For the first night all the neighbors stood out front of their houses to greet the visitors and answer questions or chat about the event. It was tradition and Tim loved a good tradition. Scott and Jackie had gone back and forth before about the best place for her to stand and they'd both agreed a few feet to the left of Santa Claws was the best shot and was far enough away from her speakers for the best audio of her conversations.

Scott pulled out his phone to check the time. Three more minutes until they started. They could faintly hear Tim's speech from down the road. Jackie, her brown curls blowing in the soft breeze looked stunning. She was glowing with excitement and anticipation. Had he really believed she would leave all of it behind to travel around with him, for his job? Had he ever really wanted that for *her*? No, he'd wanted it for him.

Pushing aside his inner monologue, he snapped a quick photo of Jackie for Twitter, then his camera was up and ready. At 5:11 each house lit up with its own music and light show. A street dead black before – even streetlights were timed to be off – became ground zero for Christmas cheer in a split second. And Scott caught it all this time. He'd thought

Jackie's face was glowing before, but at that moment it was the happiest he'd ever seen her.

The bay window lit up with the tank display. The tiny white fish glistened as they maneuvered the tank and around the tiny model houses of Christmas Lights Lane. The lights reflecting off their shiny white scales gave a look of a snowy storm engulfing the neighborhood. The bay window tanks turned into a giant snow-globe display where the snow never settled. The lights on the house pulsed to give the illusion of water moving over the siding, while the Santa Claws crab waved his two large crusher claws in beat to the movement of its Santa hat. Completing the winter wonderland was the sound of soft, Christmas jazz coming from rock speakers Jackie had set up on the beach.

Forgetting the rules, she turned from the house back to him and shouted, "We did it!" Lana had been right to make sure Jackie's reaction to the initial lighting was captured on film. It had nothing to do with their relationship. It was about the new design and a newbie experiencing the event for the first time.

He stayed for fifteen minutes and captured a few conversations Jackie had with visitors before he had to make his way across the street to Mort's house. He turned off his camera for a minute and lowered it as he moved through the crowds to Jackie.

"I have to move on to the other houses."

She was still beaming from it all – eating up the conversations she was having with visitors and tourists about her designs and decorations.

"Okay, but I'll see you later, right?"

"Absolutely," he promised.

JACKIE

*T*he night was a blur of activity. She'd stayed in her front yard meeting and greeting tourists and visitors until just before ten when Tim sounded the bullhorn and the neighborhood collectively turned off the lights and called it a night.

While she had been out front officially beginning a new chapter in her life, Sam had been doing the same across town as she told Jeremy she was leaving.

So Jackie declined the after party at Tim's house. Instead, she sat with Sam on her couch, and they sipped wine while Sam detailed out her conversation with Jeremy and what her plans were for the future.

"I don't want to put you out, but I was hoping that maybe I could stay here with you for more than just a few nights?" Sam's eyes were bloodshot from all the tears and her shoulders slumped down to a point that could only be achieved by someone who was thoroughly defeated by the world. Did she really think Jackie would say no?

"Of course you're staying with me. I wasn't offering for a

few nights, Sam. I meant for as long as you want to or need to."

"But you and Scott—"

Jackie held up her hand to cut Sam off. "Nope. No *boyfriend* would ever be more important than you and this." She studied Sam's face, debating if it were appropriate to turn the conversation to her own relationship. "Besides, he's leaving Monday. So it'll just be you and me after that."

Sam's face, already a picture of pure misery, was somehow able to look even more dejected at Jackie's news.

"Do you want to talk about it?" she offered. "Because at this point, I would love to hear about someone else's shitty love life instead of dwelling on my own." Jackie swatted her on the arm spilling white wine down the side of Sam's glass and onto the couch cushion.

"What?" she asked innocently. "I get mean when I drink sometimes. You know this about me."

"True," Jackie conceded. "And you're not wrong. We are in a bit of a shitty situation."

"Is that why Scott's not here?"

"No, he's filming the after party at Tim's. Aside from him being half a world away on Monday and having a job that will keep taking him away from me, we're perfect. In that beginning phase where the sex is white hot and we can't get enough of it."

To the outsider it may seem cruel to throw out the wild and insatiable sex comment to someone who has just left their husband, but context was key. Sam was an avid smutty book reader and even had some sort of cult following on her smutty book blog.

Even though Sam brought only one bag of belongings with her, she'd filled half of it with books whose covers consisted of nothing but half-naked men. The once barren coffee table now housed Jackie's chemical oceanography books, Scott's tome of a novel about Australia's founding, and Sam's collection of manchest novels.

"That part's amazing," Sam agreed. "It doesn't even feel like a possibility for me to experience that again. Like I used it all up on Jeremy when we were teens and didn't even know what we were doing half the time." She took a large gulp of wine. "What a waste."

"The fact that you're still reading all of this," Jackie said waving her hand at the stack of smut, "says your lady bits haven't shriveled up and died yet."

"I know. I'm in this weird place where I don't want Jeremy, but I don't want anyone else either."

"Then you'll focus on your career."

"Actually, I left Jeremy and my career today."

Jackie's raised glass paused a few inches from her mouth as she considered the possibility that Sam wasn't just going through a potential divorce and was instead going through some mid-life crisis that would end in her regretting the decisions she was currently making.

"This isn't an early mid-life crisis." Sam extended her hand out to force Jackie's glass back into motion towards her mouth. "Jeremy said I lost who I was with him, and he was right. But I did it with my dad, too, when I let him...not force, per se...but there was definitely a heavy hand guiding me towards being a vet."

"I thought you loved it..." Jackie offered as she tried to keep up with yet another bomb that had dropped in her lap that day.

"Parts of it, yes. And then some parts...putting down a beloved pet, for example. I swear I lose a tiny part of my heart each time I do it Jackie. I know it's what's best for the animal, but...I also know that it changed me. I would go home those nights and I wasn't me."

"Oh, Sam. I didn't realize..."

"No, I know. I kept it from Jeremy, too. Thought it was me being weak or something—I don't know."

"What are you going to do now?"

"Absolutely nothing for a while."

"That sounds…"

"Glorious?" Sam offered.

"Yes, it really does. Can you do that?"

"I have some money saved up. I'll be okay."

"Okay."

They spent the next few hours drinking wine and talking about everything except Jeremy or Scott.

SCOTT

When Scott let himself in the back door, it was already half past midnight. Jackie's neighbors partied hard, and Scott was beat. He walked by the living room on his way up to Jackie and noticed Sam on the couch. She had a bottle of wine nestled between herself and the couch, and a book whose cover had four half-naked men surrounding a woman who was kneeling in front of them.

He didn't want her to spill her wine in the middle of the night, so he moved the bottle to the coffee table, and he took the book to place on the coffee table as well. When he glanced at the open page, he noticed a few choice words that caught his attention and may have read a chapter or two before putting it down and heading up to see Jackie.

Striped down to his boxers, he crawled into bed and slid his arms around her. Molding his body behind hers while trying not to wake her up. Given that he was a bit tipsy and exhausted, it didn't work.

She made a cooing sound and moved her ass up and down against his already hard cock. He heard her give a soft, half-asleep laugh.

"Which one of my neighbors got you all hot and bothered?"

"Funny. I read a few pages of Sam's book. I had no idea they got that descriptive," he whispered in her ear. "Also, you're sleeping naked. I can't help but wonder if this was your plan all along. I'm merely the victim of a conniving, insatiable woman." Pulling his cock out of his boxers, he matched her movement with a rhythm of his own sliding between her legs against her already wet pussy and she moaned in appreciation. Maybe she read a bit of Sam's book before bed, too.

"But if it wasn't your plan, I'm sorry I woke you up." His hand made its way up to her chest.

"No, you're not," she answered in a husky voice that he attempted to send to his long-term memory for future nights away from her. "I didn't expect you to read Sam's book, but I admit I was hoping you would take the hint when you found me naked."

She turned her head to give him a kiss and he couldn't resist sliding his tongue in to meet hers. He needed to taste her again and commit it all to memory for when he'd be gone. She moaned into his mouth and moved her hand down his waist.

Reflexively he tightened his grip on her breasts and pinched her nipples just a hair harder. She grabbed his cock and began to stroke it as he slid up and down against her.

His teeth lightly pulled at her ear then he whispered, "I'm going to miss you." He hadn't meant to do it. He told himself whatever happened with them, they wouldn't be saying goodbye all weekend or even at the airport. It was only temporary. But there he was, sounding and acting as if he would never be in her bed again after Monday.

She wriggled in his grip and turned to face him with one

leg in between his now and one draped across his thigh – almost up to his hips.

"What are you going to miss?"

"Kissing you." He leaned in for a proper kiss full of mingling tongues and hands on each other's necks and torsos desperately trying to bring them into each other even closer than the laws of physics would ever allow.

"What else?" she asked when she finally pulled away from their kiss.

He ran his fingertips down the length of her body from her neck down to her knees. "This unbelievably soft skin that covers every inch of your amazing body."

"Hmmmm…what else."

"These perfect tits." He let the back of his finger drag up her ribs and then up the underside to her taut nipple. He captured it between his thumb and finger before leaning in to graze it with his tongue. The graze was intentional because he loved the way she'd arch her back and thrust herself towards him, demanding more pleasure than his light touch offered. As he'd expected, she leaned her chest into his waiting mouth, and he flicked and sucked and teased each nipple. His cock getting achingly hard as he took it all in: the taste of her, the feel of the silky skin, the sighs and moans she let out.

"What else?" Her voice was getting increasingly breathy as if she could barely get the words out as he continued to work her tits with his hands and mouth.

Based on the way she was rubbing herself up and down against his thigh, he knew what she wanted to hear and feel next. He gave a final lick and soft nip at each nipple before he made a trail of kisses down her stomach.

As he made his way down he said, "And I'm really going to miss these legs." His hands went to her outer thighs where the two muscles met and formed an indent running down her leg.

"But what about -"

"I'll get there." He was still planting kisses down her leg and moving into a kneeling position at the foot of the bed to reach all his favorite spots. "And this – this whole lovely, naked body in front of me that must be worshiped and adored slowly. Inch by inch so I don't miss a thing."

Still, he could tell she was torn between the romantic words and gestures, and desperately needing him to relieve the ache she must be feeling between her legs. He moved over to the other leg and started another trail of kisses and licks at her ankle moving towards her thighs. With his free hand he started to work the soft, wet folds between her legs.

"Finally. I didn't think you'd ever find the clit."

He chuckled. "Blasphemy. I've always known where that was." In retaliation to her sassy comment, he reached up and gently brushed his fingertips against one of her ass cheeks sending her into fits of giggles. Hands down one of the cutest things about Jackie was that she was ticklish on her ass cheek.

She swatted away his hand and was no longer laughing when he slid his tongue between her legs to join his fingers. Scott felt his exhaustion slipping away as he lost himself in her.

The weekend went by quickly. As the neighbors had said, the light displays ran mostly on autopilot with the timers doing all the work. Scott and Jackie crammed in an entire month's worth of holiday festivities while dragging Sam along for the ride. Sam was up and down throughout it all.

When they went to the train garden at the local fire house,

Sam was good. She even batted eyes at a few fire fighters while Jackie encouraged her to get one of their numbers. Scott felt a punch to the gut at that one. If Sam started dating again, was Jackie going to be her wingman? Would they be out at restaurants and bars looking for single men while he was half a world away without a return date in sight?

The good times with Sam were fleeting though, and mostly she was reminded of everything she was doing that season without Jeremy by her side. So Scott was careful not to be too overly romantic or touchy with Jackie when Sam was around. Sam probably sensed that they were holding back. She made arrangements to have dinner with her parents and to spend the night at their house.

"Sleeping in the spare bedroom?" Jackie asked. Sam had fallen asleep with wine and books on Jackie's couch Friday and Saturday night.

"No, on their couch. I can't sleep in a bed by myself yet. It's too big and sad. An eight-hour unrelenting reminder that I'm all alone. When I crash on the couch it feels like I'm in college again and just passed out in someone's living room."

"Once Scott's gone you can sleep with me. I'll be lonely, too." Jackie gave Sam a sideways hug and put her head on her shoulder.

Scott raised his eyebrows at them. "You're going to lay in bed together reading smutty books? Change in plans. I'm not going anywhere."

He only joked about it to keep things light. But each passing hour he felt more and more miserable about leaving Jackie. He'd first told himself that she would be too busy with her new job, so it wouldn't be a big deal for him to be away for a while. But that was too simplistic and missed all the daily details: sleeping together, texting something quick to each other (not impossible while he was away, but difficult given the time difference), spending Christmas morning together and kissing at midnight on New Year's. Hugs and holding hands. His body craved hers and from what he could tell she felt the same way about him.

Monday morning came too soon, just as he knew it would. They'd barely slept the night before. Instead, they went back and forth between having sex and laying naked in bed talking. They probably looked like shit given their lack of sleep. If Lizzy noticed when she showed up to film them saying goodbye, she didn't comment on it. She apologized profusely for having to film their intimate moment together, then hurried out once she felt she got enough footage.

Promptly at ten, Lana honked the horn of her rental car out front and he was off again.

JACKIE

The day before Christmas Eve was by far the busiest in regard to tourists flocking Christmas Lights Lane. Jackie had offered to go out with Sam to avoid hearing the Christmas Jazz from outside the house playing on repeat for hours on end. But Sam was having another bad day and wouldn't hear of it.

She was on the couch, her favorite place in the house, surrounded by books and sitting with her laptop in her lap. Jackie was in the kitchen studying and eating from a cheese tray she'd set out for them.

"We could do holiday karaoke at Pluto's, Yosemite's, or The Barn. All three are going all out this year. I'd suggest The Barn since it's right down the road from the fire house. Maybe Josh'll show up. You never know."

Jackie's tactic with Sam had been to suggest all the things she knew Sam loved that Jeremy did not. Remind her of how awesome it was to do only the things she wanted to do without worrying about anyone else. It had worked for a few weeks, but lately Jackie and Sam were running out of steam. She missed Scott, and Sam missed...someone. Some days she truly missed Jeremy, and other days she just missed being part of a pair.

"No. Josh sucks. He has bad breath and the last time I saw him he checked out some other woman right in front of me."

Sam was drinking wine again and therefore a bit more candid about her dislikes than she normally would be. She went back to typing and sipping her wine. Jackie had been dismissed.

Fine. Maybe Sam didn't want to leave the house, but she sure as hell did. She probably shouldn't have plastered Scott's face all over the walls and on her cell phone background. It was hard to ignore how much she missed him when she saw his gorgeous face everywhere she looked.

"How about we walk down to the Little Free Library?" Why hadn't Jackie thought of it sooner? Sam was covered in books and the only thing she'd wanted to do since she walked away from Jeremy was sit and read.

Success. After a few clicks on the computer, she closed it up and set it off to the side. Sam eyed up the full wine glass in her hand and Jackie thought, *oh, no. Let's not chug the wine. Bad idea.*

As if she could read Jackie's thoughts, Sam lowered the glass and walked over to the kitchen. She poured her wine into a traveling tumbler with a silhouette image of Santa Claws on it. An original creation of Jackie's that she would consider selling on Etsy or something if the documentary ever took off in popularity.

"Wine roadie," Sam said as she put on her coat and hat.

Jackie put on her winter gear as well while Sam started to collect some of her old books for donation.

"You're leaving *those* in the library?"

"Yes. I'm half tempted to put my address in them so whoever picks them up can send me a thank you card."

"Okay," Jackie sighed. "Let's go."

They each laced up snow boats at the door before heading out. It had snowed a bit earlier and was supposed to snow all the next day. They'd have a white Christmas. Unheard of in the area since they usually didn't get snow until January.

The Little Free Library was a large, enclosed bookcase just off the sidewalk at the end of the street near the church. First they had to take a few books each so they'd have enough room to unload all of Sam's books.

"Step out of the frame really quick. I need a picture," Sam said as she took a few steps back herself.

"Another blog pic?"

"Instagram and blog." She took a few pictures at different angles and with different settings on the phone.

Much like everything else in Jackie's life, it reminded her of Scott and made her smile.

"Blog hits going up?"

"Booming." Sam put the phone in her pocket and picked up her bag. It was not filled with a few secret smut books for Sam—secret because they had playful, unassuming covers—and some historical fiction for Jackie. "I now have authors requesting me to review their books. Some are even offering to pay me."

"That's amazing, Sam!" The enthusiasm was real though it did sting a little that everyone except Jackie seemed to be able to effortlessly navigate growing their social media presence.

Sam shrugged. "Sex sells."

"No, no, no. You're not being humble on this one. You rock. Admit it."

"Fine. I rock." Sam gave a genuine smile before tilting her wine roadie to her mouth once again.

"Oh, hey. What a coincidence. The Cut and Run is right over there. We should stop in for a quick drink."

Sam's smile fell. "You're a terrible liar."

"Agreed. Let's discuss that over a drink. A drink that we consume outside of my house." Sam raised the drink she was consuming outside. "With other people." Sam pointed to Jackie. "With strangers. I want to drink booze with strangers."

"Ugh, fine." Sam chugged the rest of her wine and tossed the empty travel tumbler into her book bag. "Lead the way."

But when they got to the bar, there was Jeremy sitting at a table at the front window with a woman sitting across from him. Jackie and Sam could see only the back of the woman's head; Jeremy was facing them. Jackie turned to redirect Sam back to the house before Sam saw. But before she could fully turn to Sam a snowball went flying past her face and landed against the window right where Jeremy's head was.

"Man whore!" Sam screamed. She bent down to pick up another handful of snow and stopped dead. Jackie turned to see what made Sam pause and found Chastity looking back at them. Jeremy wasn't at the bar with another woman, he was at the bar with his cousin.

The sad soggy snowball slid down the window to reveal Jeremy's morose face behind it. Sam's face was identical. Her lips started to quiver. Then she dropped the snow and turned to walk back to Jackie's house leaving the bag of forgotten books spilled over the sidewalk.

Jackie turned back to the window to see the whole bar looking back at her. "He's not," she shouted unconvincingly before stooping down to pick up her books and scuttle after Sam.

Shit. Shit. Shit. She shouldn't have forced Sam out of the house and she shouldn't have forced her to go to a bar where they could potentially run into her soon to be ex-husband.

"Shit. Shit. Shit." Sam had been quiet on the way home. Probably just trying to make it back to the safety of the house before she allowed herself to lose her shit again. It wasn't typical for Sam to yell, "Man whore," at anyone or to throw a snowball at a business. She was pacing the living room as she muttered shit over and over again.

Jackie figured she would give Sam a few minutes to decompress before she tried to calm her down or talk about what happened.

"I can't do this," Sam said when she stopped pacing. "He wasn't with another woman but he will be. I didn't want to be at the bar with him, but I also do want to be at the bar with him. Right now. I want him to hold my hand and I want to hear him say that we can still talk and be friends and that everything will be okay. But then I don't want to do that, too."

"Do you have regrets?"

She plopped down on the couch as if she barely had the energy to hold up her head. "No. I don't regret that we got married, and I don't regret leaving. But it just hurts…so much. And I'm tired of hurting."

Jackie sat down with her on the couch and they both leaned towards each other, on each other. Shoulder to shoulder and head to head.

"Should we do shots of tequila and watch Conan O'Brien?"

"Yes, please."

And so they did. Just as they'd done when they were in their late teens during sleepovers with stolen bottles of tequila they'd refilled (unsuccessfully) with water, and then later just as they'd done with Jeremy alongside them in their early twenties—their own bottles of tequila they'd legally purchased and with Jeremy as Sam's husband.

As Sam gathered the booze, shot glasses, and limes, Jackie queued up the Conan episodes and then took a quick moment to text Scott. It had been a shit day, weeks really, and she just needed some sort of contact with him. It was eight at night in Milton and noon over in Sydney, so she only half expected him to answer. Lana being Lana Jackie knew Scott couldn't pause mid-shot to answer a text.

But there was also a gnawing feeling in her gut at the way responses from both of them were taking longer and longer to get through. How at first they'd dropped everything to respond, but then as the days and weeks passed the responses took a bit longer. She would sleep through his texts or be too engrossed in a project to pause and talk for a bit.

That night she texted, *I really need to talk to you*, then set the phone on her lap on vibrate waiting for his response. Four shots and two episodes of Conan later, and there was still no response from him. Sam and Jackie had taken a turn for the worse with their new drunken status.

"Fuck guys," Sam declared.

It turned into a drunken epiphany for Jackie. "Holy shit. You're right. Fuck guys." And it was all so clear then how all guys sucked and that they would only have each other for the rest of their lives. But she was okay with that because Sam was all she ever really needed.

"And fuck Milton."

At that Jackie's head shook slightly as if trying to make sense of the connection between guys and the tiny town of Milton.

"Who's Milton? Did you fuck someone named Milton?"

"The town," Sam said as if Jackie were two years old and incapable of understanding much beyond her own name. "I can't stay here."

Jackie hadn't intended on having any more booze, but when Sam said she was leaving and offered to top off her shot glass, she gave a sad nod of "yes, please" back to her.

"Everyone's leaving me, Sam." Jackie clinked glasses with

her before downing the shot. It went down smooth which was probably a bad sign.

"I'm leaving Milton. Not you."

"When are you leaving me?"

"I'm not leaving you. I'm leaving all of this." She stood up and pulled the front door open so that only the glass storm door separated them from the outside. "I'm leaving this madness." She drunkenly pointed to the street outside filled with tourists since it was not yet ten o'clock at night even though they were smashed.

Jackie got up from the couch and closed the door before she ushered Sam back to the couch. "You love all of that as much as I do. You're leaving Jeremy. Again."

"Yes. I am."

"You don't—"

"I do. One of us is going to start dating again, and the other is going to find out. Firsthand, secondhand. It doesn't matter. I don't want to be here in town for it."

Jackie's soupy mind worked hard to put together an argument as to why Sam should stay in Milton beyond the fact that Jackie wanted her to. It was no good. The tequila was too strong.

"You went to Philly. You already went somewhere where you didn't know anyone. You made friends; you did your own thing with no outside influence at all."

Sam had a good point there. Jackie did feel like she found herself a bit when she was flying solo in Philly. She had to put herself out there to make new friends and to try new things. Didn't she want that for Sam?

"Yeah. I did," Jackie conceded.

"Well, that's what I'm going to do. Get me a globe. We'll throw darts at it to see where I go."

That was the last thing Jackie remembered. When she

woke up, she and Sam were on the couch together with some random documentary about how rice is made played on the tv. She picked up her phone to see that it was six in the morning and that Scott had never responded.

JACKIE

*C*hristmas Eve was usually a slower night in the neighborhood. Everyone had plans and family parties to attend. Parents had last-minute gifts to wrap and bikes to assemble while they quietly cursed the people who made wordless, visual instructions that were near impossible to comprehend.

But this year, with the snow the day before and the fresh coating the day of, the streets were filled with tourists and locals alike. Everyone wanted the experience of seeing the previously elusive snowy lights display.

Sam was at her parents' house for the evening and Jackie was home fixing a dinner for one when her phone started to explode with a group text from Tiny Tim. The thing nearly vibrated off the table as a few dozen neighbors promptly responded to his inquiry.

Tim: *Beautiful night. Lizzy's filming. Let's do some caroling* ☺
Mort: *Let's do Beatles All You Need is Love*
Unknown Number: *That's not Christmas*
Margaret: *It was in Love Actually which is a Christmas movie*

Mac: *Agree with Marcy. It's not holiday. Let's do Crabs for Christmas*

Unknown number: *I love Crabs for Christmas! And the Christmas Wrapping song. I've been practicing for months*

Mom: *I agree with Mort*

Every time Jackie went to type something in, a few more comments appeared before she could finish. She went back to her balsamic chicken dinner on the stove and left the phone to vibrate on the counter for a bit. Like popcorn she waited until at least five seconds passed between vibrations before she picked it up again to see what everyone had settled on. She scrolled through the comments to get the basics: everyone would meet at Tim's at eight wearing some sort of red top and a Santa hat. Mort would bring his famous wintery Moscow mule. They would sing "Last Christmas," "All I Want for Christmas is You," and "Rocking Around the Christmas Tree."

Jackie looked around the empty house full of Christmas cheer, and she was glad to have a reason to leave it all. Usually she'd fill her time with more work of some sort —a project to post to social media, learning a crafting technique she hadn't quite mastered yet, or studying up on her latest career in marine chemistry.

But she was too exhausted and unmotivated to do much beyond eat dinner while watching something on tv that would likely leave her in tears. Drinking and singing carols with her neighbors was infinitely better—though slightly jarring that it was the winning option that night.

At eight sharp Jackie muscled her way through the crowd out front of her house and in the street to make her way to Tim's. Like her, most neighbors had some sort of music to accompany their lights display so their current plan of attack was to hit up the five residences that didn't have music already. Tim being Tim, he killed his own music and decided they would start there.

"Hi, sweetie. How you holding up?" her mother asked when she reached Tim's front yard. Babs and Mort had insisted Sam and Jackie do dinner with them at least twice a week since Scott left and Sam moved in. They didn't mind since Mort was a fantastic cook, but it was obvious that the dinner was a ploy to keep tabs on them and make sure they were okay.

"I'm good, Mom. Is Mort here?"

"He's over with Tim trying to get 'All You Need is Love' added to the set list."

Jackie looked over to the far corner of the yard to see Mort, Tim, and Marcy in a heated conversation while Lizzy caught it all on film a few feet away.

"No Sam tonight?"

"She's with her family."

"Then you should stay with us tonight. I don't like the idea of you being alone in the house all by yourself on Christmas Eve and Christmas morning."

"It's fine, Mom. I'll probably video chat with Scott anyway, so I won't be alone."

"Oh, okay." Babs was not convinced —either that that would happen or that it was a suitable replacement as her family. Jackie couldn't be sure which. It made her feel irritable and antsy.

"Are we going to do this thing, or what?"

Babs looked at her watch. "Just be patient, sweetie. I'm sure we'll start any minute now."

Jackie looked around. The crowd was getting restless as well. The group of neighbors in Santa hats and red tops was attracting attention. Visitors were pulling out phones in anticipation—their fingers hovering over the record button.

"I can't deal with this tonight. I'm heading home." Jackie

started to push through onlookers again and just barely felt Babs's hand on her arm as she tried to grab her.

She easily tugged free and kept moving through the snow falling and crowds with phones around her. Scott was right to not want to be in the middle of all of this. How would she feel once the documentary aired and everything was out there for the world to see? It was suddenly apparent to her that maybe she didn't want to be the star of her own show after all. To have people shoving phones in her face at all times expecting greatness and perfection from her even on her worst days. Maybe she was getting ahead of herself slightly thinking that people would clamor for a photo or autograph from her, but still.

Music from every house, including her own, shut off simultaneously as The Beatles began to play over loud-speakers throughout the neighborhood. But it wasn't the background music of karaoke. It was the full song with The Beatles belting out how love was all they needed. *Stupid,* Jackie thought, *and still not a Christmas song despite what Mort says and despite its presence in Love Actually—a questionable Christmas movie given its terrible romantic plot lines that end in heartbreak.*

Even more certain she wanted no part of it, Jackie quickened her pace down the road. Then the chorus began and everyone around her partnered up and began to dance. Jackie froze. Something weird was happening. The phones were mostly gone, and everyone was immersed in their partner and in the dance. She looked back to her mother who was looking deep and lovingly into Mort's eyes, but also couldn't help but glance over at Jackie to see her reaction. The crowd was not due to the unseasonable snowfall; it was a flash mob. And her mother and all the other neighbors were a part of it.

Still standing in the middle of the road, and now with

Lizzy's camera just off to the side of her, the song changed to Counting Crows "Accidentally in Love." Her heart quickened. The song had been a running joke that night in Ocean City all those years ago when one of the girls insisted on playing it on repeat much to the annoyance of everyone else at the party. It was not a Christmas song, and it couldn't be a coincidence. It had to be Scott.

The dancers changed from soft, slow dancing to more of an interpretive dance karaoke style as they free danced and sang along to the lyrics. She bobbed and weaved through the crowded street back to her house. Like the parting sea they eventually moved to the side so she could make her way back. She noticed a few people here and there who had to be moved or pulled to the side by someone who knew what was going on, but it was still impressive. How had Scott ever managed this sort of stunt while he was a world away and without her knowing?

When she reached her yard, she noticed most of the people there were in white t-shirts bedazzled with images of a holiday Richard Simmons—his smiling face along with a Santa hat on his fabulously high hair. The work of Margaret, she was sure of it. She turned to see if Margaret was anywhere near, but all she saw was Lizzy amongst a sea of strangers. No Scott, either. Maybe she had it all wrong. Maybe this was just another stunt by Tim or Lana, and it happened to involve a song she and Scott had history with, and she just happened to be left out of the group text that mentioned a flash mob would be happening tonight. It wasn't probable but it was possible.

She took a few more steps towards her house then turned back to the crowd. Many had their phones out again and the Counting Crows were turned down to the level of background music. Lizzy was gone and in her place was Scott.

Gorgeous, even sexier than she'd remembered (probably due to his tan from being down under), Scott Davis. Standing in the street with a camera once again hoisted onto his shoulder and pointed towards her.

But this time he had a sign hanging from his neck with letters written in bold black marker that read: *I should never have gone to Australia.* A second later he flipped to reveal the back: *Forgive me, Jackie. I love you.*

He lowered the camera and someone from behind him took it and was promptly reabsorbed by the crowd never to be seen again. At least not by Jackie. Sam had been schooling her on all the romantic comedy tropes in her smutty books. She knew that towards the end there would be some sort of break up and the other main character would need to make some large romantic gesture to win back the love of their life. And for whatever reason, the gesture wouldn't be enough. It would be shut down and they'd need to find another way to the person's heart.

Except this wasn't some cheesy steamy book; it was her life. She didn't care or even know for sure if Scott should or shouldn't have gone in the first place. All she knew was that he was back, and he loved her. It was more than enough to win her over.

She ran and leapt into his waiting arms, almost toppling him down since her legs wouldn't go around him with that damn Candace-Cameron-Bure-like sign around his neck. Awkwardly her legs fell back to the ground, and she had to make do with her arms around his neck and her face nuzzling into his warm, citrus smelling neck. She'd been sleeping with one of his sweatshirts around her pillows each night, but she missed the real thing.

After a few seconds she remembered that they were in the middle of the street and surrounded by a few hundred strangers—many of whom had cell phones out and were filming their reunion.

"I missed you," she said into his ear. Her face still buried in his neck and shoulder.

"Me, too, Jackie."

He pulled away just a bit so they could see each other.

"I love you, and I love all of this. I love that we're surrounded by bedazzled Richard Simmons faces, that you're more handy with tools than I'll ever be, and that you're such a workaholic I practically need to restrain you some nights to keep you from being productive."

Tears filled her eyes at his spot-on assessment of her unrelenting urge to be productive at all times, and the fact that he didn't just tolerate it but found it endearing—said he loved it about her even. He loved her. She'd suspected it before he left, but the distance had left her doubting if they'd be able to survive all the barriers in their way.

"I love you, Scott," she whispered before leaning in again for another kiss. Would she ever get tired of kissing this amazing man?

The crowd surrounding them began lowering their phones and going back to enjoying the lights display, though she continued to hear crowd members mention their names and the documentary.

Scott pulled away from their kiss. "I made a bit of a deal with the Devil."

"The Devil?" Her cocked eyebrow showed apprehension. She knew it was too good to be true that there would be some sort of price to pay.

He shrugged. "Lana, actually." Her eyebrow dropped and she smiled at the comparison. Lizzy's camera was still trained on her a few feet away and she noticed Scott was mic'd up.

"I needed a few favors from her and Sam to set this whole thing up, and in exchange I promised her some extra screen time of our reunion." He searched her face looking for signs of understanding from Jackie. Confirmation that he knew the situation wasn't ideal, but it had been done with only good intentions.

She couldn't help but glance at Lizzy and the camera. Why not? Everything else was already caught on camera, why not give the audience the happy ending they'd waited so patiently for.

She nodded. "Yeah, okay." Then she chuckled at how adorable he was when the stress and worry left his face with that one comment.

She wanted to ask him the biggest question of all—if he was back in Milton indefinitely—but everything was too good at the moment to risk it being pulled out from under her.

"Tell me how you managed to get the entire town in on this without me knowing."

He gave a smug grin at how clever he knew he'd been. "It was mostly Sam. I told her last week I had made plans to come back and she made me keep it a secret. She said our relationship was like a cheesy romance and we might as well have the cliché surprise reunion to go with it."

Jackie looked around at the lights displays happening around them, listened to the mixture of music from everyone's houses, and then looked back to Scott whose perfect hair was sprinkled with the unseasonable, but timely, snowfall. White bedazzled t-shirts layered over coats still milling about around them.

"You nailed it."

"*She* did. Sam said I needed everyone in matching outfits, our song in the background, and some sort of inside joke between us." He motioned to the signs and then took them off to set off to the side.

Sam was good. Suffering through her own broken heart she still helped Scott to plan the most romantic gesture of her life. It couldn't have been easy. Jackie felt on the verge of tears again at the thought of it all.

"Margaret made the shirts?"

"With the help of some of the other neighbors. Not Tim. Lana kept him in the dark about the whole thing. He really thought everyone was going to sing carols and I think he's a bit pissed."

Jackie spotted Tim out front of his house looking irritable as he likely texted Lana.

"And what about Sam? What did you offer her in exchange for all of this?"

Scott's face turned bright red. "She wants me to pose shirtless with some of her books for her book reviews." Jackie let out a laugh. "Only if you're okay with it. She swore you would be, but I wanted to check with you, first."

She nodded her approval. "Sam's numbers are going to go through the roof. Don't worry. She'll crop out your adorable face."

The lightness left again as Jackie took a deep breath for courage. "Aside from this," Jackie tried to discreetly motion to camera to reference the fact that they were being filmed, "what else did you need to barter to get home for this and to have Lana's blessing?"

Scott licked his lips and Jackie noticed he fought the urge to glance at the camera as well. "After this I don't owe Lana anything. Ever. I quit."

Jackie gulped. "You quit?" She hadn't meant to show how excited she was, but she could feel the giant smile spreading across her face. "Are you okay? Is that what you want?" It was doubtful those questions came off as sincere as she'd wanted them to given her state of pure ecstasy.

He laughed. "Yes, it's what I want." His hand reached out to cup her chin and pull her in for another kiss, then he said, "I want you, and this crazy town. Can I stay?"

She nodded her head yes as they kissed again.

Scott pulled back to look at her again, his face serious. "One more thing."

Shit, she thought. She knew it was all too much to be true. There was still some sort of price for all the happiness she had.

"Sam said that after we publicly proclaim our love for each other, we have to privately show it with wild, uninhabited sex that results in multiple orgasms."

Jackie could feel her face turning bright red at the mention and felt the undeniable throb of desire between her thighs at the thought of having Scott in her bed again—or wherever it was they made it to once they got into the house.

"Okay, I'm just going to delete that last part there." Lizzy clicked off the camera and eased it off her shoulder. "I'm heading out to Australia tomorrow to take over for Scott, so good luck, you crazy kids. See you around."

"Thanks, Lizzy. See ya." Scott never took his eyes off Jackie. He'd likely said it because he likes making Jackie blush and he loves catching her off guard, but it must have put some ideas in his mind as well. His expression turned from wholesome and lovesick to an animal in heat as his eyes looked down to her lips and what little bit of neck she was showing.

"Well, if that's what Sam said…" Jackie's words trailed off and her finger trailed down his chest. Not that he would feel it through his parka, but she could tell he got the hint from the way he grabbed her hand and playfully tugged her towards the house. In his haste to get her inside Scott almost ate concrete when he slipped on a patch of ice on the walkway.

"I've got you," she said as she grabbed his arm to help him balance.

"Thanks, Strauss."

"I'd never let you fall, Scott."

"I know. That's one of the many things I love about you."

BEFORE YOU GO...

My biggest thanks to you for taking a chance on an unknown, indie author (that's me, in case I'm being too vague). And since you've gotten through to the end, and then some with this little blurb as well, I'm hoping I can ask one more huge favor. Please consider leaving a review at whatever fine establishment you purchased this from and on GoodReads, BookBub, or any other bookish social media outlet you peruse in your spare time. Rave about how much you loved it, or tear it down and release whatever pent-up anger and emotions you've suppressed for the past decade or so—I'm grateful either way.

HAPPY READING,

Leigh Donnelly

WANT MORE? OF COURSE YOU!

Sam needs her happy ending, too (pun absolutely intended) and she's going to get it in the small town of Deep Creek Lake. She has a rough start with the not-so-meet-cute of getting pulled over while listening to an extra steamy audiobook, but she's about to find out for herself that enemies-to-lovers beginnings often turn into the best love stories.

ALSO BY LEIGH DONNELLY

Loathe Gray

It Was Always This Way

Once You Cross That Line